6/09

Demon Can't
Help It

DEMON CAN'T HELP IT

KATHY LOVE

BRAVA

KENSINGTON PUBLISHING CORP.

www.kensingtonbooks.com

BRAVA BOOKS are published by

Kensington Publishing Corp.
119 West 40th Street
New York, NY 10018

All Kensington titles, imprints, and distributed lines are available at special quantity discounts for bulk purchases for sales promotion, premiums, fund-raising, educational, or institutional use.

Special book excerpts or customized printings can also be created to fit specific needs. For details, write or phone the office of the Kensington Special Sales Manager: Kensington Publishing Corp., 119 West 40th Street, New York, NY 10018. Attn. Special Sales Department. Phone: 1-800-221-2647.

Brava and the B logo are Reg. U.S. Pat. & TM Off.

ISBN-13: 978-0-7582-3193-2
ISBN-10: 0-7582-3193-8

First Kensington Trade Paperback Printing: May 2009

10 9 8 7 6 5 4 3 2 1

Printed in the United States of America

Acknowledgments

I always have very special writing friends who are there for me and help keep me sane.

I want to thank Erin McCarthy for the phone chats and frequent pep talks. Julie Cohen for more phone chats and pep talks. F. Paul Wilson for the "daily damage reports." And convincing me that a writing routine isn't totally evil. Thanks to Carmen Ross Weed for being a great and supportive friend.

I must, as always, thank The Tarts.
You ladies rule.

And thanks for Kate Duffy for being a great editor, and a patient one.

Chapter 1

"Are you sure you feel up to this?"

Jo finished draining the fettuccine and glanced over at her friends. Maggie leaned against the kitchen counter, waiting for an answer to her question. Erika sat at the small bistro-style table, concern drawing her finely arched brows together. Clearly she was waiting, too.

Jo smiled, knowing she probably appeared a little tired. "Of course. It's just pasta, not a five-course meal. Why wouldn't I feel up to making my friends dinner to celebrate my new place and my new job?"

"Well, I know you said that you were already working long hours. And you've looked a little . . . pale recently," Maggie said.

Jo supposed the reflection that greeted her in the mirror these days was pale, drawn, and fatigued. But she'd made a huge move, found an apartment, and started a new job in the course of a month.

"I am a little tired," she did admit, but then gave them another smile. "But I like the work at the community center and I love being in a new city. And being with you two again, of course."

She gave the pasta a final shake, then dumped it into a pasta bowl. She turned to the simmering pot of white wine clam sauce, trying to ignore the wave of nausea as the garlicky scent wafted up to her in a billowing cloud of steam.

She hadn't been feeling well, and she knew that fact was evident on her face. But she would be fine. That had been her mantra now for the past couple months. And it would be true. She just needed to get her life back in order. She liked order.

She busied herself with pouring the creamy sauce over the pasta, then returned to the oven to take out the garlic bread, which, again, did nothing to steady her queasy stomach.

"Here we go," she said with a forced smile as she set the bowl of fettuccine and platter of bread on the table. "I know you two always loved this meal when I made it for you back in D.C."

"Mmm, it looks great," Erika said, staring at the pile of white steaming pasta as if it might turn into a multi-tentacled creature and attack.

"It does look good," Maggie agreed, giving it her own askance stare. "And it smells good, too," she added, when she realized that Jo was regarding her with skepticism. Maggie's forced smile still didn't convince Jo, but she accepted the praise and sat down.

"Then dig in." Jo took a sip of her ice water, waiting for her guests to get their servings first.

Erika chose a piece of bread, while Maggie took two small helpings of the pasta. They looked at each other as they did so.

Not for the first time since moving down to New Orleans, Jo felt as if her two friends were sharing some private, wordless communication.

Maggie took a bite of the food, actually more like a nibble. "Mmm, plenty of garlic." She nodded approvingly, but then her glance flicked back to Erika. Erika's lips were pressed together as if she was suppressing a chuckle.

Jo glanced back and forth between her friends, again feeling as if she'd been excluded from an inside joke. When she moved here, she'd expected her relationship with her long-time friends to be as it had always been. But it had changed.

Jo supposed it was natural for Maggie and Erika to have a special bond now that they were married to brothers. But some-times, like now, Jo felt as if Maggie and Erika shared some-thing more, something private. Jo supposed she couldn't say much about that. After all, it wasn't as if she wasn't hiding something from them as well.

She pushed that thought away, focusing on scooping up her own portion of the meal. She needed to think about first things first—wasn't that what her grandmother had always said? And her grandmother had been a wise woman, a woman Jo had always trusted, loved, and admired. First things first.

And Jo suspected she was being oversensitive about her friends anyway—another side effect of her big move and ex-haustion. She just wanted to get her life back in order. She seemed to be a font of mantras and mottos at the moment.

And she *was* very pleased to be back with her friends. She'd been close to Maggie and Erika since freshmen year in college, and they'd always been like sisters. Adopted sisters who'd become so important to her.

"Is Vittorio playing with the Impalers tonight?" Jo asked Erika, feeling the need to steer her thoughts away from places she didn't want to go. And given how smitten her friends were with their new spouses, she felt certain this would be a topic the two women couldn't help but discuss. The two new hub-bies and their Bourbon Street band, the Impalers.

"Yes," Erika said, nibbling her bread.

"He's playing for me tonight," Maggie said. "Although I think he's going to take over playing bass. Dave is talking about leaving."

"That's good, right?" Jo said.

Erika nodded, setting her bread aside and picking up her fork. "He loves being back, playing with his brother. And I'm enjoying it, too. I have a hot, sexy musician husband—but mostly it gives me time to work on my art."

"When you're not down there being a groupie," Maggie said with a wink.

"Like you can talk," Jo teased.

Maggie shrugged. "I never denied that I was Ren's biggest fan. But don't forget, I'm with the band."

"So you are still enjoying playing, too?" Jo asked, realizing this was actually the first time since she got here they'd had time to talk about day-to-day life. See, no wonder she looked so exhausted. She'd not stopped since moving out of her apartment in D.C.

"I do. It's like a dream," Maggie's smile was dreamy. "Who could have guessed how things would have changed for us with that first trip here?"

Jo smiled, forcing herself to take a bite of the pasta, the clam sauce slimy on her tongue, the fettuccine turning to paste against the roof of her mouth.

There really wasn't any way to tell how one event could change the course of your life, Jo thought, but she was working very hard to get her life back in control. No more surprises for her.

They all ate silently for a few moments, or rather picked at their food, lost in thought.

"So," Erika asked slowly, poking at the pasta with her fork, "isn't the community center a lot of work compared to your job at Potomac Prep?"

Jo smiled, immediately knowing what her friend was really angling at. "Don't you mean, isn't a job at St. Ann Community Center a big step down from Potomac Prep?"

"That isn't . . ."

"Yes, it is," Jo cut Erika off good-naturedly. "And yes, it's definitely a step down prestige- and money-wise, but it was still the right move for me."

Maggie set down her fork and reached out to capture Jo's fingers, squeezing them. "Why the change?"

Jo stared at their joined hands. This was the moment to tell them. To admit what had her running from Washington, D.C., but she couldn't. The words wouldn't come. Almost as if once she admitted it, it would be true. All true.

It is true, whether you like it or not. But then she pushed the thought away.

She set down her fork, and pushed the plate away from herself. Clearly no one at the table had an appetite. Her first dinner party in her new place, and it was less than a success. So much for just having a normal evening with her two best friends.

She hesitated still, trying to get the words to come, but they didn't. Instead she forced a smile.

"Isn't it enough that I was feeling left out? Missing my two best friends?"

Erika moved her plate aside, too, and shifted so she could join her hand to Jo and Maggie's. "It's definitely enough."

They stayed like that, her friends' fingers cool against her skin. A calming coolness that suppressed the nausea that seemed to be just at the back of her throat at all times.

Their kind, caring touch didn't hold back the tears that threatened to spill over at having them here. She pulled her hand away to sniff and grab her napkin, using the paper to wipe her eyes.

"I guess I really am overtired," Jo said with a watery laugh.

Both Maggie and Erika gave her sympathetic smiles that didn't really help the emotional overload. Jo swiped at her eyes again and swallowed back more tears.

"Let's get out of here," she said with strained brightness.

"Where?" Erika said, with a surprised laugh.

"Let's go see your boys," Jo suggested, needing to think about something besides herself for just a few moments. Loud rock and roll and other people seemed like just the thing.

"Really? You feel up to it?" Maggie asked with such concern that it made Jo pause. She glanced at Erika, seeing the same worry creasing her pale brow. Almost as if they sensed a problem.

Ridiculous.

"Of course," Jo said, already rising from her seat. "Don't you want to go see your boys?"

"If you want to, of course we do," Erika said also standing.

Jo was counting on that.

Maksim Kostova knew all about Hell. After all, he'd been a resident of the place for all of his existence. The eighth circle to be exact. But the real Hell had nothing on this bar on the corner of Bourbon and Toulouse.

Sweat clung to his skin and the all-too-familiar strains of a Kansas song pounded around him, making his head ache. He mindlessly plucked a plastic cup from the tower of them and headed to the beer tap.

If this place, or rather the man currently playing keyboards on the stage across the room, wasn't the only link he had left to his missing sister, Maksim wouldn't be here.

But he was starting to lose hope. Every night, he waited, expecting that Vittorio, or someone affiliated with Vittorio, would give him another hint, or maybe even the answer to what happened to Ellina.

So far, that hadn't been the case. Vittorio knew nothing. Maksim was confident about that. He'd known when he'd found the scrap of paper with Vittorio's name written on it in Ellina's handwriting that any connection was a long shot. But it was his only tie to anyone, and he kept hoping that someone Vittorio knew would know something, anything. A half human/half demon didn't just disappear. Vittorio was Maksim's last thread, however, tenuous. He didn't have anywhere else to look.

He finished pouring a light beer for a man, who had been bellied up to the bar for hours. As Maksim slid the plastic cup toward the man, it was on the tip of his tongue to tell the barfly that light beer wasn't going to make an iota of difference to his enormous girth. Not when he'd already had nine or ten of them. But instead of sharing that dieting tip, he said, "Put it on your tab?"

The man nodded, but for the first time since he arrived, his attention was on something other than his beer. Maksim followed the man's stare toward the open doorway to his left.

Three women strolled in, all of whom he recognized immediately. The first two were Ren and Vittorio's wives. But it was the third woman who caught Maksim's attention.

Maksim had met Jo Burke a few times, although the woman always acted as if she only vaguely remembered him with each introduction. That rankled him. Women did not forget him. Just ask any of the moony-eyed chicks who came here night after night to watch him tend bar. He had as many groupies as the band did.

What needled him even more than her indifference was that he wasn't even that into mortal women. So where did she get off ignoring him? It should be vice versa.

Mortal woman just didn't know how to get their freak on. Not the way his demon appetites craved. Oh, he would use them for easy entertainment when there was wasn't someone better to do. But paranormal paramours were always more interesting.

Still for whatever reason, aloof Jo Burke had managed to capture his notice and curiosity, probably *because* she didn't seem interested in him. And Maksim did so love a challenge. Well, as long as he won in the end.

"Hi, Maksim," Maggie greeted, taking a barstool across from him. Ren's wife had to be the Pollyanna of the vampire world, but Maksim liked her despite it.

Erika wasn't as warm. Of course she had good reason. He had been inside her head, a neat little demon trick he had. Not that she knew that, exactly. She just knew she wasn't very comfortable around him. But then having someone inside your head didn't exactly make you feel comfortable. Not that it mattered to him whether Erika liked him or not. She didn't have any information about Ellina, which was the only reason he'd jumped into her mind.

Still Erika managed a tight smile and a mumbled hello.

But by then, all his interest was focused on the third woman of the group.

When had she gotten into town again?

"Hi there, ladies. What can I get you?" His gaze stayed on Jo as he spoke. He breathed in and something about her, something he couldn't pinpoint, caused need to fire through his body like jet fuel ignited in his veins. The sensation literally took his breath away.

Unnerving, to say the least.

Jo's dark eyes locked with his, her expression steady and remarkably unaffected by him. Again, he was struck by the fact that she didn't seem to react to him in any way. No recognition, no happiness or dislike, nothing. Certainly no highly flammable substances shooting desire through her limbs.

"I'd love a club soda," she said dropping onto a stool beside her friends. She then turned to watch the band, dismissing him.

Maksim only half-heard what the other women ordered, irritated again by Jo's utter disinterest in him. Disinterest was a novelty, and he was discovering it was not one he particularly cared for.

He grabbed three cups and started filling one after the other, his glances going back to Jo every now and then.

She remained with her back toward him, her attention on the band. What was it about her that drew him? And damn, did it draw him. Right now, he wanted to just reach over the bar, grab her, pull her over to him, and lick her entire body.

Good Lord, he was a demon, not a mindless caveman.

"So, when did you get in?" he asked with casual politeness, forcing himself to keep the caveman out of his behavior. He set down the soda, then leaned forward on the bar, waiting for her to turn around. She did, but still didn't react to him, even with him bringing himself as close to her as he could with the long, wooden bar between them.

Instead she nonchalantly lifted her drink and took a lengthy swallow. She moaned with appreciation, the sound low and deep in her throat. She savored the soda water like it was a fine wine, her eyes closed, her lashes looking impossibly long and dark against her cheeks. Her lips parted once she'd swallowed, looking rosy pink and wet with moisture.

Maksim's already reacting body managed to react even more, an erection pressing against the unforgiving material of his jeans. His muscles clenched with pure need.

The response maddened him further, especially when she opened her eyes, set down her drink, and regarded him with her usual impassive stare. All bliss disappeared behind a no-nonsense gaze.

"I got in last week." She took another sip of her drink, again closing her eyes with appreciation.

For a moment, Maksim didn't understand her words, already forgetting that he'd asked her a question. Of course that was before his raging hard-on and the fantasies of making her look as blissful as the icy soda did.

God, he was actually feeling like he was in competition with a carbonated beverage. Pathetic.

Just then, Maggie's laugh drew their attention toward her. Ren, Vittorio, and the rest of the band were off the stage, and Ren had come up and captured his wife around the waist, catching her off guard.

"Come outside," Vittorio said to the women. "We can talk easier without the music." He gestured toward the speakers now playing recorded Top 40 pop tunes.

They all gathered their drinks and headed out to the sidewalk, where they could chat until the band was finished with their break. Jo followed them, not even looking back.

Maksim stared after her as she disappeared outside, confused and frustrated. What was it about that woman? And how was it she didn't seem to notice he existed? He was no fool. He knew he was attractive to the opposite sex—sometimes the same sex, too, although that kind of "getting his freak on" didn't appeal. The point being he knew he was good looking. He'd made that a fact when in the mortal realm.

As if to prove his point, a woman who'd been trying to get his attention all night approached him, blocking his view of the doorway where Jo had just exited.

"Hi," she greeted him with a wide smile and a flip of her long blond hair. "I was wondering what you are doing after you get off work."

He didn't react right away, still mystified by Jo's lack of reaction. Finally he focused on the woman. She was very pretty, curvy, and soft. And there was no question about the interest clear in her light blue eyes.

Now, Maksim was never one to waste time on futile ventures. He liked challenges, yes. But he wasn't wasting time chasing someone who didn't want to get caught.

Okay, this was in fact the first time he could recall meeting someone who didn't want to get caught, but still he didn't believe in working too hard. After all, there was always something, if not better, then just as good coming around the corner. And this was plainly one of those moments.

He smiled at the blonde, who practically glowed back at him, thrilled with his attention.

"I'm getting off work around two. Why? What do you have in mind?"

The blonde giggled. "Well, I can think of a few things."

His smile broadened. "I can, too." Then he extended his hand. "I'm Maksim."

She slipped her fingers into his. "Jenna."

See, he could forget about dark-eyed, dark-haired mortals just as easily as that.

But even as he told himself that, his gaze returned to the doorway that Jo had walked out.

* * *

"When did that guy start working here?"

Erika frowned at Jo, then glanced around the street where they stood with the band. "What guy?"

"The bartender." Jo remembered his name, but she couldn't even bring herself to say it. For some reason, she felt as if remembering his name would show too much . . .

Well, just too much.

Erika still frowned.

"I think she means Maksim," Vittorio supplied even though Jo didn't realize he'd been listening.

"Oh," Erika said, her tone not exactly negative, but not exactly amiable, either. "He's been working here for . . ." She glanced at Vittorio for an answer.

"A couple months," he said. "Right after we got married, he started here."

Jo nodded. She remembered him at Erika and Vittorio's wedding. He'd looked stunningly handsome in his expensive, designer suit. He'd just screamed money, power, and sex appeal. He still did—even slinging beers.

"I wouldn't have pegged him as being a bartender for a living," Jo said. "He seems too . . ." She couldn't find that right word.

"High and mighty," Maggie suggested.

"Yes," Jo agreed. "That's it exactly."

"Oh, he's definitely not from around here," Ren said with a enigmatic smile, making Jo realize that everyone was aware of the topic of conversation.

Jo didn't quite know what Ren meant by his statement or how it tied in to the man's demeanor. And his accent stated he wasn't from Louisiana—or even the U.S. She'd been more focused on the fact that he seemed like the type who was waited on—not doing the waiting.

She could easily picture him in one of those ritzy nightclubs, the ones with dress codes and guest lists. Five-star restaurants and yachts with sexy women in bikinis. She certainly didn't see him working behind a bar in the French Quarter.

So what was he doing here, then?

"Are you interested in him?" Maggie said after everyone had moved on to the subject of whether Drake's guitar solo in Poison's "Talk Dirty to Me" was too long.

Jo blinked. "Interested in him? Hardly."

Maggie nodded, seeming to readily accept her words, then she added, "He's interested in you."

Jo shook her head. "No, he isn't."

"Trust me, he is." Maggie stated, and Jo couldn't decide how her friend felt about the observation.

But then, she wasn't sure what her feelings were, either. Jo wasn't completely oblivious. She noticed the way the man watched her. She'd noticed it the past times she met him, too. But at the time she'd been too involved in her own issues to give it any thought. And frankly she didn't have time to think about it now, either.

Plus, Maksim—and at least she didn't have to pretend she didn't know his last name because she didn't—wasn't the type of man she found attractive.

Okay, that wasn't strictly true. Maksim Whatever-His-Name-Is was the type of man all woman found attractive. Truthfully, he was probably the most stunningly beautiful man she'd ever seen. Well, one of the most beautiful.

For a moment, her mind returned to her own problems and the mess she left behind in D.C. *But you didn't leave it all behind, did you?*

She shoved those thoughts aside and glanced in the doorway, catching a glimpse of Maksim serving a large, fruity-looking drink to a curvaceous blonde.

So sure, she'd noticed Maksim. He was hard to miss with his unusually pale green eyes that reminded her of peridots. His sexy smile that turned up just slightly at one corner. And his body, tall and lean with broad shoulders and—

All right, she sighed, closing her eyes just briefly, trying to block out the image of him. So she'd noticed him. He was a gorgeous man. But she also knew his type. Along with all that masculine beauty, she knew he had an ego the size of St. Louis Cathedral, and she had no use for that. Absolutely no use.

And in the end, he'd have no use for her, either. She'd learned that firsthand. Again, she told herself not to think about it. She had other things to focus on. Like work and friends and starting a new life. Starting a new life . . .

A wave of nausea, sudden and intense, hit her, and she looked around, panicked, deciding if she should rush to the restroom. *Calm down. Calm down.* She swallowed several times and the feeling gradually subsided.

Erika appeared at her side. "The guys are going back in for one more set." She studied Jo. "Are you okay?"

Jo nodded, not quite sure she was ready to speak. She swallowed again, then pulled in a slow, deep breath.

"I'm fine." She forced a closed-mouth smile.

Erika still watched her, her finely arched brows drawn together with concern.

"Are you sure you want to stay?" she asked.

Jo nodded. "Sure." She wasn't ready to be alone with her thoughts at the moment. She'd long ago realized that keeping busy was the best way to avoid things she didn't want to think about. Busy was good.

"Okay," Erika said, her voice uncertain. She glanced at Maggie again. Another knowing look shot between them. This time it irritated Jo.

"I'm fine," she repeated, more firmly, and her friends didn't say anything. They just followed her back into the dark bar.

A group of partiers boogied on the dance floor. The air was hazy and seemed to glow, smoke lit by neon beer signs. Jo ignored the overwhelming scent of cigarettes mingling with stale beer and headed toward the back of the bar to an empty round high-top table. It was a little quieter away from the stage. And she couldn't easily see Maksim from this angle. Noticing his eyes and body and smile wasn't doing her any good.

Men were not a part of her future. She was done.

"So tell me more about the community center," Maggie said, and Erika leaned forward to hear over the band, who'd started again.

"Well, the center is woefully understaffed," Jo said, gladly grasping onto the topic of work. "After Katrina, a lot of the employees and volunteers just didn't return. The building isn't in great condition, either, but at least it didn't suffer any major damage. But even with the lack of staff and facilities, there are more kids there than ever.

"And the kids are great. Well, mostly great. There are a few troubled ones, which, given the area, is to be expected. But they are the kids who need this place the most."

"So will you start looking for staff as soon as you can?" Erika asked.

Jo nodded. "Volunteers, mainly. We just don't have the money to take on full-time employees. Yet. I've been looking into our funding options, what grants I can apply for. Once we know about that, I can start hiring. But my first order of business is coming up with volunteers to help out the kids in our daycare and aftercare programs. We have a lot of kids whose parents can't afford a lot for daycare. And I need to make them the priority at the moment."

Maggie smiled. "I think that's great. And the work seems like something you will love."

Jo nodded. She did love it. She needed to have that sense of helping others. And she loved working with kids. Seeing kids overcome and flourish even against such unfortunate odds. Nothing felt better.

For a moment her mind wandered again, straying to things she didn't want to deal with.

"Yep," Jo said, straightening in her seat, shaking off the sudden sweep of sorrow that filled her. "So St. Ann Community Center will be back on its feet in no time, as long as I can find some volunteers to help me."

"Can I get you ladies some drinks?" said a voice, deep and velvety and tinged with an exotic-sounding accent, from right beside her. Jo started, clapping a hand to her chest.

"Sorry," he said, smiling at her reaction as if it pleased him in some way.

Jo felt irritation rise in her chest, replacing the rapid beat of her heart. He probably thought she was affected by his sudden nearness. Because of some sort of uncontrollable desire, rather than genuine surprise.

She stared at him, trying to ignore the scent of him that managed to blot out the other smells of the bar. Something spicy, like burning incense, earthy and very arousing.

She immediately pushed back her stool and stood, making sure her vacated seat was between them.

"Nothing for me," she managed, then turned to her friends. "I have to run to the restroom."

She didn't look back or wait for her friends' reply as she hurried toward the back of the room and the door labeled LADIES.

Once inside, she leaned against the graffiti-scribbled wall, offering messages of "love 4 eva" and "for a good time call" and "New Orleans rocks!" She didn't pay any attention to the plethora of yearbook-like captions, and instead focused on trying to get her wayward body under control.

She was not attracted to that guy. She wasn't. He wasn't her type and while he might be handsome and sexy and even smelled like sex—really good sex—she wasn't going there. There was just no way in hell. Her life was already too complicated without another self-important, insincere and too-good-looking-for-his-own-good male in it.

And what was she doing thinking about men, period? Hadn't she sworn off them? Hadn't she just left D.C. because of a relationship that went horribly wrong?

She let her head fall back against the marker- and pen-scrawled wall. A wave of nausea hit her and she swallowed several times. Anger and disgust also threaten to gag her.

How could she even be attracted to anyone? Not when her life was in complete upheaval, and she was running away from her past. And her lover, who had somehow managed not to mention—and she'd managed not to notice—that he was married.

Chapter 2

Maksim glanced to where Jo had disappeared into the restroom, for the first time feeling just a tad hopeful that she did in fact feel something for him. He couldn't quite decipher what, but she had reacted, and he was taking that as a good sign.

Damn, when had he ever been the type to settle for any old reaction from a woman? He was used to adoration. Attraction. Full-blown carnal lust. Not a reaction that could range anywhere between tepid interest to overwhelming disgust.

Disgust? Over him? That seemed unlikely. But he wasn't sure. How irritating.

Instead of analyzing her reaction any further, he turned his attention to her friends, taking this moment to discover a bit more about the mortal who'd somehow become an odd fixation to him. A fixation that was increasing by the minute.

Did he mention he wanted to lick every inch of that woman?

"So did I just hear that your friend is working down here?" He kept the comment casual as he used a rag to wipe down the table. "Didn't she live somewhere else? Somewhere on the East Coast?"

"Yes, she just moved down here from D.C. about a month ago," Maggie said.

He noted that Erika frowned at her friend. Oh yeah, Erika wasn't going to give him any information. Which meant, go little Pollyanna vampire, go.

He smiled widely at Maggie, pouring on the charm. "So she's living here? Working here?"

Maggie nodded, completely oblivious to Erika's disapproving look. "Yes, she's the new director at the community center on Esplanade."

"That's great," he said with a smile designed to reveal nothing.

"I don't suppose you'd know anyone who'd be willing to volunteer there?" Maggie said, only to be cut off by a sharp shush from Erika.

Maggie frowned at her friend, confusion clear in her eyes.

"Volunteers," Maksim said slowly, his smile widening. Oh, he'd be willing to volunteer for a thing or two with sexy Miss Jo as his director.

Instead he shrugged. "Not right off the top of my head, but I'll think about it."

Maggie smiled. Erika frowned—even more if that was possible.

"So more drinks?"

Both women declined, which gave him no real purpose to hang around. Even though he would have liked to ask more about Jo, he didn't want to be too obvious. He excused himself and headed back to his prison behind the bar. Although tonight, it didn't seem quite so bad. Amazing what a new project could do for his outlook.

"What were you thinking?" Erika asked as soon as Maksim stepped back behind the bar.

Maggie blinked at her friend, confused by her question, but more so by the terseness of her tone.

"What?"

"Do you really think he's the kind of guy we should be asking about volunteers? Who would he know aside from other demons? Are you trying to get some minions from Hell to help Jo with her daycare?"

Maggie grimaced, seeing her point. "I didn't really think about that. With all the paranormal folks in this city, I sometimes forget the people around us aren't—well, really people."

Erika nodded. "I sometimes forget that about ourselves," then added, "But we shouldn't be giving him any info about her. He's very interested in Jo; it's in the air like cheap, really stinky cologne." Erika glanced at him. "It's like he's scenting, staking claim on her."

"Maybe he is." Maggie followed Erika's gaze, watching Maksim take a drink order from a buxom brunette in a dress that barely covered her equally rounded derriere. Then she added, "That *was* a stupid move. Sorry."

They were silent for a moment.

Then Erika said, "Do you think she even knows?"

"About us?" Maggie asked, not needing any clarification on who "she" was.

"No, about herself?"

"Oh. I'm not sure," Maggie said, then considered Jo and her situation. A very surprising situation to say the least. "But I don't think we can bring it up. We need to wait for her to do that."

Erika nodded.

Maggie sighed. "I really shouldn't have said anything to Maksim. I just figured given he had more access to daywalkers than we do, he might know someone. I know he's a dem—" Maggie's mouth snapped shut as she noticed Jo standing behind Erika. Erika must have seen the direction of Maggie's gaze, because she turned to glance over her shoulder.

"Hi," Jo said, not hiding her curiosity over the subject. "Who are we talking about?"

Jo waited for her friends to explain, finding the small bit she'd overheard quite—peculiar—to say the least.

"We're talking about Maksim," Erika stated. "Maggie told

him that you were looking for volunteers at the center, and I just didn't think that was a good idea. I don't trust him, Jo."

"I didn't think it was a big deal," Maggie said, although she didn't sound defensive, just contrite. As if she agreed that perhaps he wasn't terribly trustworthy.

Jo sat back down and gave her friends a comforting smile. "I don't think you have to worry about sharing that info with him. He doesn't strike me as the Good Samaritan type anyway."

He didn't strike her as the good anything. She fought the urge to look in his direction. Except maybe good in bed, and she knew where that type of guy got a gal.

"That's true," Erika agreed, and Maggie nodded.

They all fell quiet as the Impalers started another song, "I Want You To Want Me."

"So is that what you call us boring people with normal day jobs?" Jo asked suddenly over the chorus.

"Huh?" Maggie asked, and Erika raised an eyebrow in question.

"Daywalkers? Is that musician lingo for us boring people with nine-to-five jobs and regular sleep hours?" Jo said.

"Oh." Maggie laughed. "Yeah. That's just a private joke among the band members."

Jo nodded, then said after a few moments, "And you started to say that Maksim was a deem . . . A deem what?"

"Oh," Maggie said, looking decidedly awkward. She glanced over to Erika.

Again with the shared looks, although this time, it almost looked as if they were silently discussing their answer.

"He's a de—de—" Maggie gave Erika another pained look.

"A demon," Erika announced. "You know, with the women." She winced when she was done.

Jo glanced back to the bar, where Maksim stood, hands braced on the countertop, watching her. She wondered why her friends seemed so reluctant to say that.

"Oh, you don't have to tell me. I have no doubt."

* * *

"Girl, this is cracked. Totally cracked."

Jo finished entering in the last numbers into the community center's expense database. Then she blinked trying to focus on her daycare director, but impressions of small rows of numbers scrolling down her computer screen still blurred her vision. Even after several more blinks, she still couldn't see what her daycare director was talking about.

"What's broken now, Cherise?"

The woman placed a hand on her ample hip and rolled her dark eyes at Jo. "Nothing's broken! Except this whole teacher situation. Which is cracked!"

Jo sighed, realizing now what had Cherise all worked up. Cherise was the only full-time employee she had, and she was a darned good one, with the energy and patience of three women, but she wasn't three women, and she needed help.

"I got twenty-eight kids out there, and I can't do it alone."

Jo nodded, knowing full well that was the truth. She was amazed Cherise could do as well as she had been.

"I'll be right out to help," Jo said, sliding her glasses up and turning back to her computer to save her latest entries. Entries that revealed they were further away from getting another full-time daycare teacher than she'd hoped.

She clicked Save, and the ancient computer hummed and rattled and did this pausing thing that 50 percent of the time resulted in a total freeze-up.

"Mmm, girl, you can't take on director of this place *and* my assistant. That's two full-time jobs, and this place isn't ever gonna get ahead without you trying to get us some funding and finding volunteers and setting up better programs." Cherise raised an eyebrow after she was finished, as if daring Jo to deny those facts.

"I know," Jo agreed with a sigh. "But for now, we have to do what we have to do." She rose, a wave of lightheadedness making her catch herself on the edge of the desk.

"You all right?" Cherise took a step toward her, but Jo raised a hand to stop her.

"I'm fine. Just not getting enough sleep."

Cherise crossed her arms across her plentiful bosom and made a tsking sound. "Not eatin' enough, either, if you ask me."

Jo laughed. "I eat."

Cherise raised that dark eyebrow that spoke as loudly as the woman herself.

"But I'll eat more," Jo said dutifully.

She followed Cherise to the large room they used as the daycare "classroom." The walls were decorated with flowers and butterflies and bees that Cherise had made herself, probably three or four years ago. The edges were curled, the colors faded, but they were better than nothing. And Jo chose to see the curling as more of a 3-D effect than the signs of age.

She grimaced. Well, she *tried* to see it that way.

At several worn wooden tables, kids between the ages of two and five sat eating their snacks. Well, "sat" made the state of affairs sound orderly and peaceful, when in fact most of the kids squirmed and pushed and chattered away. Very little snack eating seemed to be involved.

Lettie, a woman who had to be eighty-five if she was a day and who was nearly totally deaf stood sentry over the wild scene. Occasionally she'd point to one of the children with a long, bony finger and gesture for them to sit down. The child would obey, for about a half a second, then he or she would be again wiggling off the bench, giggling and ignoring the old lady. Which, half the time, Lettie didn't notice anyway, because she was darned near blind, too.

But she showed up almost every day, and beggars couldn't be choosers. Which Jo repeated yet again to Cherise, when her full-time teacher muttered, "Damned, Lettie. The old bat is practically a mummy."

"Can't even leave to use the bathroom without all hell breakin' loose," Cherise said, then headed toward the two tables, clapping her hands loudly as she approached the kids. "Everyone find your places!"

As their drill sergeant had returned, the children found their seats and snacks, although there was still plenty of fidgeting and giggling.

Jo moved forward to pitch in. She wrestled with a couple juice boxes and drink straws. She opened a yogurt. She wiped a runny nose or two. As she moved around helping where she could, frustration replaced any sense of satisfaction in giving her assistance.

All Cherise managed to do with these kids was glorified babysitting. She just didn't have the time or the help to do projects with them. They colored and played in the courtyard. They had some puzzles and some games, but these kids needed and deserved a daycare that would get them ready for school.

Jo set the yogurt she'd just opened down in front of Damon, a particularly cheeky little four-year-old.

"I can't eat that," he informed her adamantly.

"Yes, you can," Jo said. She knew that Damon's mother was alone and every cent she had was precious to her. No food could go wasted, just because Damon was feeling contrary. She pushed the yogurt toward him and waited while he reluctantly picked up his spoon and dipped the very tip into the pink custard, then put it in his mouth with a horrendous twist of his face.

"Jo?"

Jo straightened, her heart grinding to a complete stop as she recognized the voice, even as she told herself she couldn't. Slowly she turned.

Maksim stood in the midst of the curled, faded flowers and bees, sporting designer slacks and a perfectly tailored shirt that showed off his flawless physique to a tee.

A slow smile unfurled over his equally perfect lips as he saw her shock.

"Hi."

Jo blinked. Was that all he could say? What the hell was he

doing here? Her first impulse was to shove him out of the shabby classroom that just managed to further showcase his utter perfection.

Instead she pushed at the edge of her glasses and scowled at him.

"What are you doing here?"

Maksim's smiled deepened as if she'd greeted him with warmth rather than shocked disdain.

"I was in the neighborhood."

Jo's scowl creased into a frown. Was he serious?

"Well," she said slowly since it was clear he'd lost his mind, and might have trouble comprehending. "I'm at work, so I really don't have time to chat at the moment." She jerked her head toward the children. For the first time since they'd arrived this morning, all their little attentions were focused on Jo and her unexpected visitor.

Leave it to children to pay attention when you don't want them to, Jo thought, praying they'd lose interest quickly. Of course, they wouldn't.

"Actually," Maksim said clearly undaunted by the miniature audience, "I really didn't just stop by for a visit." He smiled again, and held out his hand. For the first time, Jo noticed he held several papers.

She stared at them for a moment, then reached out to take the pages. Carefully, she studied them, flipping through one page then another then another.

She knew her eyes must have been the size of one of the flowers on the wall when she finally looked up at him.

He didn't wait for her to speak, or maybe he realized she couldn't.

"As you can see, I have plenty of experience working with—" he smiled at the kids, who still watched him as if he was a superhero come to life, "these little—fellas."

He reached out to scruff the boy closest to him on the head. He smiled broadly at the child, but Jo noticed this time it seemed a little more strained.

She continued to gape at him. He wasn't really saying he wanted to volunteer? He didn't really have experience? He couldn't. He just—couldn't.

"Let me see this?" Cherise appeared at her side, snatching the résumé out of Jo's numb fingers.

After a few seconds, she let out a low whistle. "Gorgeous and experienced." Her chatty little eyebrow rose. "You must have dropped right out of heaven."

Maksim grinned and extended a hand. "Something like that."

Cherise readily seized his hand, grinning back at him with moony, dark eyes as if she was half in love with him already.

The image of her no-nonsense daycare director practically deifying this man was the thing that snapped Jo out of her daze.

"Excuse me," she bit out to Maksim, roughly extracting Cherise's hand from his. She dragged the much larger woman out of the room, discovering strength she wouldn't have thought she had.

"What are you doing, girl?" Cherise said as soon as they were in the hallway.

"We are not hiring this guy," Jo stated.

"I know that."

Intense relief flooded Jo's body to the point she almost sagged against the wall.

"But we are sure as hell going to get him to volunteer until we can afford to hire him." Cherise leaned back to sneak a peek in the doorway. "Mmm, mmm, mmm." Her chatty eyebrow rose, again speaking volumes about what she thought of the man.

Jo couldn't help peeping around the corner herself, just in time for Maksim to notice her. He waved and she jerked back out of sight, this time allowing herself to lean against the wall.

"No," she said to Cherise. "No, no, no."

"Why ever not?" Cherise asked, which was a fair question.

And one that Jo couldn't answer honestly. She couldn't tell her daycare director that he couldn't work with her, because Jo was worried she was too attracted to him. How professional was that? Not professional in that least, that's how.

Cherise held up the list of places he'd worked and volunteered. Big Brother/Big Sister, a basketball coach for mentally handicapped children, a counselor at a camp for kids who were terminally ill.

"How are we going to find anyone better?"

Jo stared at the sheets. They weren't. He was a dream. He was.

"He isn't what he seems," Jo finally said.

"You know him?" Cherise's eyebrow said she was willing to listen if Jo had some facts about the guy.

"I've met him a few times before," she said, realizing that hardly sounded incriminating enough. Especially for the virtually perfect volunteer.

"So do you think these things are made up?" Cherise waved the paper slightly.

"Maybe," Jo said, grabbing onto that suggestion, although she again didn't sound as convincing as she thought she should.

"Well, they'd be easy enough establishments to contact."

Cherise was right. Of course. Her and her always accurate eyebrow.

Jo nodded, then took the résumé from her. She would tell him that she needed to contact a few of his past employers and then let him know. That was a reasonable way to get him to leave, and then, once she wasn't so completely discombobulated by his presence, she'd come up with a believable reason to reject his offer to volunteer.

Walking back into the room on legs that she hoped looked steadier than they felt, she crossed directly to him.

She forced a smile. "Maksim, this résumé is very impressive."

He nodded, and she noted his humble expression didn't quite meet his eyes. See, he *was* up to something.

"So—" She paused as she felt a tug on her arm. She glanced down to see Damon at her elbow.

"Wait just a moment, Damon," she told the boy.

She returned her attention to Maksim. "So, as I was saying—"

Again there was a tug on her sleeve, this time more insistent.

"Damon," she said, but stopped when she saw the boy's pallor and the expression on his face. Out of instinct, Jo stepped aside, just as the boy heaved. Vomit spewed from the boy's mouth in a flying spray, all of the chunky, foul-smelling stuff landing directly on Maksim's shirt and pants.

Jo stared, stunned, absently noting that at least Maksim's polished black Kenneth Cole shoes had remained unscathed.

Jo started to open her mouth to say . . . Well, she didn't know what, when nausea swelled in her own stomach. Then his expensive Kenneth Coles weren't so unscathed anymore.

She retched again.

Chapter 3

"I told you I couldn't eat the yogurt," the nasty little creature who'd just covered him in vile, slimy stench said almost smugly before the large woman, who Maksim was really beginning to like, whisked him away.

Couldn't eat yogurt was an understatement. The dreadful little beast had puked in Exorcist-sized proportions—all over one of his favorite shirts, no less. But Maksim's attention was drawn away from his soiled clothing to the woman who'd added to the disgusting mess.

Jo still stood in front of him. Well, stood implied that she was on her feet; it was more like she leaned heavily on the table where the children squealed and gagged and pointed at the disaster clinging to his $200 hand-tailored shirt from Milan and his $300 Armani trousers.

But he disregarded both his destroyed clothes and the creatures surrounding them, who sounded like a flock of agitated farmyard birds. Instead he stared Jo, a strange sensation he didn't quite understand making him feel—like he needed to help her.

Shake it off, man, he told himself. No piece of ass was worth this.

But instead of leaving, he reached forward to balance her. She jerked away, nearly slipping off the edge of her precarious perch. Even though she was stubbornly and stupidly avoiding his touch, he wasn't willing to let her fall.

Instead he pulled her to his side, keeping her away from the side Damon had covered, with more than just yogurt, he might add.

"Where's the bathroom?" he asked.

She gestured, with a weak wave of her hand toward the hallway. Maksim walked her in that direction, supporting most of her slight weight. His instinct was to carry her, but he suspected she'd really be irritated by that, and not just because she'd be unavoidably covered in what he was.

When he reached the hallway, he looked both ways, then spotted the door labeled GIRLS. He headed toward it, expecting to find the large woman in there with the little puke machine. But instead, the gray-tiled room was empty. He led Jo to the sink and held her until she seemed to have herself braced against the edge.

She stood there for a moment, her fingers gripping the white porcelain so tightly, they were nearly the same color.

"Can I get you anything?"

She shook her head, then winced as if the gesture caused her pain. If possible, her skin drained even further of color until she seemed to blend in with the gray and white of the lavatory.

"I just need a minute." For a brief moment, her dark eyes met his in the mirror. He saw embarrassment there, but also a flash of something else. Something that looked remarkably like despair. Then they dropped again, her focus returning to the sink that seemed to be the only thing holding her upright.

Maksim watched her for a second longer, making sure she was truly steady on her feet. Then he began unbuttoning his shirt, easing the ruined mess away from himself.

"What are you doing?"

Maksim paused, the garment off one shoulder, meeting her eyes again. "I'm getting out of this thing." He finished slipping out of the shirt and dropped it in the trash can near the sink.

When he looked back to Jo, she was still staring at him in

the mirror. He considered pretending not to notice, but he couldn't pass up seeing her expression.

But he didn't see in her eyes what he thought he would. Instead of surprise, or interest, or even disapproval, her gaze was flat, emotionless.

"You're not planning to take off your pants too, are you?"

"Not unless you want me to," he said, wagging his eyebrows, then added once she didn't react—yet again, "No, my pants aren't too bad. My shoes, however . . ."

That gained him a pained wince. "Sorry."

He shrugged. "Vomit happens." Had he really said that? Normally he'd be very, very unhappy about something like this, and an unhappy Maksim was a bad thing. But right now, all the could seem to care about was Jo.

Her eyes lingered on him a moment longer, then she realized he was watching her watching him. A slight flush of pink tinged her pale cheeks and she looked down.

Again, moving her head seemed to disorient her and her knuckles whitened as she held fast to the sink. He stepped closer, just in case.

She lifted one of her hands to the faucet, her fingers pausing there as if the act of just turning on the water was too much for her at the moment.

Maksim leaned forward, his bare chest brushing against her shoulder and arm as he placed a hand over hers and twisted the water on. The rush of water echoed through the stark room.

Her eyes moved back up to find his in the mirror. They locked for several moments, and he began to wonder if the loud rush reverberating through the room wasn't the swell of his own longing coursing through him like churning white water. His yearning and the look in her eyes, finally a spark of something, some response, left him coiled and breathless. And filled with a need to . . .

Immediately he dropped his hand from hers and backed away as if she'd scalded him.

"I'll let you freshen up," he mumbled and continued to

walk backward away from her. Her dark eyes followed him, that despair there again. Calling to him. Pulling at an emotion in him he didn't understand, but he knew he didn't like.

He turned and left the room.

Maksim didn't stop until he was outside the community center, standing on the cracked, uneven sidewalk, his breathing irregular, his thoughts jumbled. He'd finally gotten a reaction from her, but it wasn't the lust he wanted. It had been heartbreak, desperation, fear—and maybe lost somewhere in those emotions was a hint of attraction. So why in the world had that reached out to him, made him want to protect her? To make those feelings disappear? Help her?

A man in a dirty sleeveless undershirt and denim shorts tottered down the street. He grimaced at Maksim as he passed, revealing missing teeth and grime accenting his frown lines.

Maksim narrowed a look back, the vagrant's disdainful reaction snapping him back into his normal frame of mind. When was he *ever* the object of someone else's derision? He knew he was a superior species to these lowly mortals, and most mortals instinctively knew it too. How dare some filthy transient look at him as if he was beneath him?

Then he glanced down at himself. No shirt, vomit-spattered pants and shoes, and a look of complete bewilderment in his eyes.

What the hell? He was standing here, on the sidewalk, covered in stench, musing over a mortal woman like some uncertain teenage boy. And, damn, he was never uncertain—not when it came to his wants. Not about anything. And he'd sure as hell never been a teenager. So what the hell was wrong with him?

He made a disgusted noise deep in his throat as he glanced down at himself again. No piece of ass in Hell or on Earth was worth this.

He should just leave. But instead, he found himself striding to the side of the building and ducking into an alley that ran the length of the community center and the building next door.

He stopped and glanced over his shoulder. No one was around. Remaining very still, he closed his eyes and concentrated. He knew if anyone were to watch him, he'd look like an image in a camera going in and out of focus. An effect they'd most likely blame on their own vision. But there was no point in taking unnecessary risks.

When he opened his eyes again, his soiled clothes were gone, replaced by a new tailored shirt and designer trousers. His shoes were Roberto Cavalli. The defiled garments were on the ground around him. He carefully stepped over them as if they were a heap of vermin liable to jump up and cling to him. He'd loved that outfit, but it was replaceable. Most things were.

Being able to materialize things was one of his favorite demon tricks, although damned irritating at times, because he could only materialize things he actually had somewhere. Because, frankly, if he could materialize a stiff drink, he would.

He stepped back out onto the street, smoothing down his shirt, then adjusting the cuffs. Now, he'd go back in, remember why he came here. And it wasn't to help a wounded mortal.

It was to get laid.

Jo splashed another handful of water on her face, relishing the way the cold stung her skin, taking her mind off the events of the past few moments. She cupped water in her hand and lifted it to her lipes, rinsing her mouth again, swishing the cold water for several seconds. Then she splashed her face again. And again. She had to gather herself and get back out there to work, but she couldn't make herself leave the bathroom.

She just wanted to hide. To not deal with anything.

No, she had to get back to work. That would help. It always did.

One more splash, then she fumbled around for the paper towel dispenser, finding the lever and pumping it several times. She pressed the crumpled paper to her face, even appreciating the roughness of it on her cheeks and forehead. The discomfort of icy water and scratchy paper towels was something tangible to focus on, a welcome distraction from what had just happened. And she wished she was referring only to the vomiting. Because ridding her stomach of its contents on a man's ridiculously expensive footwear wasn't bad enough. No, she'd actually stood there doe-eyed as he'd taken his shirt off, wanting the man with every fiber in her being.

She nearly swooned when the man's bare chest had come in contact with the skin of her arm. She'd longed for him to wrap his muscular arms around her and hold her and kiss her and . . .

And what? Take care of her? Make her past disappear? That wasn't going to happen.

She tossed the damp towel into the garbage can near the sink on top of Maksim's soiled shirt. The image of him peeling it off flared in her mind, hard muscles covered in smooth, golden skin.

She straightened, taking a deep breath, pulling herself together. This was ridiculous. She moved to the mirror to tuck loose hair back into the knot on the back of her head and wipe away any remnants of water-smeared makeup.

She pulled her glasses out of her pocket, hoping the dark frames would distract from the worst of it. She dropped her hand and stared at her face, not seeing herself, but Maksim. The memory of his reflection staring back at her. The look in his eyes.

She could have sworn she saw tenderness in his stunningly vivid eyes. She looked down at her hand. The hand he'd held as he'd helped her turn on the water. His touch had been gentle, kind.

Her gaze lingered on her hand, which tingled. From the water, she told herself. Then she frowned at herself in the mirror. What was she doing? She couldn't think of him as some gallant knight who'd come to her rescue.

He wasn't that. She knew it. She did know his type. Only too well.

But for a moment . . .

"Enough," she growled, the word echoing through the tiled room.

Get a grip.

Pulling in a deep breath, she realized as much as she didn't want to see him, she had to muster up her courage and go apologize to the man. She'd apologize, and then tell him that, while his résumé was impressive, she just didn't have a position for him.

She couldn't have him around. It wasn't possible. And if she was lucky, he'd already left and she could just call him to tell him all this anyway. She doubted he was waiting around out there shirtless and covered in barf.

How would she explain that to her daycare parents?

And that was what had to be her focus. The center.

When she walked back into the daycare room, Cherise had somehow managed to get the floor cleaned and the children on their threadbare mats for nap time. Even Damon was calm and lying with his favorite toy, a tattered dog with one missing eye. Lettie sat in a metal chair at the now vacant tables, her chin on her chest, dozing. She enjoyed nap time most of all.

"Are you feeling okay?" Cherise asked in a hushed tone.

Jo nodded. "For some reason, seeing what happened—just got to me."

Cherise nodded. "A chain reaction. It happens to the best of us."

Jo nodded, appreciating the woman's gesture to make her feel less mortified.

Jo glanced around again, relief flooding her.

"Did Maksim leave?"

"No, I'm right here."

Jo spun to see him behind her, leaning on the door frame leading to the hallway. Damn, couldn't, just this once, luck be on her side?

Her eyes scanned down his body, taking in his newest collection of designer apparel.

"I had clothes in my car," he said, in response to her lingering stare.

Her cheeks burned. She'd wished that was what she'd been pondering, when in truth, her mind had moved on to the way the cut of his shirt accentuated the broadness of his shoulders and chest and how his pants emphasized the narrowness of his hips. Even his feet caught her attention.

She forced herself to meet his gaze. One of his dark eyebrows rose as if he could read her mind and knew she hadn't even wondered where he got the new clothes.

Great, another one with tell-all eyebrows. He and Cherise could probably hold a whole conversation with nothing but movement of their brows.

"I'm—I'm glad you had—some—other clothes to change into." She clenched her teeth briefly, irritated with her fumbling speech. *Just get out what you need to, and then get back to work.*

"And I'm sorry for . . ." There she went again, stammering. "For getting sick on you."

Maksim shrugged. "No big deal. That sort of thing happens."

Jo nodded, then pulled in a breath, preparing herself for what had to be done. For her sanity.

"And I'm very impressed with your résumé—"

Maksim nodded and again with the raised eyebrow. This time it said, "But of course."

"But," she said, trying to keep her voice steady and firm, "I just don't have any positions at this time to offer you."

Jo waited for Maksim's indignant response, but he never even got a chance to react. Instead it was Cherise's outraged voice that responded.

"What?" Her voice was loud and sharp enough to cause a few of the children to stir on their mats. She bustled away from the kids, joining Jo and Maksim.

"Have you gone crazier than a gull at a crawfish festival?" she asked in a hushed but no less emphatic tone.

Jo frowned at her employee, really wishing in this case, she'd just let her eloquent eyebrow do the talking for her. And even then, only *after* Jo had gotten rid of Maksim.

No luck of any sort was on Jo's side today, because Cherise added, "We don't have room for him? Look around here. We got nothing but room."

Jo's frown deepened, and she willed Cherise to just stop. Stop talking. Stop standing with her hands on her hips, which meant she wasn't messing around. Stop looking at her like she was an utter fool. To just stop.

Instead of stopping, the feisty eyebrow joined in, arching so high it nearly touched her hairline.

"If you don't take this guy on as a volunteer, I'm going to let Lettie handle free-choice centers from now on."

Jo's mouth dropped open. Now that was low. Free-choice centers was the wildest part of the day for the children. They got to move from learning station to learning station and without proper supervision it was utter chaos. Not an easy time for Cherise and Jo to handle—impossible for the nearly catatonic woman slumped in the chair over there with her mouth wide open and a steady snore emitting from it. The children would destroy the place. Given the hands on the hips and the sky-high eyebrow, Jo didn't think Cherise was bluffing.

Jo turned back to Maksim. He watched them, a smirking, closed-lip smile turning up the edges of his mouth. His vivid green eyes sparkled.

He was loving every minute of this.

Oh, she could not do this. She couldn't let him have a position here. She stared at him for a moment, trying to think of any loophole, any possible out, that neither he nor Cherise could debate.

Nothing came. His résumé was impeccable. He'd handled

the whole upchuck fiasco with grace. He wasn't giving her any reasonable flaw to back her decision.

She was stuck. With a résumé like that . . .

Wait . . . that *was* one heck of a résumé. A dream résumé, really. He had to have faked his past work experience and references. He had to have.

Her initial opinions of him couldn't have been so far off. He *wasn't* a knight in shining armor.

Her eyes narrowed as she regarded him, taking in the newly changed, crisply clean, still expensive, still designer name clothing.

If this guy had ever worked with a kid in his life, then she wasn't just the director of this community center, but of the whole freakin' world.

He'd made the whole thing up. She knew it.

She smiled back at him, feeling in control for the first time since he'd stepped foot in the center.

"Cherise is right. How can I possibly turn down such a great candidate?"

Maksim's smile deepened, although she couldn't quite read the look in his eyes.

"Well, I am glad you came to your senses, woman," Cherise stated, her hands no longer on her hips.

"Me, too," Maksim said, his rich voice low, but drawing Jo's attention back to him as surely as if he'd shouted.

Jo's heart sped up, and something simmered warm and intense in her belly. She gritted her teeth, forcing the feeling aside.

"So, I'll give you a call tomorrow to iron out your schedule, and what works best for you," Jo said, keeping her voice aloof and all business.

"Any time works for me." Again his voice was low and sultry washing over her like the humid Louisiana heat.

She nodded, determined not to let him see she was reacting to him. Damn it.

Finally, after none of them had said anything for several seconds, Maksim nodded.

"See you tomorrow, then."

Jo opened her mouth to tell him she hadn't said she'd *see* him, but that she'd call him. Then she decided against it. He'd find out soon enough that she'd guessed at his little deception.

A Good Samaritan—yeah, right. He was looking to get laid and had no problem using small children and the goodness of others to do so.

She wouldn't see him tomorrow or ever again, if she had her way.

And she would.

Chapter 4

Maksim already had his cell phone in his hand, when it began vibrating and then playing his ringtone—"Highway to Hell." He knew he wasn't going to have to wait long for the first call. He'd seen the moment when realization and then satisfaction had glittered to life in Jo's dark eyes. She thought she'd found a way to get rid of him, legitimately.

"Hello, Maxwell Edison speaking," he answered easily, all traces of his natural, deep, accented voice gone. He waited, just a tad anxious.

This was the only dicey part of his plan. He was going on the assumption that Jo would just go down the list of references in exact order. He could tell she was a systematic person. A person who liked tidiness and control. Well, he liked control, too.

So, right now, it was good he had it.

"Hello, Mr. Edison. My name is Josephine Burke. I'm the director of the St. Ann's Community Center in New Orleans."

Maksim liked the sound of her full name. "And I was just calling to check on a reference submitted by a Maksim Kostova, who is interested in volunteering for us."

"Oh, Maksim, how is he?" Maksim concentrated on the task at hand and manipulated his voice, making him sound a fine Southern gentleman. "He's truly missed here at the Chattanooga branch of the Special Olympics."

"He appears to be—fine."

Maksim wondered what she really wanted to say. Not fine, he was sure. He smiled.

"Well, Ms. Burke, I can safely give you one of my highest recommendations for Maksim."

There was a pause on the other end of the line, then she said, "Thank you, Mr. Edison."

"No, thank you. And please give my regards to dear old Maksim."

Another pause. "Yes. Of course."

Maksim hung up the phone. Demons did have all sorts of neat little tricks, such as changing voices, changing appearances. The phone, however, had actually been a little trickier, and certainly more mundane. He'd had to purchase other numbers and then set those numbers up to be forwarded to his regular cell phone number. He didn't have that much faith in his cell phone provider, but so far so good.

Clearly he was too obsessed with this woman. Phone redirecting and fraudulent résumés were way beyond the usual effort he made for sex. But he just knew Josephine—and he did so like her full name—Josephine Burke would be worth the effort.

The phone vibrated, then ran again. This time he stepped off the street into an alley, before answering. A 6'3" man emitting a perfectly female voice was bound to gain some attention out on the sidewalk.

"Good afternoon, Sunshine Hills Day Camp. Loretta Martin speaking."

This time Maksim gave his voice a more clipped New England cadence.

Again, Jo gave her little spiel.

When Maksim spoke again, he couldn't help softening the clipped tone to one of fond remembrance.

"Oh, Maksim Kostova, my, my. Of course, I'd be glad to recommend him to you. Do I ever miss that man."

Jo made a noise on the other end of the line in response.

Maksim grinned. This was fun. Jo clearly felt something for him. He wasn't quite sure what, but he was going with attraction and maybe a little jealousy.

"He was the best—and I mean best—volunteer we've ever had here."

There was a pause. "Great. That's all I needed to know."

But Maksim couldn't resist adding, "Tell him I'd love to hear from him."

More dead air, then a slight cough on the other end. "I will do that. Well, thank you for the information, and have a good day."

Maksim flipped the phone closed. Maybe he shouldn't have made ole Loretta so obvious, but he couldn't resist.

A few moments later the phone rang again. He half-expected Jo to give up on the last reference, but he should have guessed she wouldn't. He could already see that wasn't her personality.

"Good afternoon, Eleanor Rigby."

Maksim's newest female persona was met with silence. Uh-oh, perhaps he was getting too heavy handed, both with his praise of himself, and also with having all his fake names stolen from Beatles tunes. Eleanor Rigby. That was definitely heavy handed. He should have gone with Desmond or Molly Jones. More subtle.

Well, that would teach him to concoct elaborate plans to get laid whilst listening to his sister's vast Beatles collection.

But after a minute, Jo spoke. "Hi, yes, I'm calling to inquire about one of your past employees. His name is Maksim Kostova."

This time Maksim paused before answering. "Maksim Kostova." He pretended to ponder. "Hmm, oh yes. Maksim

Kostova. Let me see, I believe he worked in our organization from . . ." He pretended to ponder again, then said in his best kindly old lady voice, "I believe it was 2002 to 2006. Maybe 2003."

"You were correct the first time." Jo sounded very disappointed.

"That's right. Yes, he did a wonderful job for us. He was a team leader for our mentoring program. Just great with the kids. A hard worker. We were very sad to lose him."

There was another of Jo's pauses. "It sounds like he will be perfect for us, then."

Maksim waited for amusement and delight to hit him, but they didn't. Instead he was almost—sorry. The resignation in Jo's voice wasn't what he wanted to hear. She didn't want him there. She didn't want him around her, period.

"Well, thank you for your time." Jo's voice pulled him out of his thoughts.

"You're welcome," he managed to say, catching himself before his voice slipped back to normal. Her end of the line went dead.

He stared at his now silent phone, looking at it as if the small device was something he'd never seen before.

What he was doing was wrong.

Then he snapped the phone shut. Of course it was wrong. He was a demon, damn it. Demons were not known for their good deeds and moral fortitude. He was the ruler of the Eighth Circle of Hell. Not Dudley-Do-Right.

Slipping the phone into his pocket, he smiled and headed back to the street. She'd come around. They always did. It wasn't as if she wouldn't enjoy herself once he got what he wanted. She'd love every minute of it.

He'd show her the best time of her life. And surely, that made up for the uncertainty she was feeling now.

So, see, in a strange way, he was doing a good deed.

Maksim whistled to himself as he strolled back to his sister's apartment.

Jo stared down at the résumé. That hadn't gone at all as she'd hoped. She'd really believed these references were faked. I mean-Eleanor Rigby-really? Now she just felt rather stupid. And egotistical, too. Had she really believed he'd gone to such great lengths just to be around her?

Maybe she was too jaded. She couldn't spend her whole life assuming all men were like Jackson. But she could have sworn Maksim was a chip off the same block. He had the same air about him as Jackson. The designer clothing, the confidence that bordered on outright conceit. The surety that he could have whatever he wanted.

And God knows Jackson never would have volunteered his time. Oh, he'd have donated money—then he could claim altruistic motivations. But get his hands dirty? No way. Jackson wasn't into things getting too messy. She knew that very well. Somehow he always came out smelling like roses. While others cleaned up his messes.

She sighed. No matter how hard it was, she'd been lucky. She'd escaped a real disaster with that man. She was still dealing with the aftermath he'd helped create, but at least she wasn't going to have to deal with him. The liar.

Her attention returned to Maksim's résumé. With her fingertip, she traced the place where he'd signed the cover letter. His penmanship curled and sweeping, but unquestionably masculine.

Maybe she was putting too much of Jackson on Maksim. It really was the ultimate in arrogance to believe this man falsified references just to get to her.

She shook her head, chuckling to herself. Clearly Jackson hadn't wounded her ego that badly.

And Cherise was right. Turning down someone as experienced as Maksim would be utterly stupid and self-defeating.

They needed help. So she was going to let her own feelings about the man go. She had to give him a chance. This could be a changing point for her. A real way to get the center going on the right track.

Really, Maksim Kostova, now she knew his full name, could be a godsend.

Chapter 5

"**D**o you even know what you're doing?"

Maksim paused, focusing on where the tiny angled straw was supposed to fit into the small rectangular box labeled JUICY JUICE. He narrowed his eyes as the bane of his existence gazed up at him with wide, dark eyes.

Damon, the puker, blinked innocently. Pure evil hidden behind youthful artlessness.

"Yes, I do," Maksim muttered, returning his attention to the stupid little box. How hard could this be?

"It goes right there." Damon reached up and tapped a dirt-caked finger on the top, and Maksim was glad he didn't have to drink the juice after this kid had repeatedly touched it. Maksim just hoped that grimy fingernails didn't make him vomit like yogurt had.

"I showed you yesterday," Damon said, then followed the statement with a long-suffering sigh.

Maksim gritted his teeth and shoved the straw in as if he'd known where to insert it all along. But as he jabbed it into the tiny foil-covered hole, clear, sticky juice gushed out of the bent straw, covering his hand and the cuff of his sleeve.

Damon giggled. "I told you to cover the end of the straw too. You suck at this."

Maksim glared at him, then shoved the juice in the kid's

direction. The little boy accepted it, still sporting a pleased smile.

Maksim suppressed a growl.

"How are things going?"

Maksim whipped around to find the reason why he'd decided to engage in this stupid plan standing in the middle of the room. Or course the reason was becoming more distant with each passing minute.

This was the first time he'd seen Jo since agreeing voluntarily to interact with these vile little creatures known as human children. It was truly a wonder that humans didn't eat their young. And to think he wasn't even getting paid for his hell.

But amazingly, things looked much better upon the appearance of Jo. And he now easily recalled what his payment would eventually be, and it was something far more appealing and pleasurable than money.

His eyes wandered slowly over Jo. The light green sundress she wore swished around her long shapely legs and displayed the curve of her bare shoulders.

Oh yeah, he suddenly remembered why he was here. Covered in fruit punch, and snot, and grimy handprints. Okay, he was still a little bitter, but Jo would so—so—make it up to him.

"Ms. Burke," Damon called, before Maksim had even gathered his thoughts enough to respond to Jo's question.

Jo immediately turned her attention to the small boy, walking over to the table, where he sat looking all wide-eyed naiveté. The little deceiver. Maksim had nothing on this kid.

"Mr. Kostova doesn't even know how to open my juice even after I told him yesterday."

"Is that so?" Jo glanced at Maksim, her eyes twinkling with amusement.

Children were evil.

But even as he thought that, not for the first time today,

Maksim forced a sheepish, yet boyishly charming smile onto his lips. "I must admit, I've never been good at those things."

Jo's eyes flickered just briefly to his mouth. Then she met his gaze, her dark eyes unreadable as usual.

"Not a big juice-box-drinker, huh?"

Maksim chuckled, making sure the sound was rich and full, designed to vibrate deep inside her. "No, not often."

He smiled charmingly again.

Jo smiled back, although a little tentatively. But he realized that was the first genuine smile he'd ever received from her, which suddenly made the awful events of the morning much more tolerable.

"Things are going great," he said, returning to her original question. He took a step toward her, half expecting her to back away, but she held her ground.

Jo smiled back, the gesture still reserved, but the smiles were coming more readily. Perhaps he would be able to charm her more easily than he'd thought. Though why he'd doubted that fact seemed silly to him now. He was a demon—he had good looks, and deceit on his side.

"How is your day going?" He took another step toward her.

"Great," she said, her eyes flicked down at the space between them, clearly gauging how close she'd let him get. "I've been able to get a lot of paperwork done."

He would imagine that was true. She'd been sequestered away in her office, door closed, for two days now. He wondered how much of her disappearance was work and how much was just avoiding him.

"Maksim is doing great," Cherise called over to Jo from where she helped some of the other kids with their lunches. "The kids just love him."

Maksim had to admit he liked Cherise. She was sarcastic, outspoken, a blatant flirt, and still his biggest advocate. What wasn't to like?

And Cherise spoke the truth. The children did love him. To

torment him. To crawl him all over him. To talk incessantly to him in lisps that were virtually impossible to understand— if he'd really wanted to, which he didn't.

Again he plastered on a smile. "They are great kids." His lying skills were usually impeccable, but his declaration sounded insincere, even to him.

Jo didn't show any signs of doubting him. Again she gave him a smile. Man, he was doing well today.

"Well, I thought while the children were busy with lunch, I'd go over what days and hours you'd like to help out. It would be easier for me if you had a set schedule, if that is okay with you?" Jo said.

In her office. Alone. Oh yeah, he'd love that.

"Great," he said.

Jo nodded, then headed toward the hallway. Without looking back, she led him to her office.

The room was tiny, which he liked. The tight space brought him into a much closer proximity to her. The only pieces of furniture in the room were a rickety, cheaply made desk with an ancient-looking computer on it. An equally old office chair covered in worn, ugly, brown tweed sat on one side, while two metal folding chairs were positioned on the side closest to the door.

Spread on the desk were several piles of paper, revealing that while she may have been avoiding him, she was busily working, too.

She gestured to one of the gray metal chairs as she slipped around the desk. He sat down, the metal creaking under his weight. She braced both hands on the arm of the desk chair and gingerly eased herself down.

"The hydraulics are broken," she said by way of explanation to his look. "Sometimes it just drops."

He nodded, not really interested in the chair. He was far too distracted by the delicious scent of her permeating the room—a warm, inviting perfume like vanilla and cloves that made his mouth water and his muscles tighten with need.

He fisted his hands on his knees as he looked at the pale gold skin of her bare arms, imagining that her thighs were the same color. Her belly paler, her breasts, too.

A hungry growl rumbled low in his throat, but he caught himself and disguised it with a cough.

"Are you okay?"

"Just a little tickle," he said, coughing again for effect.

She nodded, then turned her attention to her computer. Her fingers, which were long and elegant with short nails and no-nonsense clear polish, moved easily over the keyboard, somehow looking graceful even in such an ordinary action. He imagined those same fingers gliding over his bare skin, touching him everywhere.

His erection, which had risen as soon as he'd stepped into the room and was surrounded by her scent, pulsed in his trousers.

"Just give me a minute here," Jo said as she frowned at the computer, clearly willing the archaic machinery to perform whatever action she wanted. Then she bit her bottom lip, and all his attention was on her white teeth sinking into the pink pillow.

He wanted to nip the soft, rosy flesh there. He wanted to bite her all over, to feel her skin under him, against him, around him.

"Maksim?"

He snapped his attention back to her, and away from his very vivid and very naughty fantasies of nibbling every inch of her body. He'd just reached her inner thigh, too—damn it. But he pushed the image away, which was not easy, and said, "I'm sorry. I missed that."

Jo shifted in her seat and crossed her legs as if she knew what direction his thoughts had been headed in. South—very deeply south.

She shifted again. "I've made up a calendar for the remainder of this month. What days were you thinking you'd like to come in?"

He offered her a small smile, intended to put her at ease,

but then followed with, "What days do you want me?" the words said quietly, full of innuendo.

Pink tinged her cheeks, but her features remained unaffected. Maybe she wasn't going to make this easy. And maybe that's why she fascinated him so.

She turned her attention back to the monitor, but not before he noticed her pulling in a slow breath through her nose. That could be trying to get her reaction to him under control. Or annoyance. He wasn't sure which.

"Well, we could use your help any day. It's really whatever is best for you."

"Hmm," he pretended to consider. "Let me take a look."

Before she could respond, he rose and came around to her side of her desk. She pushed her chair to the side, offering him space, but the cramped quarters wouldn't allow her much distance. He watched as she tucked away a strand of hair, which had fallen free from the loose bun at the back of her head. Her hand returned to the desk, fidgeting with the edge of the keyboard.

He wished he knew what was making her so antsy. Oh, he knew it was his nearness, but was it because she didn't like it, or she liked it too much?

For a fraction of a second, he considered going into her head to find out. He hesitated, standing at the edge of her mind like a stranger outside a fenced property with a NO TRESPASS-ING sign posted. Even with the warning, he could scale the railings and jump inside. But just like with trespassing, there would be consequence. Not for himself, but for her.

For once he heeded the warning. Instead he did lean down, letting his shoulder bump hers. His cheek just inches from hers.

"Hmm." Again he pretended to consider the calendar. When in fact he was breathing in her scent, taking it deep in his nose and lungs like a powerful hit off an opium pipe. He held it there, then slowly blew out.

His breath touched her, ruffling that strand of hair that had fallen loose again. Her fingers fiddled more quickly with the edge of the keyboard. She lifted her other hand as if to touch the stray hair his breath just touched, but caught herself. She pushed up her glasses instead.

Maksim grinned. She wasn't oblivious to him. He leaned in closer, pointing to the screen.

"I could do every morning." He turned to her, his mouth now just inches away from hers. "If you would like."

For just the briefest moment—if he'd blinked he would have missed it—her gaze flicked to his lips. Then her eyes shot back to meet his. They were so dark brown they were almost black. Pink colored her cheeks further.

"What—what about your job at the bar? Aren't you going to be tired?" she managed to say, her voice sounding a little breathy.

"It will be fine. I don't require a lot of sleep. And being here is very satisfying to me." Or it will be. And very satisfying to her, too.

Again her eyes flashed to his lips, then she gave up looking at him altogether and turned her focus to the computer.

"Of—of course, the center would love the help," she said.

He smiled. Oh yeah, this would definitely lead to his satisfaction.

"Great. Then I will see you every morning." Every night, too.

Jo breathed in slowly through her nose. What had she just agreed to? Seeing this man every day? She pulled in another slow, even breath, telling herself to shake off her reaction to this man's proximity.

Sure, he was attractive. And he had—a presence. But she wasn't some teenage girl who would fall to pieces under a cute boy's attention. Not that cute was a strong enough word for what Maksim was. He was—unnerving. To say the least.

But she wasn't interested in him. She decided that quite definitely over the past two days. Of course that decision was made secured away behind her closed office door.

But either way, she should have more control than this.

Apparently *should* and *could* were two very different things. And she couldn't seem to stop her reaction to him. Her heart raced and her body tingled, both hot and cold in all the most inappropriate places.

"So every morning?" he said, his voice rumbling right next to her, firing up the heat inside her. "Does that work for you?"

She cleared her throat, struggling to calm her body.

"Yes—that's great," she managed to say, surprising even herself with the airiness of her tone. "I'll schedule you from eight a.m. to—" she glanced at the clock in the lower right-hand corner of the computer screen, "noon?"

That was a good amount of time, getting Cherise through the rowdy mornings and lunch, and giving him the go-ahead to leave now. She needed him out of her space.

If her body wasn't going to go along with her mind, then avoidance was clearly her best strategy. And she'd done well with that tactic—although she'd told herself that wasn't what she was doing. *Liar, liar, pants on fire.*

"Noon is fine," he said, still not moving. Not even straightening away from the computer. And her.

"Good," she poised her fingers over the keys and began typing in his hours. "Then I think we are all settled. You can take off now if you like."

When he didn't move, she added, "You should go get some lunch. You must be hungry." She flashed him a quick smile without really looking at him.

This time he did stand, but he didn't move away. Instead he leaned against her desk, the old piece of furniture creaking under his tall, muscular weight.

"You must be hungry, too. Would you like to join me?"

She blinked, for a moment not comprehending his words, her mind too focused on the muscles of his thighs so near her.

The flex of more muscles in his shoulders and arms as he crossed them over his chest.

She forced herself to look back at the computer screen.

"I—I don't think so," she said. "I have a lot to do here."

"But surely you allow yourself a half-hour lunch break."

She continued typing, fairly certain whatever she was writing was gibberish. "I brought a lunch with me, actually." Which was true. Not that she was hungry at the moment. She was too—edgy.

"Come on," he said in a low voice that was enticing, coaxing. "Come celebrate your first regular volunteer."

She couldn't help looking at him. He was smiling, the curl of his lips, his white, even teeth, the sexily pleading glimmer in his pale green eyes.

God, he was so beautiful.

And dangerous.

Jo shook her head. "I really can't."

He studied her for a moment. "Can't or won't? What's the matter, Josephine? Do I make you nervous?"

Jo's breath left her for a moment at the accented rhythm of her full name crossing his lips. But the breath-stealing moment left as quickly as it came, followed by irritation. At him and at herself.

She wasn't attracted to his man—not beyond a basic physical attraction. And that could be controlled. It could.

"You don't make me nervous," she said firmly.

"Then why not join me for lunch?"

"Because," she said slowly, "I have a lot of work to do."

Maksim crossed his arms tighter and lifted one of his eloquent eyebrows, which informed her that he didn't believe her for a moment.

"I don't think that's why you won't come. I think you are uncomfortable with me. Maybe because you are attracted to me."

Again the eyebrow lifted—this time in questioning challenge.

"That is ridiculous. You are so not my type."

Maksim shrugged as if her rejection didn't bother him in the least. It probably didn't. Men like Maksim knew other women were only a charming smile and smooth line away.

More irritation rose in her chest—even as she told herself she should be thankful that he was accepting her dismissal so easily.

"Well, if I'm not your type, then lunch should be no big deal. Just some shared food and company between coworkers."

She almost pointed out that she was in essence his boss, but caught herself. Now wouldn't that sound petty? And defensive—and she wasn't on the defense.

"No, thank you." She shifted in her chair, attempting to dismiss him completely.

"I think you are uncomfortable with me. And if not because you are attracted to me, then why?" he said, as if just pondering the theory aloud. He didn't move.

Finally, after it was clear he wasn't going to leave until he'd sorted out a satisfactory solution in that far too pretty brain of his, she let out an annoyed groan. She rose, her body brushing briefly against his as she did so. She ignored the shock wave of awareness, and pushed her chair in with a little more force than necessary.

"Fine. I'll go to lunch with you."

"Great," he said.

But Jo didn't miss his smug smile as he moved around the desk toward the door.

Why did she have the feeling she just got totally played? Played right into his little plan?

Chapter 6

Maksim walked beside Jo, trying to keep the self-satisfaction out of his tone. Really, he was jumping the gun, being too overconfident. Oh, he knew he'd get what he wanted—eventually—but Josephine Burke was a tough cookie. She still wasn't acting like she was ready to fall into bed with him. He'd just barely gotten her to go eat a meal with him.

He was making headway—and frankly he was finding the chase fun. But only to a certain point. He wouldn't be patient forever.

"So do you have a favorite place around here?" he asked.

"I don't really know," she said. "I haven't been here long enough to explore much. I haven't really had the time, either."

"You've been working a lot, then?"

She nodded. "Yes."

They both fell silent for a few moments.

"How about you? Do you know a good place?"

"Sure." If there was one thing he knew, it was food. And frankly, it was the only thing he liked about New Orleans. "I know a place just a couple blocks from here."

He took the lead, picking his way around the broken and uneven patches on the sidewalks. He glanced back to make sure she was okay. Her cheeks were flushed from the heat. Stray locks of her long, dark hair clung to her sweat-dampened skin, bringing to mind what she'd look like after he'd spent a night pleasuring her.

The vivid picture of that eventuality slipped away as he noted the way she was carefully picking her way along the rough, eroded concrete, her open-toe sandals making the sidewalk even more precarious.

He slowed his pace and opened his mouth to ask her if she was all right, when the toe of one of his Ferragamos hooked on a jagged piece of concrete. He caught himself, but not before Jo grabbed his arm to help steady him.

"Are you okay?" she asked, seeming to steal his quesion from his mouth.

Maksim nodded, but his mind whirred. When was he ever clumsy? When did he trip? That answer was easy. Never. Well, never until this moment.

But he'd been distracted. By Jo. And not just a sexual distraction, either. He'd been concerned for her—so concerned he wasn't paying attention to what was most important. Himself.

He paused, trying to comprehend what the hell was going on. And he studied Jo. She was a lovely woman—for a mortal—tall, elegant with dark eyes that seemed slightly sad and soulful. Her lips were neither too wide nor too thin. But they were prettily shaped, bowed at the top, fuller on the bottom. And when they turned up in a real, unguarded smile, his heart pounded in his chest and he filled with delight.

Annoyance rose up in him like a flash flood. Anger with himself and with Jo. When did he consider things like what a woman's smile did to him? He was a tits-and-ass man. He liked pretty faces and rockin' bodies. He gave great thought to how they would feel wrapped around him, naked. Not at the melancholy in their eyes.

What was the deal with this woman? Why was she having this effect on him? He was admittedly as shallow as they came. His attraction never bordered on poetic and protective.

"Are you sure you are okay?" Jo touched his arm, the first

time she reached out to him in anything resembling friendship. It should have pleased him, but all he could think was something wasn't right here. Something was different and dangerous and unnerving about this woman.

But when she didn't remove her fingers, some of that agitation left him. Her fingers were warm and gentle on his skin. Soothing.

But only for a moment, then raw need filled him, and he found that response more comforting. Normal.

He mustered up a sheepish smile, even though he was still feeling uneasy. "I'm fine, just feeling like a klutz."

Jo smiled. "I can't believe it wasn't me. I trip over my own feet. And these sidewalks are treacherous."

Maksim forced his smile to deepen, even though concerns still plagued him. But he did feel unadulterated lust, too. A good sign. To comfort himself further and to keep his mind on the goal, he looped her arm around his.

"I guess it's good you agreed to accompany me. I clearly need the help." He gave her a wink.

She smiled, shaking her head at his flirting. But she must not have found it threatening, because she didn't pull away; instead, she fell into step with him.

He smiled down at her, giving the gesture all his charm. Okay, so he was reacting to her more than he did other mortal women—other females in general—but that just meant that he wanted her badly.

Keep your eye on the goal, boy. That's all that matters.

"Here we are," he said stepping into an alcove and opening the door.

"This is lovely," Jo said looking around the open courtyard, which was filled with greenery and flowers, as she pulled out her chair. Maksim moved around behind her, holding the chair for her, pushing it in as she sat.

"Thank you," she mumbled, glancing back at him just for a second, but once again he couldn't quite read her reaction.

He took the seat to her right. Not across from her—that

was too far away. And he wasn't messing around anymore. He didn't have the time to waste. Obviously he wasn't going to be able to function normally until he'd nailed this woman.

Even as he used the rude, impersonal term, his mind rebelled against it. He wanted to have sex with her, that was for certain—but . . .

He gritted his teeth. He was doing it again! Just stay focused. It didn't matter what he called it as long as he got this woman in his bed.

"The menu looks great," Jo said, drawing his attention away from his strange debate with himself.

He hadn't even opened his own. He did, making himself concentrate on his second-favorite thing after sex. Food.

"Do you come here often?" Jo looked around again, smiling appreciatively at the greenery and quaint appeal of the place. "It's so beautiful."

He glanced around, too. It *was* lovely here and made lovelier by Jo's presence.

Stop it!

"A few times," he said, studying the menu—gathering his idiotic wits. "The walnut chicken salad is delicious. Great raspberry dressing."

She made an approving noise, then snapped her menu closed. "That's what I'm getting. It sounds wonderful."

Maksim watched her as she took a sip of her water. She really was beautiful—and his desire for her bordered on desperation.

"It is wonderful," he agreed. Then he smiled, offering her the brunt of his charisma. "I'm so glad you decided to join me. And agreed to let me help at the community center." He lifted his water glass in a toast.

Her smile slipped slightly, easily picking up on his shift to supercharming. Not the reaction he'd hoped he'd get. But she did join him, clinking her glass against his.

She took another sip, regarding him over the rim, for once her eyes easy to read. She was uncertain. Not the emotion he wanted—but better than the closed-down, shut-away look she could get.

Some of her guard had dropped with him, but it was on a hairpin trigger and could shoot back into place in the blink of an eye.

He shifted in his chair, subtly pulling back, giving her space. "How did you start working in this field?"

Jo leaned back a bit, too, unconsciously relaxing along with him. Her reaction gave him hope that he wasn't totally out of control. He could still manipulate the situation to suit him.

"Well, I double majored in social work and education in college with a minor in English," she said.

He whistled, honestly impressed. "Very industrious."

Jo shrugged. "I've always liked to keep busy."

"I'd say."

"I worked as an English teacher for many years in Washington D.C. I was also a student advisor at a private secondary school."

"A private school. That sounds a lot cushier than St. Ann's Community Center." As clearly motivated as she was, why would she take on a job that would never pay a large salary nor raise her to a prestigious position?

As soon as the words were out, he regretted them, suspecting they would put her on the defensive. But to his surprise, she laughed.

"Oh, it was definitely cushier. But I really needed to get away—" She let her words just end, hiding it behind taking a sip of her water, and Maksim knew she'd been about to say something she'd rather not.

"I, umm, just really needed a change," she finally said. "And I also needed to do something that made me feel more fulfilled. Truthfully, teaching *Macbeth* and *Beowulf* to overprivileged, overindulged kids wasn't rewarding in the least."

"So struggling to get help and money from a community that doesn't care does fulfill you?" This time he clearly didn't keep the derision from his voice, because Jo's smile faded into a frown.

"Of course it's fulfilling. These kids need that community center. They need an advocate. They need the volunteers—like you," she said pointedly. "And I need to know I've made a difference in the world." Her frown deepened. "I mean, isn't that why you've done the things you've done?"

For a moment, the "things" he'd done popped into his mind. None of them for the betterment of humanity. None of his actions designed to make a difference to anyone but himself.

"Well, yes," he said, though. "Yes, of course that's why I do the things I've done."

Something akin to guilt made it hard to swallow, but he did, forcing it down with a smile.

She regarded him for a few moments, then turned her attention to the waiter, who appeared with a wrapped loaf of warm French bread. They placed their orders, although Maksim couldn't have said what he got.

What the hell was wrong with him? Why did her desire to make a difference, and his utter disinterest in doing so, bother him? He shouldn't be giving it another thought. So she was a "save-the-world" type. He should be just hoping that meant she'd be more than generous in bed. And he'd make her feel very, very fulfilled.

Maksim cut off a piece of the bread, offering it to her. Jo accepted with a mumbled thanks.

They both ate silently. Maksim focused on Jo; she focused on her bread, her water, anything but him.

"Did you like living in D.C.?" he asked, grasping for any topic of conversation when he realized she wasn't going to speak first. And seduction just didn't work when the person you were trying to seduce was more attentive to a piece of French bread than you.

"I did, yes."

She didn't continue, and Maksim knew there was more to the story than her short response was revealing. But as had been the case since meeting this woman, he couldn't read her features. Had she left simply for a change? Or had she left because she had to leave?

Somehow he didn't think prying would get him any further toward what he wanted from her. Still he did wonder, was it something that had happened back there that made her dark eyes appear melancholy so often?

"Did you grow up there?" he asked, avoiding the more interesting question of why she left.

She shook her head. "No, I actually grew up in a small town in western Maine."

"Was that nice? It must have been beautiful—and cold. I like cold."

She smiled at that. "It is very beautiful—and definitely cold." The topic of her hometown seemed to be a good and safe one, because she continued, warming up to the subject of her childhood and life in Maine, talking even as the waiter left their lunches.

"So you pick blueberries with a rake?" Maksim asked in between bites of his crawfish étouffée, after she told him about her multiple summers spent doing something called "blueberry raking."

"No," Jo said with an impish smile. "You pick blueberries with your hands. You *rake* blueberries with a rake."

Maksim smiled back, enjoying her relaxed demeanor. The way her lack of wariness allowed her dark eyes to glitter with humor and delight. The way she used her hands to tell her story, animated, uninhibited. The way her smile made her whole face light up. No melancholy, no reservation.

And he wouldn't delve back into why he liked all those things so much. He was enjoying himself too much to overanalyze.

"Okay," he said slowly, trying to comprehend such a strange thing to do as a job. "So you use this rake, and what? Rake them into a pile?

"No!" Jo laughed. "I've already explained this twice."

Maksim shook his head, giving her a perplexed look. "I just can't imagine there isn't a better way to get blueberries."

"Well, there isn't. You use this rake, which has tines and a metal back. You slide the tines under the bush and pull up." She imitated the action to clarify. "The berries come off in the rake and gather at the metal back."

"Are you sure?"

Jo laughed again, the sound rich and warm, circling around him like the fit of a perfectly tailored suit. "Yes!"

Maksim laughed, too, realizing he wasn't even pretending to enjoy her story like he so often did with women he planned to seduce. He liked her company—how odd.

"I think you've made this up," he said, grinning.

"I haven't." She smiled, too, as she speared pieces of her salad and popped them into her mouth. She chewed merrily.

He watched, feeling something—so strange. A tugging at his chest, at his gut.

She took another bite of her food, clearly enjoying it.

"I like a woman who likes food as much as I do." Maksim almost groaned at his comment. If he did know one thing about human females, they did not like men—or anyone, really— to remark on their eating habits. Especially that they *liked* food.

Jo finished chewing, and Maksim waited for her annoyance.

Instead she speared more of the salad, dripping with the delicious raspberry dressing. "Food is one of my favorite things."

She popped the lettuce, chicken, and dressing into her mouth and chewed with relish.

He laughed.

She smiled, mouth closed around her food, letting her eyes drift shut to show just how much she did indeed love to eat.

Instantly Maksim's mind alit with flashing images of her under him, her eyes shut, an orgasm making her arch and writhe against him. Legs splayed, wrapping around him.

His laughter stopped, desire ripping through him with an intensity that was breath-stealing.

Jo opened her eyes, her own amused expression fading as she met his gaze. He knew she saw the unrestrained longing there, but he couldn't seem to temper it. The need was just too powerful.

She swallowed, but didn't break her gaze away from his. They stared at each other, him wanting her, her aware of that fact.

Nothing in her expression gave away how she felt about his obvious desire. Not even a hint. Her face was placid, emotionless like a doll's, waiting for him to react.

Finally he did. He reached down to his lap for his napkin. Raspberry dressing glinted pink and shiny on her lower lip. He touched the corner of his napkin to the spot, wishing it was his mouth on her berry-flavored lips, instead of a stiff piece of fabric.

At first she didn't move, allowing the contact. Then his thumb strayed away from the napkin, stroking the soft curve of her bottom lip. At the touch of skin to skin, she jerked back, her chair squeaking on the flagstones at the abruptness of her movement.

She pressed her own napkin to her mouth as if to blot out the brief, grazing caress.

"Did I get it?" she asked, her voice frustratingly even and unemotional.

And something inside Maksim snapped. He couldn't handle her indifference any longer. Without a second thought, he entered her mind, ignoring the NO TRESPASSING sign, scaling the fence surrounding her thoughts and emotions.

Chapter 7

Jo's head spun from Maksim's slight touch, nothing more than a fleeting brush of his thumb against her lip. Probably accidental at that. Certainly nothing to warrant such a strong reaction, but she hadn't been able to stop herself. She had to pull away. It made her think and want things she absolutely couldn't.

She tried to stay calm, to react normally, but as soon as she'd asked him if she'd gotten whatever was on her lips off, her head started spinning even more.

Now she couldn't seem to focus her eyes. The restaurant shifted and blurred around her like she was peering through a kaleidoscope. She braced her hand on the table to ground herself. But that didn't seem to help.

She closed her eyes, not daring to open them for several seconds. When she finally did, she saw Maksim watching her. His own face bleached of its natural healthy color as if he was feeling the same nauseating vertigo. Confusion clouded his peridot-green eyes. And he continued to study her as if she were a complete stranger unwelcome at his table.

But instead of asking him what was wrong, she used the edge of the table to help herself stand. She didn't understand his reaction, but she couldn't focus on that.

Nausea churned in her stomach, threatening to make her retch.

"I need to use the restroom," she mumbled, glancing around for a sign to point her in the right direction, finding it on the far side of the courtyard. She didn't wait for Maksim's response as she headed that way, weaving slightly.

Once inside the ladies' room, she leaned heavily on the bathroom door, pulling in a gulping breath to calm her roiling stomach. She remained that way for several seconds, then straightened again, using the wall to balance herself.

Moving carefully, afraid another wave of nausea would hit her or she might jar her head more, which still felt muddled and heavy, almost as if she had somehow gotten a concussion, she made her way to one of the stalls.

Shoving the door closed behind her, she again propped herself against the stall wall. She closed her eyes, willing herself to calm down. The nausea had subsided, thank God. But her head. She pressed a hand to her temple. What a strange feeling as if her brain was too—full.

She rested there for a moment, eyes still closed, not moving.

Finally the strange sensation dwindled slowly away. Still she didn't move. She wasn't ready to go back out to Maksim. She didn't want to face him. Embarrassment replaced the nausea—just a different type of sick feeling. Embarrassment and dread.

She knew she'd seen desire in his eyes. She knew he wanted her. While that was awkward, what was worse was that she wanted him, too.

With just the likely unintentional brush of his thumb, she'd wanted him with an intensity she couldn't deny. Just that easily. What the hell was wrong with her? She prided herself on willpower. On control.

Although she couldn't recall why now. She hadn't been in control of anything for so long, she wondered if she'd only imagined her restraint. Look at her, she was in this restroom, fighting yet another bout of nausea, because things were happening to her that she couldn't alter.

She wasn't going to think about any of this right now. She was going to get herself composed. She was going to go out there and thank Maksim for a nice meal. And she was going back to work. That was the best strategy.

She ran a shaky hand over her face, but didn't move. Instead she rested her forehead on the stall door. Just another moment.

After a few seconds she heard something. Like the pattering of bare feet on the tiles. But she hadn't heard the door open.

Frowning, she lifted her head. And she could have sworn the three-stall restroom was empty. Even in her agitation she'd managed to make note of that. Maybe she'd been wrong.

She stepped away from the door slightly, listening. The footfalls had stopped. Jo held her breath, a sudden shiver of apprehension making her skin tingle and hair stand up on the back of her neck.

The bathroom was freezing, she realized, trying to slough off the strange sensation as just that, a matter of temperature. Cold tiles and humming air-conditioning.

Then she heard another movement, like an impatient shuffle. Carefully, silently, Jo backed away from the door more, until the backs of her legs made contact with the toilet.

She stared at the door, waiting. Her breath held, her heart racing.

This was ridiculous. She should just call out and see if anyone was there. Or just exit the stall. She opened her mouth to ask who was there, but no words formed. She willed herself to reach for the latch on the door, but her hands stayed limp at her sides.

When, after a few seconds, she heard nothing more, she bent just a little, peeking out underneath the door as much as the narrow stall would allow. Underneath, a few feet from the door, she saw small bare toes. Bare feet, just as she thought, facing her stall.

Real fear filled her, even as she tried to tell herself she was being ludicrous. It was a child. Probably nervous, maybe because she's being allowed to go to the bathroom by herself for the first time.

But without shoes?

Well, that was apparently the case, and surely lurking in her own stall wasn't putting the child at ease. Still Jo couldn't seem to bring herself to move.

Just as she'd managed to raise one of her hands and start reaching out slowly for the latch, the feet turned as if to exit the bathroom. Jo stared at the crack between the door and the stall wall. A flash of dark hair and multicolored clothing crossed past the narrow gap. Rainbow stripes.

A chill coiled down her spine like a long, creeping snake. She shuddered, watching the space around the door. She listened. No sound. No footfalls. No opening of the door. Nothing.

She forced herself to release her pent-up breath, blowing out long and slow. Then she flicked the lock open, her hand darting out and jerking back as if she expected something to grab her.

This is crazy. She was acting crazy.

But as with the lock, she shoved the door, then braced herself for something to jump at her. But the restroom continued to be silent.

She stepped out of the stall and looked around. White sinks that could have used a better scrubbing lined the wall beside the stalls. Gray and white tiles covered the floor and walls. A trash can threatened to overflow with crumpled brown paper towels. A paper towel dispenser hung on the wall—with an empty roll inside. And nothing else.

No child in rainbow clothing. No one.

She frowned, still searching, looking under the half-closed doors of the other two stalls. Had she imagined everything?

Was that part of the nausea and the strange ache in her head?

Great, hallucinations were just what she needed—as if she didn't have enough to contend with. Jackson, her new and still changing life, Maksim.

Oh no, Maksim. He was probably wondering what happened to her. Well, that made two of them.

She glanced around one more time, realizing that some of the bone-deep chill had left her. As the coldness seeped away, so did some of her fear.

She didn't want to stay there any longer, however. She hurried to the door, her sandaled foot slipping, and she caught herself on the door handle. Water, she immediately realized. Probably from people washing their hands, and being forced to shake them dry, because there were no towels.

She looked down. Yes, water. But not splattered drips like one would expect from wet hands being shaken dry. Each puddle had a form, a distinguishable shape.

Small, wet footprints.

She yanked open the door and dashed back into the restaurant, pausing just briefly to get her bearings. Spotting Maksim, she beelined right to the table.

"I—I just realized that I need to get back to the center," she told him without any pretense of composure or good manners.

She expected him to argue, to ask if she was okay, to tell her to have a seat and finish her meal. He only nodded, his thoughts clearly miles away.

Some of her anxiety faded at his distant reaction. He'd been trying to win her over, to charm her. What happened?

Then she reprimanded herself. She didn't want his interest in her. He just made her altogether too stressful life even more so.

"Okay," she said. "Let me give you some money toward lunch."

"No," he said, his voice sharp and abrupt. Then he added more softly, "I've got it."

"You're sure?"

He nodded again.

"Okay. Thank you."

Another nod.

She hesitated, feeling like there should be more to say, but then she gave up. She couldn't take any more weirdness. She just needed out of there.

"Bye, then."

"Bye." The word was mumbled vaguely as if he was back to that place miles away.

Maybe he was experiencing the same strangeness that she had. Maybe. But she didn't care, honestly. She wanted to be back at the center, surrounded by the noise and bustle of the children, back to worrying about finances and volunteers and new programs. Not feeling—frightened.

Maksim watched Jo weave her way through the maze of tables like a professional barrel racer. He should have stopped her, tried to get inside her head again, but he'd been too stunned. What had he just happened?

Not anything he'd ever experienced before. He'd entered Jo's head—and there had been nothing. Just a blackness. Not an emptiness like she didn't have any emotions, any memories. It was a like a veil, a thick haze that he couldn't see through. He couldn't reach through.

"Are you done, sir?"

Maksim frowned at the waiter, taking a moment to comprehend his question.

"Oh. Yes. We're done."

The waiter picked up the plates and told Maksim he'd be back with the check, but Maksim already paid no attention to him. What was different about Jo? He'd never had that happen. So was it about her? Or maybe it was him.

Maybe his powers weren't working correctly. That had never happened before, either, but he supposed it was a minute possibility.

To check, he focused on the waiter, who was now heading back to the kitchen, his hands full of dirty dishes. Maksim concentrated, then ducked into the kid's head for just a brief moment. Long enough to know the kid was bored, ready for his shift to be done. He needed to stop at Walgreen's after work for some condoms. Which he hated to use. But he did want to get it on with his new girlfriend, a girl he'd met last week at a place called Krazy Korner. And she wouldn't do it without a rubber.

Maksim stole back out, before he got a clear look at the kid's impression of the girl. Just a brief snippet of short shorts and tall, black boots. Maksim didn't want to stay too long. He didn't want to mess up the kid's head too much, which it invariably did.

As it was, the poor guy had dropped one of the plates he was carrying the moment Maksim had hopped in his head. The remainder of Jo's salad spread across the flagstone, a jumble of greens and dressing and broken glass. Much like the muddle of thoughts going on in Maksim's own head at the moment.

So his powers weren't faulty. The kid's brain had been like an open book, or more accurately a wide-screen television. The images had been clear, easily accessed like channels flipping to offer one glimpse after another of his thoughts and feelings. So why hadn't that happened with Jo?

Maksim didn't wait for the waiter to return with the bill. He was now busy cleaning up the mess of the dropped plate and wondering what had just come over him, and why his head felt so strange. And Maksim didn't have time to waste— even though technically the mess was his fault.

Maksim stood and fished in his pocket. Pulling out a hundred-dollar bill, he dropped it on the table. That would more than cover the meal and compensate the kid for the extra mess.

Maksim strode out of the restaurant, heading north on Dumaine Street. He didn't slow his pace until he reached the row of shotgun houses lining both sides of the street.

He stopped in front of the one painted pink with faded green shutters the color of mint ice cream. The trim work was pale yellow. Leave it to his sister to live in something that looked like it should be out of a fairy tale. Or an Easter basket.

He rooted around in his pocket for the key. Once inside, the gingerbread house colors didn't end. The front room was lavender with gold brocade furniture, leading into a short hallway the color of blue cotton candy.

He dropped his keys onto the coffee table and headed down the fluffy blue hallway, walking into the one somewhat palatable room in the whole place, Ellina's study.

He flipped on the light. At least the walls here were a tolerable shade of deep orange that was only mildly reminiscent of living inside a pumpkin, but did manage to look decent with the dark oak bookcases and desk.

Across her desk were all the notes and papers she'd been working on when she disappeared. His sister was a writer. Research books about the occult. With a distinct focus on demons. Go figure.

But he didn't go to her desk. He'd been through all her notes so many times in his search for her that he knew they wouldn't have the answer he needed right now. Instead he went to her bookshelves, scanning the titles. *Demons For Dummies*. Nice, Ellina. *Demonic and Loving It*. Maksim shook his head. *The Everyday Guide to Demons*.

He grabbed that one. Then he spotted one called, *Demons: Their Abilities and Their Downfalls*. That could be of use. Of course, it did bug him that his sister, half demon herself, thought it was wise to give the human world insights into the downfalls of demons. Couldn't she let them believe they were all-powerful?

Ah, well, in this case, he needed some insight into his own downfalls, which until today, he would have said he didn't have. Maybe Ellina had researched what was going on with him. Because in all of his existence, Jo was the first mortal he hadn't been able to read.

He flipped to the back of the book, running down the index. *Trapping. Banishing. Cleansing a demonically possessed item.*

He checked the index several times, but nothing she mentioned actually addressed the quandary within the demons themselves.

"Lot of good this will do me," he muttered, tossing the book on the floor. "I know how to banish myself back to Hell."

He thumbed through the other book with no more luck than the first. Not for the first time he wished Ellina was just here.

He paused looking through the book and glanced around the empty room.

Where are you, Ellina?

He needed her, and not just to help him with this dilemma. He was worried about her. More than worried. But so far all leads had ended up going nowhere. So he stayed here and waited.

Feeling helpless was not something a demon handled well. He hoped Ellina had at least put that fact in one of her books. Because he was feeling decidedly helpless about his sister. And about Jo.

Why would Josephine Burke, a mere mortal, have the ability to keep him out of her head? He didn't understand. And why did this particular woman keep bringing up previously unknown feelings?

Whether he wanted to admit it or not, Josephine Burke was affecting him like no one else ever had.

He suspected if he could just have her, then things would calm inside him. Clearly the oddity of not being able to read her mind wasn't curbing his desire for her.

Seduction was still his plan. In truth, he knew he was helpless to take any other course of action.

Chapter 8

"You do know you should go home, don't you?"
Jo looked up from reviewing the grant proposal she'd started and restarted several times. So much for her determination to concentrate on her work. She'd been staring at the same paragraph for—well, who knows how long.

"Have all the parents come to get the kids?"

Cherise nodded with an indulgent smile. "Hours ago. Now Mary is here with a few others to set up the room for Wednesday Night Bingo."

"Oh, good." Jo acted as if she wasn't unnerved by the loss of time, but she was still shaken about the event of lunchtime. She'd also completely forgotten that tonight was one of the events for the older adults.

It was only the second week the event had been implemented; one of Jo's first ideas for fund-raising and something to get the older adults back to the center. She supposed she could forgive herself for forgetting about it. If that was truly why she'd forgotten.

"You're leaving now, too, right?" Cherise said pointedly.

"You know, I think I will stay and work on this a bit longer."

Cherise grimaced and her hand went to her hip. Jo readied herself for one of Cherise's blunt lectures.

"Girl, you've looked like hell all afternoon. And you've been acting all sorts of strange."

"I know." Jo didn't bother to deny it. She had no idea how she looked, but she knew she'd been acting weird.

She'd been unable to completely dismiss or shake off that eerie feeling that had overcome her in the restroom. Even though she had mostly managed to explain away what she'd seen as a confused child who was too scared to use the restroom by herself.

With bare feet. Which were wet.

This was New Orleans—and Jo had already seen far weirder things than wet, barefoot children in a restrooms.

As much as she'd fixated on the odd event in the restroom, she'd obsessed more about her reaction to Maksim's brief touch. Her whole body had sparked to sexual life with that innocuous brush of his thumb on her lip.

And no matter how she broke it down, the reaction did not please her. She'd wanted him. Desperately.

And then add the nausea and the strange headache, and well, she was sure none of it had done wonders for her behavior. Or her appearance.

"I think you'd better get some rest," Cherise said, then held up her hands, guessing Jo would reject her suggestion. "I'm just saying."

Jo smiled, appreciating the woman's concern. "I'll head out in a few minutes. I promise. I'm just going to finish this up."

"Good," Cherise said, "because you've got the coloring of an uncooked beignet. Get some rest."

Jo wasn't sure what an uncooked beignet looked like, exactly, but she knew it wasn't good. Not in this instance.

"When was the last time you got a good book, went outside, took in a little sun, and relaxed?" Cherise asked in a motherly tone.

"I could ask the same of you," Jo said. Cherise often stayed as late as Jo, and usually was the first one here in the morning.

"Well, all the stresses of this place don't fall on me. I just handle the kids."

"No small feat."

Cherise's eyebrow indicated that she wasn't going to be one-upped away from her point. "I'm not playin' here. You need to get some rest. Real rest."

Jo nodded, quietly accepting that truth. "I will."

"Okay, I'm trusting you on that."

"Good."

Cherise shook a finger at her. "Don't stay too late."

"I won't." Jo laughed at her friend's doggedness.

Again the eyebrow shot up, stating she didn't believe Jo in the least. But then the larger woman bustled away, muttering something about "damned stubborn people" as she went.

Jo smiled, appreciating the concern. And Cherise was totally right. Unfortunately, taking on St. Ann's hadn't allowed much time for relaxation. And while she could go home and work on this in the morning—because of Maksim's help with the kids, ironically—Jo just didn't believe she'd get any quality rest.

Her mind was just too agitated. And despite the creepiness of the restroom incident, it was Maksim who kept popping into her head. So she thought it best to just keep busy.

Of course, forty-five minutes later, it was clear that work wasn't going to be the solution to calming her circling thoughts. Sighing, she saved her document, booted down her computer, and gathered her things. She didn't want to go home, but sitting here, staring at her monitor, fingers positioned over the keyboard but never moving, wasn't doing her any good.

She flicked off the lights and locked her office door. As she passed the main gathering room, gray-haired men and women sat at the tables where the children had been earlier. More tables had been set up as well. All full.

Well, at least one of her programs was going well.

The attendees had several bingo cards lined up in rows in front of them. They squinted with concentration as Mary called the numbers. Then their gnarled hands would fly over the cards with astounding speed as they punched the numbers they had with fat, round markers designed solely for the purpose of this pastime.

"Bingo!" one of the men shouted, grinning like he'd won the multimillion-dollar lotto. He waved the card over his head in victory.

Jo smiled, feeling a little better. Bingo might not seem like a major achievement to most people, but Jo saw it as a step in the right direction. The more she got people into the center, the more they would realize what a valuable resource they had—right here in their neighborhood.

Another person, a woman this time, with white, white hair and dark skin, yelled out "Bingo!" wiggling in her seat like one of the preschoolers who'd sat there earlier today.

Jo laughed at the woman's glee. She watched for a moment longer. Mary spotted her and waved. Jo waved back, then headed to the front door.

Humidity nearly bowled Jo over as she stepped outside. It was only May; she could only imagine what the heat and humidity were going to be like in July and August. Of course, D.C. could be pretty darn uncomfortable during the summer months, too.

Even with the events of the day, Jo was still much happier to be here then back in that city—where everything reminded her of Jackson. Now talk about uncomfortable.

Glancing up and down the street, allowing herself to acclimate to the heat, she debated what to do. She glanced at her watch. It was nearly seven. Was she hungry? She should be. Lunch was hours away now, and she hadn't eaten much of it before everything went very strange.

But she didn't seem to have much appetite. She'd force the issue later, if necessary, which it frequently was these days. For now, however, she was going to walk and see where that led.

After wandering for a while, window-shopping, she stopped into a convenience store to get a bottle of water. Even though the heat was oppressive, she still couldn't bring herself to go home.

Instead she sipped her water and strolled to Jackson Square. Finding an empty bench, shaded from the setting sun, she sat and watched the tourists ambling past. They browsed the artwork being hawked by local artists and wandered in and out of some of the shops lining the square. Residents hurried along with more determination than the visitors, heading to work or to meet friends or just wanting out of the sticky heat. Fortune-tellers under beach umbrellas sat in lawn chairs at card tables, waiting for their newest marks.

Jo watched over the top of her bottle as a young woman, about college age, who was traveling with several other friends, approached one of the fortune-tellers. The older woman in a multicolored caftan and rings on every finger greeted the girl with a motherly smile and gesture for her to sit down. The girl did.

Jo watched, trying not to make a face about the scene. The college kid was just doing it for fun. A cool thing to tell others about when she returned to wherever her hometown was. And Jo shouldn't care.

But Jo didn't like things like that. The occult always freaked her out. She told herself she wasn't a believer, but she still found things like psychics and mediums to be very unnerving.

After all, who really wanted to know the future? That was a terrible burden. A terrible burden.

Jo turned her attention to a woman dressed up like a fairy in a red tutu with black and silver wings. Her face was painted in dramatic makeup with false eyelashes, pale powder, scarlet rouge and lipstick, then the whole effect brushed over with iridescent glitter. She posed on a wooden orange crate, remaining utterly motionless, a living sculpture. At the base of the box was an open violin case, waiting for tourists to throw in change.

At first, Jo considered the woman's attempt at entrepreneurism quite absurd. As she watched her hold her position for minute after minute in the muggy, relentless heat, Jo reassessed her initial thoughts. That was a tough way to make a buck.

Absently she wondered if the woman really played violin, even though she didn't see any instrument, just the case. Jo took a sip of her water, then debated going to get the fairy girl a bottle of water, too. The poor thing had to be miserable.

Jo stood, deciding that while *she* would rather have the water, the fairy would probably prefer a buck or two. As she walked toward the street performer, if the woman could really be called that, Jo opened her purse and rummaged around for a couple dollar bills.

She glanced up, just long enough to make sure she didn't run into anyone as she searched. It was also long enough for something unnerving to catch her eye. A fleeting glimpse like a flash on a television screen. A child with dark hair clad in rainbow stripes, thin arms, and legs bare.

Her head snapped back up, but she saw nothing. Tourists wandering past the statue girl, some regarding her with interest, others more captivated by the square itself. Jo spun, taking in all of the square, searching but seeing the child nowhere. She'd looked back up too quickly for the child to disappear, to run down a crossroad, or slip into a store. It was just fractions of a second, but she wasn't there.

She imagined it, she told herself. She had to have. Someone else's clothing reminded her of a rainbow. That had to be the case—she just *thought* she saw something.

That was all. She shivered.

Picking up her pace, she tossed the dollar bills in the fairy's violin case, then she hurried down St. Ann. She didn't want to go home. She needed to be with her friends.

Still peering around herself as if she expected the child to reappear at her elbow, she doubled her steps until she came to the large barnlike door that led to Maggie and Erika's court-yard.

They'd given her a key when she first moved here, which she hadn't used. They'd even offered for her to live in Ren's apartment house, which was quirky and now charming, a renovated historical building that had once been slave quarters and a carriage house.

She'd never considered taking them up on the offer, because she'd felt a little like she'd be an intruder on their wedded bliss commune, and that just wasn't where she wanted to be after the bombshell of Jackson and his own wedded, albeit not blissful, state.

Now she wished she'd accepted the offer. The idea of going back to her empty apartment did not appeal. Not when she was having these weird hallucinations. How did she even explain what she thought had happened without sounding nuts? And so what if the images had been real? It was just a kid. Hardly worthy of getting all creeped out about. But she was creeped. Something about the image of that little girl was so familiar. So eerie.

She twisted the key in the lock, then shoved the heavy door open with the aid of her shoulder. Entering the courtyard always made her think of what it would be like entering the lush inner bailey of a castle. Gardenias, azaleas, and magnolia trees were all in full bloom, the scents mingling into a heady mixture, reminding Jo of sweet perfume and romantic, breezy summer nights.

She tugged the door closed and relocked, then rubbed a hand across her sweaty brow. What she'd give for a breeze. She turned to look at the carriage house straight ahead, then the first-floor apartment to the left. Both places were quiet, all the windows dark.

Jo had been pretty sure that Maggie and Erika wouldn't be up yet, but she thought it was worth a try. They lived their husbands' schedules now—which made sense. Maggie played with the Impalers a few nights a week. And Erika's job as a sculptor gave her the freedom to work whenever she wanted. Their schedules didn't do Jo any good now.

She considered knocking on their doors and seeing if she could wake one of them up, but then she thought better of it. Instead she wandered over to the wrought-iron patio table situated under the sweeping limbs of the magnolia. Collapsing into one of the chairs, she pulled another one over and put up her feet.

Her feet were a little swollen from the heat. Again, how would it be in the full heat of the summer, and when . . .

She frowned, looking in the direction of the vacant apartment. She thought she heard something. She listened, then saw a small bird hopping around in the leaves, searching for food.

Smiling, she relaxed back in her chair. She didn't feel the apprehension she had earlier. That was good.

She supposed that now that she was sheltered in her friends' beautiful, lush courtyard with said friends, while asleep, nearby, her fears seemed rather silly.

She rested her head on the back of the chair and let her eyes drift shut. Suddenly she was exhausted, which happened to her nearly every day of late. A wash of bone-deep fatigue that siphoned away all her strength. And today had been particularly stressful and tiring.

She must have dozed, because she was groggy and confused when something brushed against her leg. Another brush, and she started, suddenly wide awake. She pulled her legs up onto the chair, terrified.

Then she laughed, the sound abrupt and surprised, as the culprit, Erika's moody black cat, wandered leisurely into view, sitting down and watching her with eyes that glowed golden in the waning light.

"Well, hello, crazy thing."

She leaned forward to scratch the side of the feline's neck. He angled his head, offering her better access. Jo smiled, surprised the temperamental beast was allowing the attention.

She rubbed the cat for a few more seconds, then straightened up, stretching the sore muscles in her lower back. She was a mess—dog-tired, sore, apparently a nervous wreck.

Raising her hands over her head, she stretched, angling her head from side to side to get the kinks out of her neck. As she dropped her arms, she spotted her.

A pretty woman with long wavy black hair and pale eyes and skin stood on the other side of the courtyard, watching her from the growing evening shadows. Jo sat up, peering at the woman.

"Hi," she called.

The woman tilted her head as if she didn't understand what Jo had said. Then she looked behind her as if she thought Jo was talking to someone else.

Jo frowned, finding the woman's reaction strange. Who was she? Had Ren rented out the apartment he'd originally offered to her? He must have—the courtyard doors were locked now and had been when she arrived.

"Are you renting the upstairs apartment?" she asked.

Again the woman looked at her as if she didn't understand. Maybe she really didn't speak the language. So Jo pointed to the upstairs. "Do you live up there?"

The woman followed her gesture, but didn't respond. She did, however, step closer, and Jo had to reassess her initial opinion of the woman. She wasn't just pretty, she was stunning.

"I'm Jo," she said slowly, emphasizing each syllable, feeling a little stupid, because she still wasn't sure if it was a matter of the woman not comprehending her. Although what else could it be?

The woman's eyebrows drew together as she studied Jo. Then she gestured to herself, patting the base of her throat. She opened her mouth to speak, but no sound came out. Not even a rush of air.

"You can't talk," Jo said with dawning understanding.

The woman touched her throat again, and nodded.

The poor woman.

Just then, the door to the carriage house opened behind Jo. She turned in her chair to see Maggie coming out, still wearing a pair of silky red pajama bottoms and a matching cami.

"Jo, what are you doing here?"

"I just came to visit before you all head to work. But everyone was sleeping, so I just decided to relax out here."

Maggie joined her at the table.

"And I was meeting your newest tenant."

Maggie frowned. "Who?"

"Your newest tenant." She gestured toward the place where the woman had been standing. But she was no longer there. Jo peered around the courtyard, searching for the woman. She was nowhere.

Maggie looked around, too, clearly trying to understand what Jo was talking about.

"We don't have a new tenant," she finally said to Jo. "It's still just Erika, Vittorio, Ren, and I living here."

Jo studied the shadows and vegetation for a moment longer. "But I just saw a woman in here. Long dark hair, pale skin."

Maggie gave her a quizzical look. "I don't know. Unless she wandered in off the street somehow, she shouldn't be here."

Jo stared at Maggie, not really seeing her friend. She had seen the woman—as clear as day. She'd interacted with her.

What was going on? Was she losing her mind?

"I guess I must have—dreamed it," she finally said to Maggie. "I—I did doze off for a bit."

Maggie nodded, giving her an understanding, almost sympathetic look. "That must have been it."

It must have, Jo told herself again, trying to convince herself of that theory. But she couldn't quite do it. She had seen the woman.

She glanced around again, but there was no one but herself and Maggie there. Then she noticed a small black shape sitting in the place where Jo had last seen the lady.

Erika's cat. He blinked at her, his golden eyes there, then

gone for a moment, then back. The wise, unreadable gaze like that of a shrewd, watchful owl.

Jo stared at the animal for a few moments, getting the strange feeling he was watching her with purpose.

"You're right," she finally said. "I had to have been dreaming."

But the explanation didn't lessen the eerie feeling that had returned to her chest. What was happening to her?

Chapter 9

Jo put off going back to her place as long as she could. But she couldn't avoid her new home like she was avoiding D.C. This was her new beginning—such as it was so far.

She dropped her purse by the front door, then kicked off her shoes. She paused as a loud hum filled the room, but she quickly realized the noise was the window unit air-conditioner in her living room.

She shook her head, telling herself she couldn't let every noise, every imagined image out of the corner of her eye, terrify her.

She wandered to the kitchen, going straight to the fridge. She had to eat even though she still didn't feel hungry. Grabbing a container of plain yogurt, she went to the cupboard, and pulled down a box of granola. Then from another cupboard, she got a bowl. Once she'd created her concoction of yogurt and granola, she sat at the small café table to eat.

She took several bites, then pushed the bowl away, even as she told herself she should finish it. She had to.

Instead she rehashed the visit with her friends. Maggie and Erika hadn't done much to ease her mind. Both of her friends had watched her with wary, worried eyes as if they expected her to have a full blown breakdown right there in front of them.

Which wasn't completely out of the question.

But she hadn't mentioned what she'd seen or the uneasy feelings she'd had all day. Nor had she told them that Maksim was now volunteering at the center. She told herself, even now, it was because she didn't want them worrying about any of it. Which was true about the hallucinations, but that didn't explain why she didn't tell them about Maksim. She didn't have an answer for that one, she just hadn't wanted their opinion, she guessed.

She'd chatted in a stilted way about grants and programs, and they responded in kind, as if they knew she had other things to tell them, but they didn't want to pry. Jo appreciated that. She would share everything—she wouldn't have much choice eventually.

Jo had actually been relieved when they had to go to work at the bar. Erika had asked her to stay with her while she worked on her latest sculpture, but Jo turned her down, knowing the visit would just continue to be awkward.

Having them fretting about her wasn't help get her mind off all her problems.

So here she was, willing her whirring thoughts to quiet. Which wasn't great, but what could she do?

Go to bed.

She decided that she might as well. She might not sleep, but at least she'd be resting in her bed. And that was better than poking at her unwanted dinner or pacing around her apartment.

She placed her bowl in the sink, then headed to her bedroom. Digging through one of her dresser drawers, she found a pair of pajama bottoms and a tank top. She tossed them on her bed, which she hadn't made up that morning, because she was late. She considered making it up now, but didn't have the energy—and she was crawling right back into it, although the rumpled bedding seemed like another reminder that she wasn't doing well getting her new life in order.

She sighed and headed to the bathroom to wash her face

and brush her teeth. The narrow hallway leading to her living room, kitchen and bathroom was lined with built-ins. She had managed to get all her books and pictures put away. That was a good start to organization, she supposed.

She stopped, taking a moment to admire something that she did have a handle on. Tidy shelves—it wasn't much, but at the moment she'd hold onto anything she had.

She straightened a picture of her, Erika, and Maggie on their first trip to New Orleans, taken at Pat O'Brien's, big smiles, and big umbrella drinks in hand. How things had changed since that trip. She sighed, then moved on to straighten the picture staggered slightly behind it. Her fingers paused on the frame.

Oh my God. She picked up the picture, studying closer. It was a picture of Jo and her little sister, Kara, holding up sticks with toasted marshmallows on the end. A picture taken only days before Kara died. Jo wore a pale blue bathing suit with yellow and white daisies dotting the material. Kara also wore a bathing suit—rainbow striped.

Jo set the picture down as if the pewter frame was searing hot, even as a stark chill ran down her spine. She backed away from the photo, telling herself if she *had* seen a child in rainbow stripes today, it wasn't a bathing suit. It wasn't anything more than a coincidence. It certainly wasn't Kara.

No. No, that was insane. Insane to even consider.

She forgot the bathroom and headed back to the kitchen. The bright lights and yellow paint instantly made her feel calmer. But she didn't want to be alone. She was too shaken.

She glanced at the digital clock on her microwave. It was after 9:00 P.M. Maggie would be at work for hours yet.

Erika. She'd call and ask her to come over here. She didn't know what she'd tell her friend, but she needed company. She scrolled through her phone, finding Erika's number. She pressed the call button, and waited for the number to autodial. The phone rang once and then went straight to voice mail. She hung up and tried again with the same result. The second time she left a message for her, then hung up, debating what to do.

She could walk back over to Erika's. But the idea of being outside in the dark, already nervous, really didn't appeal. She flipped back her phone, scrolling through the numbers, looking for someone to call and talk with until she calmed down.

Cherise's number came up, and she considered calling her, but decided against it. Cherise had three children and was likely busy with them. She could call her mother—but Mom never really calmed her. In general, her parents just made her more tense.

Then she stopped scrolling on a number without a name. Maksim's number. She had it in her phone from when she'd called him to tell him he had the volunteering position, but she didn't bother to type in his name yet. Before she thought better of it, she pressed the green dial button. She watched somewhat dazed as it pronounced it was calling.

"Hello." She heard Maksim's deep voice even before the phone was to her ear. She didn't speak. She just held the receiver to her ear, trying to decide if she should speak or if she should just hang up.

"Hello? Jo, is that you?"

She was silent a moment longer, then said, "Yeah, it's me. How did you know?" Her voice sounded funny, breathy, hoarse.

"I saved your number when you called me the other day. Are you okay?" he asked.

Of course he had, just like she had. "Umm—yeah."

There was silence on his end, then, "Why are you calling? Did you need something?"

God, she should just hang up.

"Jo?"

"I—I just . . ." What was she doing? What was she supposed to say?

"Jo, something is wrong. It has to be; otherwise, you'd never call me."

His wry tone made her laugh slightly.

"Yeah, you got me there."

"Thanks."

She laughed again at the flatness of his voice.

"So what's going on?" he asked.

She should just tell him it was something about the center. She needed him to work longer tomorrow. Something. But she didn't.

"Nothing," she said, "I'm just—being silly."

"Well, you could use a little more silly, I think."

She smiled. "You are probably right."

"Glad to hear you are being agreeable. I'll be right over."

"No," she said quickly. She didn't know how she'd react to him being here now, when she was tired and vulnerable and not thinking clearly. "I was just having a little problem with nighttime nerves. No reason to come over."

"What has you nervous?"

"Just my own overactive imagination," she said, feeling like an idiot. Had she really called Maksim Kostova, of all people? After all her vows to keep herself removed from the man? Even after the awkward ending of their lunch today? Like *he'd* be the one to calm down her agitation.

She had to admit he was making her feel better. She didn't understand why. They barely knew each other, but he was helping.

Dangerous. Very dangerous, she warned herself. She shouldn't even accept friendship from this man. Not when she knew how his slightest touch could make her feel.

But she made no attempt to end the phone call.

"Did something go bump in the night?" he asked.

"No. Not exactly. Just thought I was seeing things. But it's nothing."

"Sure you don't want me to come over and take a look around your place for you?"

"No. I know it was my imagination. I just—I just needed a

little conversation to calm me down and convince me I'm just being foolish."

"Wow, and I was your chosen voice of reason." He sounded infinitely smug. That was Maksim she knew. She could even picture his self-satisfied crooked smile.

"Well, you weren't my first choice," she informed him.

"I have no doubt about that. Was it Maggie or Erika?"

She smiled. "Both. But Maggie's at work and Erika has a crappy cell phone."

"Lucky for me." His voice resonated low and sexy. She shivered. And not from anxiety.

"And I figured you'd be around," she added, trying to dispel some of the longing that at least she felt.

"You sweet talker, you," he said, that voice of his the one that was so sweet. So much for changing the mood with levity.

"I'm not so sure how lucky it was for you," she said determined to get things back to a less sexy ground. "Now you know your boss is a nut job."

"No, not a nut job. But you could probably use a good night's sleep."

Jo laughed a little derisively. "That is the general consensus."

"Mmm, don't you love unsolicited advice? Sorry about that."

Jo didn't say anything, for a moment caught up in how lovely his voice was, deep and rich with that subtle accent warming her even through the speaker of a phone.

Dangerous, her mind warned again. At this minute, she didn't care. She needed someone, and Maksim was a good someone. A really good someone.

"Jo? Are you still there?"

"Yeah. Just zoning out." Thinking about you.

"Are you going to go to bed?"

"Yeah," she said, even though she suspected sleep was still hours away. "I think I will."

"Good. Get some rest."

There was silence on the other end. Then he said, "I'm glad you called me. Even if I was only your third choice."

Don't go there. Don't go there. And she didn't know if this warning was for him or for herself.

"I'm glad I called, too. Good night."

" 'Night."

Maksim hung up the phone, frowning. Wow, he hadn't expected that.

He set his phone on Ellina's desk, where he had been all evening, continuing to try and find out something about what happened with Jo this afternoon. Still to no avail.

What had Jo thought she'd seen? He hadn't pressed the subject, because he got the vibe she wouldn't tell him even if he had.

But surely this was a good sign. She was willingly turning to him. That was definitely good. How far away could he be from getting her where he wanted her?

The question now was did he push his hand a little further? Or did he hold? Sit back and let her come to him again?

He stood, grabbing his phone and his keys. He went directly to the kitchen, opening the freezer and grabbing a pint container of ice cream. Then he headed to the door.

"I guess I'm not sitting back," he muttered to himself as he started walking toward Esplanade.

Chapter 10

Jo was in the bathroom washing her face when she heard the rap on her door. She patted her face dry, tossing the facecloth over the edge of the sink, then headed down the hall to the front door.

Who was it? It was times like this when she really wished she had one of those little peekholes in her door. Instead, she stood with her hand on the doorknob, waiting to see if the person was still there.

Another loud rap nearly made her hop out of her skin. She clapped a hand to her chest, then called, "Who is it?"

"The Good Humor man."

Jo frowned, even though she recognized the voice. She pulled open the door, the wood sticking on the uneven floorboards.

"Maksim?"

He leaned in the doorway, holding out a container of ice cream. "You better let me in. We're having a Chubby Hubby meltdown."

Jo stared at him, utterly confused both by his appearance at her place and by his words.

"Chubby Hubby?"

He wagged the ice cream at her, and she saw the name. "Ah. Well, we wouldn't want that."

She stood back to allow him in.

"What are you doing here?" she asked, following him as he strolled to the kitchen and put the ice cream into her freezer.

"I just thought you might still be nervous, and I wanted to make sure for myself that you are fine." He turned and smiled, his pale eyes roaming over her. "You look fine."

She blushed, realizing she was standing there in a tight black tank top sans a bra and baggy plaid pajama bottoms. Her face was newly scrubbed, and her hair was in a ponytail. She probably looked like a teenager ready for a slumber party.

A very vivid image of a slumber party with Maksim popped into her mind. None of it fit for teenage consumption.

Maksim's smile deepened as if he could read her mind. Again his gaze grazed down her body, and she fought the urge to cross her arms over her chest. She didn't like this. She felt totally caught off guard. Unprepared for him. But instead of covering herself, she walked over to the cupboards and pulled down two bowls.

"We shouldn't let the ice cream go to waste. Since you took the time to bring it over." She kept her voice calm, but she didn't meet his gaze.

"I agree." He said, leaning on the kitchen counter, watching her bustle around, which did not help her feel in control. His eyes on her, nor her frantic bustling.

Plus she had the feeling he was imagining other ways of how to not let the ice cream go to waste. Or maybe she was just projecting that on him. She certainly had a few ideas of her own.

"Don't go there," she muttered softly to herself.

"Go where?"

Figures the man had good ears along with all the other good parts of him.

She shook her head. "Just talking to myself. I do that." She said the last part pointed like a warning—something he should be wary of.

He wasn't. "I do, too."

She nodded, busying herself with her search for her ice cream scoop, which she wasn't even sure if she'd unpacked yet. Or if she'd even brought it with her.

"Damn it," she muttered, bracing her hands on the counter, Maksim's sudden appearance and her own flustered reaction overwhelming her.

"Are you okay?" he asked, suddenly beside her, his large warm hand on her bare shoulder.

"I can't find my ice cream scoop," she blurted out, feeling ridiculously close to tears. Then she looked up at him, her vision slightly blurry with the threat of waterworks she was trying desperately to suppress. "I'm sorry."

Maksim's eyebrows drew together over his green eyes, confused and taken aback by her reaction. For which she couldn't blame him.

"That's okay. You can just use a spoon."

His solution was so simple and so sincerely said, that Jo laughed, even as stupid tears rolled down her cheeks.

Before she could say anything, explain her utterly crazy behavior, Maksim scooped her up in his arms, hesitating only for a second as he got his bearings and located the living room.

He headed to the couch, and she expected him to set her down among the overstuffed cushions. Instead he sat down with her cradled on his lap.

The action was so kind, so caring, and Jo couldn't seem to stop herself. She broke down, sobbing against his chest, while his strong arms held her.

Helpless. Yet another feeling that, being a demon, Maksim was not familiar with. Okay, he did feel helpless about his sister—and her disappearance. But not helpless like this.

He stared down at Jo as she pressed her face against his chest and cried like her heart was breaking. And he felt very helpless—and overwhelmed.

He tightened his arms around her, each racking shake of her slight body pulling painfully at something in his chest.

"Shh," he whispered. "Shh, it's okay."

Her fingers curled in the front of his shirt, holding on to him as if she'd come apart if she didn't cling to him. He held her fast, mumbling that everything would be fine over and over, hoping she was okay.

Finally her crying subsided to small hiccups, but still she didn't lift her head.

"Jo?" he asked softly, "are you okay?"

"Not really. But I'm trying."

He was silent, not sure what to say. Finally he said, "A spoon really will work just as well."

Jo began to shake again, and he closed his eyes, silently castigating himself for bringing the ice cream scoop up again. Clearly it was upsetting for whatever reason. Then Jo raised her head, and he saw she was laughing.

He blinked, thoroughly bewildered.

"I'm sorry," she said amid her giggles. "A spoon will absolutely work fine. I guess it was just the last straw of a very stressful day."

Maksim considered that. "And did crying help?"

Jo nodded. "A lot. But it didn't help your shirt much." She brushed at the large wet patch she'd created. Maksim caught her hand, holding her fingers.

"Since meeting you, I'm getting pretty used to being covered in bodily excretions."

Jo made a disgusted noise, then laughed again. "Now that's hot."

"Definitely," Maksim agreed, looking down at her, finding her wide smile breathtakingly beautiful. Without further thought, his lips captured that lovely mouth, needing to feel it against his. To taste her. To feel her breath as his own.

Jo froze as Maksim kissed her, startled by the suddenness of it. Then his lips moved against hers, velvet heat slow and sensual, and she melted into him. He nudged her lips apart, his tongue brushing fleetingly, taking small tastes of her. She sampled him back, savoring heat and the sweet tang of his breath.

His hands, broad and strong, splayed across her back, keeping her tucked tightly to him. Her own fingers slid up his torso, caressing the hard muscles of his chest and shoulder, then over the column of his neck to the sharp cut of his jawline.

She moaned as one of his hands left her back and came up to cup the back of her head, angling her so he could deepen the kiss even further. She allowed it, loving the feel of him hard against her, yet his lips silky smooth, his tongue hot.

She loved him taking control.

Control. The word flashed in her mind, then dissolved like ice-cold water in her veins. The hand that had been caressing the cut of his jawline, the hair at his temples, stopped. Then moved back to his chest, as she levered herself away from him. She half-scrambled, half-fell onto the sofa away from him.

"I'm—I'm sorry. I—I shouldn't have . . ." She was breathless and her words came out in a dazed jumble. "I—that was, umm, I'm sorry."

Maksim's breathing seemed calmer, his wits more gathered, which made her feel even more stupid for being a blithering idiot.

Then he wiped a hand over his face, and she noticed his hand was shaking. Seeing that he was affected, too, made her feel better—not that it should. Nothing should be making her feel better. What was she doing?

"You don't have to be sorry," he said, his voice husky and even more accented than usual. "I don't want you to be sorry."

"I—I just don't think this is a wise idea for us, Maksim. I've got—a lot that I'm trying to deal with, and I—I just can't."

He nodded, but she didn't get the feeling he agreed.

"I think you are great. And I do appreciate you being here for me tonight." God, her words sounded lame to her own ears. Especially when she did want him. She so wanted him.

But she couldn't go there. She couldn't lose control of herself again. Too much was at stake for her now.

He nodded again, then laughed, the sound dry and humorless. "I don't usually get the 'it's not you, it's me' speech."

"Maksim," she started, but didn't really know what to say. She couldn't really comfort him. That *was* the speech she was giving him, and it was for the best.

He rose then, wiping his hands down the front of his pants as if smoothing away any wrinkles would help him gain control of the situation. She understood that feeling. She'd lived that way her whole life. Keep things ordered, keep busy, and that would keep things safe and keep her in control. She didn't like to lose control.

Every time she ever had—she'd paid for it. She closed her eyes; she was paying now.

She opened her eyes when she heard Maksim's feet on the wooden floorboards. He was leaving—and her first instinct was to stop him.

No. Let him go. It was for the best.

But instead of going to the door, he walked into the kitchen. She heard the refrigerator door open. The suction of the seal releasing sounded very loud in the quiet apartment.

He was taking his ice cream. She supposed she couldn't blame him. As all over the map as her behavior was, if she were him, she'd probably take her ice cream and go, too. He'd probably decided he couldn't get away from her fast enough.

And that was a good thing, she told herself. Then she wished she believed as much as she told herself she should.

He returned to the living room, and she saw she was right. He had the pint ice cream container in his hand. Then she noticed he also held two spoons in the other.

He lifted the items in the air. "Let's have some ice cream."

"Maksim," she said slowly, not wanting this to be any more difficult than it already was.

"Just ice cream, Jo."

She stared at him. Somehow she didn't think there was anything as simple as just ice cream with Maksim.

Just tell him no.

"I bet all you've eaten tonight is some of that awful-looking mush in the bowl in the sink," he said, then waving the ice cream temptingly.

She smiled despite herself, shaking her head at both his accurateness and his persistence. "And ice cream is a better meal than yogurt and granola?"

"It definitely tastes better. And this happens to have peanut butter and pretzels." He scanned the label. "Let's see it has vitamin A, calcium, of course, iron, and even vitamin C." He gave her an impressed look. "That's pretty healthy."

Jo shook her head again, then held out a hand for one of the spoons.

Maksim couldn't believe he was fine with this. Relieved and content even. That sitting here on her sofa, with nothing touching but their knees, alternatively taking spoonfuls of ice cream from the container he balanced between them, was enough for him. Was this what he'd fallen to? And as a demon, one would have thought he'd already fallen as far as he could go.

"This is good," Jo said, taking another large scoopful. She'd eaten over half the container, which pleased him, too. Another oddity. Pleasure from feeding her. Strange.

She nibbled at the creamy confection, savoring each bite.

"See. Much better than that other stuff." He grimaced at the thought of her earlier snack.

"I like yogurt and granola."

"I'll forgive you."

She regarded him, narrowing her eyes speculatively. "You don't look like you'd have a sweet tooth. You look like a low carb/high protein guy who spends most of his time in the gym."

He took a bite of his own ice cream, relishing it before he answered, "Is that a compliment or an insult? I can't decide."

She laughed, the sound stroking over his skin. Then she

licked her spoon clean. He watched, finding each lap of her tongue intensely, painfully arousing, imagining that small pink tongue licking over his flesh, savoring him.

Oblivious to his desire, she set the utensil down on her coffee table.

"That was wonderful. Thank you." She leaned back against the pillows of the sofa looking like a content cat, her eyes growing drowsy, her eyelids heavy.

He wished he'd done more than share a container of ice cream with her to make her feel so satisfied, so sleepy.

"I'm sorry," she said, her voice slurred with exhaustion. "I'm falling asleep on you."

He nodded, even though he wasn't sure if she was looking at him from under her dark lashes.

"Yeah. Well, I think you need some rest."

"That's the general consensus," she repeated with a sleepy half smile.

Maksim watched her for a moment, then finished off the last of the melting ice cream, wondering why he wasn't more irritated with the evening's chain of events. He'd wanted to sleep with this woman—not watch her doze on the sofa. He'd wanted their kissing to continue, but he'd let her stop without even forcing the issue.

And he wanted her right this minute with an intensity that was a little frightening, but instead he eased off the sofa, being careful not to jar her, and put both spoons in the sink and the empty container in the trash.

He walked back in the living room and again studied her. She now slept. He supposed he should be insulted. It was bad enough she was turning him down—but clearly she was wasn't struggling with the same raging desires he was. He wouldn't be sleeping tonight, that was for sure.

But instead of feeling angry or resentful or even annoyed, he felt—okay. She needed her sleep. He knew that. And there was always tomorrow. It wasn't like he was giving up. He was just giving her a break. For tonight.

He grabbed a fleece blanket from the place where it was folded on the back of the sofa, and draped it over Jo.

Then he did something he couldn't say he'd ever done in his life. He kissed a woman's forehead.

"Good night," he whispered, and left the apartment.

Chapter 11

"I'm not ruining my marriage over this."

Jo stared at Jackson, trying to comprehend several things all at once. Awful, confusing, heartbreaking facts that she'd refused to see.

"I'm not ruining my marriage for *you*."

Jackson stared at her for a moment, his eyes narrowed, his mouth pursed into a thin line, looking at her as if she were nothing more than dirt marring the perfection of his ideal life. A life that included a wife and children.

How hadn't she known? Was she really that naïve? Or had she just not wanted to see? Had she ignored the signs that were right in front of her?

Jo tried not to cry as she turned away from him and ran. But she didn't make it far before she dashed blindly into someone. Someone tall and muscular, his arms coming around her.

She looked up. "Maksim?"

Maksim smiled at her, the crooked curl of his lips, taking her breath away. Then he kissed her. A wonderful, slow, deliciously sexy kiss. He tasted like vanilla and chocolate and need.

She wanted more of him, but he backed away from her. She held out her hand, but he kept moving away. Then he spun, walking fast, as if he wanted to get away from her as quickly as he could. She followed.

"Maksim, wait. Wait!"

He turned back to her, and he was holding a baby. A perfect apple-cheeked angel with vivid green eyes and curling wisps of dark hair. He looked down at the child, cooing to the her in his rich accented voice. He smiled at Jo and she joined him in admiring the beautiful child. Jo's chest swelled with such happiness and intense love as she looked at Maksim and this baby together.

From behind him a woman with pale skin and black hair stepped forward to look at the infant, too, longing on her face. And Jo's joy was replaced by a terrible sense of helplessness and despair.

Jo started to reach for Maksim, to pull him away from the other woman, to pull him toward her. But she didn't move fast enough. Maksim drifted away from her. Away from the other woman.

Now he walked over to a girl, about ten years old, wearing a maillot bathing suit striped like a rainbow after a summer shower.

Jo couldn't see her face; she stood sideways to her, head down, long brown hair shielded her from view. Maksim handed the baby to the girl. Then the girl turned to face Jo. She lifted her head from looking at the baby and regarded Jo with dark, heartbreaking eyes.

Surprise, then confusion, then happiness rippled over Jo, one after the other in dizzying speed.

"Kara?" Jo stepped forward, holding out her hand to touch the girl. "Kara, is that you?"

The girl backed away.

"Please, Kara." Jo chased her, but the girl continued to drift backward.

Jo looked around wildly. "Maksim! Where are you?"

He was there, watching her. But he floated away, too, until

they all faded from view like they were sinking into the depths of dark gray water.

Jo woke, gasping for air. She glanced around, trying to figure out where she was. She was on her couch. She'd been eating ice cream with Maksim and she must have fallen asleep.

Outside, the sun was just beginning to rise, banishing the shadows from her room. But not banishing the shadows of her past. Not banishing her fears.

She glanced around, looking for Maksim, but she could tell right away he was gone. And all that was left was a sharp, piercing sense of sorrow and regret and fear.

She pulled her knees up to her chest and wrapped her arms around them, rocking slightly She tried to close in on herself, trying to keep those awful feelings at bay.

She stayed that way for minutes, for hours, she didn't really know. Until finally, she forced herself to get ready for work.

"You look awful."

Jo stopped unlocking the door to her office and glanced over to see Maksim, leaning against the wall, his intense green eyes taking in every detail of her appearance. She wished she could say the same for him, but as usual, he looked magnificent.

"And I was worried things would be awkward this morning," she said wryly to his brusqueness.

"Well, you do."

His words stung, even though she knew they were true. But what hurt worse was the sweet, considerate, tempting Maksim of last night seemed to be gone.

"I get it," she said, shooting him a fuming glare. "Don't you have other things to do besides critiquing my appearance?"

He didn't respond, nor did he move. She returned her attention back to her office door and the damned key that she couldn't seem to slide into the lock.

A large, strong hand slipped over hers, taking the key from her fingers. Jo watched, growing angrier by the moment as

Maksim easily slid the key in the lock, twisted, then pushed the door open. He moved his tall frame away from her to allow her to pass.

Jo held out her hand for the key, not saying anything as he dropped it back in her hand. She walked into the office, tossing her purse onto one of the metal chairs. She flipped on the lights and then moved to put the decrepit desk between them.

Maksim stayed in the doorway, his big, powerful body taking up most of the entrance. His presence there somehow made the already tiny room feel all the smaller.

Today he wore faded jeans, which must have been his concession to the work he was doing, but she was sure they were still expensive, still brand name. The strategically worn material clung to his narrow hips and emphasized the length and muscles of his legs. He also wore a black T-shirt. Somehow the simple garment also managed to perfectly display the width of his shoulders, the muscles in his arms and chest, and the flatness of his stomach.

How was that fair? Jeans and T-shirt and he looked amazing. She'd actually bothered with makeup, a hair dryer, and hair spray. She'd even picked out her least wrinkled skirt and shirt, and she was still being told she looked awful.

"You should take the day off," he stated, his voice still cold and slightly patronizing. His behavior hurt. Why was he acting so antagonistic? It didn't make sense, not that she was sure she wanted Mr. Nice Guy back either.

"Well, I don't think that's your position to say. Besides, I can't go home. I have a grant proposal that has a deadline of tomorrow. Not to mention, I'm fine."

Maksim raised an eyebrow. "You don't look fine. I take it you didn't stay asleep after I left last night."

She fought the urge to shush him, just in case Cherise or one of the parents were around this morning. Instead she scowled at him.

"I slept." Some.

She dropped onto her chair, forgetting that the old piece of junk could be dicey on the best of days. But under her grace-less collapse, the air hissed out of the hydraulics, and plummeted nearly to the ground. She gasped, flailing slightly as Maksim disappeared out of sight behind her computer monitor, and she was suddenly seated at eye level with the desk.

She fought back a groan. Well, that certainly helped her look together and in control, now didn't it?

Before she could wrestle out of the awkward, lowered position, Maksim was around the desk, grasping her elbow and helping her to her feet.

Once standing, she found herself face-to-face with him. Or more like face-to-chin as he had several inches on her. And his wonderful, sensual kiss was suddenly painfully vivid in her mind.

As if he was recalling the same thing, his gaze moved to her lips, but he remained still, and Jo couldn't read the look in his eyes.

Then the hand he had cupped around her elbow released her, and she expected him to back away. Instead the hand that just left her moved up to tuck an errant piece of hair back behind her ear. His fingertips grazed her temple.

Her breath whooshed from her at the slight touch. She stumbled back, frightened by the intensity of the longing shooting through her. He caught her again, his long fingers curling around her upper arm.

"Careful," he said, this time his voice was low, not filled with the terseness of earlier. He tugged her back toward him. Her chest grazed his, just another brief touch, but more desire roaring through her.

"Shouldn't you be in helping Cherise?" Jo said, grasping onto the only thing she could think of to get him away from her. She needed him away.

He glanced at her lips again, then nodded. But he didn't move.

"Then you'd better get in there," she managed, even though

her voice sounded reedy and breathless. "You don't want an annoyed Cherise after you."

Jo was surprised when he released her, moving around the desk to the door. She hadn't expected him to go so easily.

He did stop in the door, regarding her again with unreadable green eyes. "Are you really okay?"

She hesitated; her exhaustion, the abrupt change in his behavior toward her, the events of yesterday—and especially last night—were too much for her. For a second, she allowed herself to long for the support of his strong arms again, but she pushed back the moment of weakness. She didn't understand this man, and the truth was, it didn't matter even if she did. Her life was too complicated to include him anyway.

She nodded. "I am a little tired, but I'm fine."

He studied her a moment longer, then left the room.

Jo heard several of the preschoolers shout, "Maksim" in adorable, childish lisps as he entered the main room.

Jo tried to ignore the way their greeting tugged at her heart, telling herself it was lack of sleep making her sentimental. Making her long for things she shouldn't.

She leaned down and wiggled the lever under the seat of her chair, gradually getting the blasted thing back to a normal height. She eased herself down on the seat—then just sat there.

What was she doing?

What was he doing?

Maksim leaned against the wall, pretending to watch the children at play, but his thoughts couldn't seem to leave Jo. She looked awful—pale and drawn. And even more disconcerting was the fact that he cared. And not because he was seeing this as another step in getting her into bed. He was genuinely concerned for her well-being.

It was freaking him out.

He'd gone home last night and decided this had to come to

an end. He'd sat with a mortal woman, a mortal woman he wanted more than he'd ever wanted another being in his life, and he'd *just shared ice cream with her*. Then he just went home—because she'd fallen asleep. Something was really, really wrong with the whole scenario. And he wasn't pleased with any of it.

Were these strange emotions, strange behaviors, a side effect of jumping into her unreadable mind? He was somehow bound to her or something? He didn't know. All he knew for certain was that he wanted to be back to his usual self. Feeling—stuff—yeah, he didn't like it.

He liked his callousness, his shallowness, his greediness. He liked being in control, and right now, Jo was in control of him. And he had to figure out a way to stop this. All of this.

He'd gone to her this morning to show to himself that he could stop this. He could push her away. He could walk away. Then he'd seen her, and he couldn't.

Oh, he'd been rude to her, but he couldn't keep going. She looked too exhausted, too stressed. And frankly none too happy to see him.

She didn't like to lose control any more than he did. And something was really upsetting her. He didn't think it was all him.

He'd considered jumping in her head again while he'd been holding her in her office, but then couldn't bring himself to do it. He was pretty sure jumping into her mind had done some sort of damage to her. She didn't look well—at all. And frankly, he thought the jump had done something to him, too.

"Look at this."

Maksim blinked, glancing around. He'd completely forgotten where he was. He looked down to see Damon, the evil puker, standing in front of him with something dangling from his hand.

Maksim narrowed his eyes, trying to make out what swung there like a pendulum. All he could see was a chunky, cheaply made chain, huge against the boy's small fingers.

Even though he knew it would be easy enough to just say, "that's great, kid," he found himself reaching out and catching the item. The chain was heavy in his hand, but he could see the thick links were plated with silver—maybe silver. Hanging at the end was an E encrusted with paste diamonds. Several of the crystals were missing.

"My daddy gave this to me."

"Really?" Maksim turned the piece of heavy, hideous jewelry over in his hand. "It's definitely something."

Damon nodded proudly. "Yep, he sent it to me."

Maksim nodded, dropping the aesthetically offensive item, allowing it to again swing.

"Wow, that's nice gift. What does the E stand for? Your last name?"

Damon laughed, the sound so full of pure joy. His dark eyes twinkled. "No, silly, it's for *excellent*!"

"Oh." Maksim nodded as if he should have guessed that.

Damon ran off, thrilled with the cheap, damaged present. Maksim frowned, unable to imagine why such a thing would make him happy.

"Can you believe his father sent *that* to him for his birthday?" Cherise said, appearing at his side, clearly misunderstanding Maksim's confounded look. "A five year old—and that's what he gets from the father who has only deigned to see him once since he was born. And it's not even a D for Damon. Or T for his last name."

Maksim frowned deeper. What was that kid's last name, anyway?

Cherise clucked her tongue, and for a moment, Maksim thought it was because he didn't remember, then she continued.

"Well, at least he sent him something, I guess," she said, but Maksim got the feeling that she wasn't really buying her own justification.

She bustled off to break up a shoving match between two girls over a toy shopping cart with only one wheel.

Maksim returned his attention to the group of kids Damon had rejoined, finding him still grinning from ear to ear, clutching his gift.

How strange. Humans were so strange about what they found sentimental and important.

He watched Damon a moment longer, then let the thought go. But not before he felt an odd tugging. A feeling he didn't understand.

He groaned. Oh no. No, no. Wasn't it bad enough he was feeling stuff over Jo? He couldn't start feeling sympathetic to all humans.

Even their evil little offspring.

No way.

Chapter 12

Jo had to admit this felt like her longest day of her life. She'd managed to complete her grant proposal and found a grant that would provide computers to nonprofits.

She should have felt good about that, especially since racing thoughts and exhaustion had made the already tedious task of technical writing all the more challenging.

But she'd managed to keep thoughts of Maksim at bay. She'd even managed to convince herself that his odd behavior this morning was good. A reminder that she had no business being interested in him. Her reasoning had mostly worked. Sort of.

Either way, she'd gotten some work done and now all she could think about was getting some dinner and heading to bed; with any luck, she'd get a good night's sleep.

The center was quiet as she hit save on the computer, then searched her desk drawer for a disk. She shook her head as she fumbled with the small square storage device. No one used floppy disks anymore.

She was so pleased she found that grant for computers. Then they could offer some basic computer courses in the evening. And the preschoolers could even get familiar with using a mouse and how to use the icons. This was an computerized world, and it would do the kids good to have a little experience with them. Maybe she could even have some tutoring for high school kids, too. Computers would help all the way around.

Jo was still considering how she could offer tutoring at the center when her contemplation was interrupted by a sound in the hallway.

She paused, her finger on the eject button of the computer. She listened. No one should be here. On Thursday nights she had no adult or seniors' events scheduled, due to lack of help.

Again she heard the noise. The shuffle of feet, or more a pattering like small bare feet on the worn linoleum. Goosebumps dotted her arms and a chill skittered down her spine. Fear rose in her throat, strangling her.

You're hearing things, she told herself. No one was here. Cherise had locked the doors when she left. She was just imagining it.

Then she heard the same sound, this time closer to her door. As if someone was creeping closer.

"Hello?" she called, shifting her chair so she could see around her computer and out the door. The glimpse of hallway from the half-closed door was dingy gray, the sunlight waning but not quite gone. Her call was met by silence.

She shivered, icy cold seeming to fill her room. Her small office, which was usually stuffy, suddenly felt like a meat locker. She released a slow, scared breath, and moisture misted the freezing air.

She leaned a little further over her desk, trying to see if she would make out any shadows, some kind of movement.

And what if she did?

Glancing around, she reached for a ballpoint pen, holding it tightly. Not much of a weapon, but better than nothing.

What if what she was hearing wasn't a person? What if it wasn't flesh and blood. What if . . .

She didn't let her thoughts finish.

"Hello?" she cried again, determined to prove to herself her fear was unfounded. If anyone was there, it was someone with a good explanation

"Is anyone there?"

This time her question was met with a distinct response. The slap of feet on the floor, heading away from her office.

She forced herself to rise and go around her desk. Pen poised in front of her, she peeked out into the hallway. The corridor was empty, nothing but scuffed linoleum, finger-print-smudged off-white walls, and fading light.

Jo stood there, trying to understand, trying to explain away what she heard. But after a few moments, she gave up. She just wanted out of here.

Hurrying back into the office, she shut down her computer, grabbed her purse, and turned off the lights. Looking neither left nor right, she went to the front door and twisted the lock open. She stepped outside, the warm evening air instantly calming her.

She rummaged through her purse, looking for her keys.

Just your imagination, she told herself. Nothing but exhaustion and overworking. And probably hunger, too.

She laughed slightly, the sound a little panic-stricken. Her thoughts sounded like Ebenezer Scrooge's in A Christmas Carol, right before seeing his deceased business partner, Jacob Marley. The noises back there had to be caused by a blob of mustard. Or an old potato.

She was really losing it.

She finally found her keys and secured the door. Just as she was pulling the key from the lock, she caught movement through the window. Someone or something was in there.

The hallway was dark, darker now because she was in the light. But she knew what she saw. Dark hair and rainbow stripes.

A startled sound escaped her and she turned and ran.

*   *   *

Maksim had been waiting outside the St. Ann Community Center for hours, telling himself that the endeavor was a stupid one. He was hot. He was bored. His butt hurt from sitting on the concrete stoop he'd been using as a bench. He was feeling more than a little foolish.

And he was hungry.

None of these problems led to a friendly or reasonable demon. And an unhappy, irrational demon was usually bad news.

But some of his discontent and crankiness vanished as soon as he saw Jo leaving the center. He stood, about to follow her, because in all his time of sitting there, waiting, he still hadn't formulated a decent plan of what to do when he finally saw her.

He only knew he needed to see that she was okay. All morning she'd remained in her office, but he hadn't been able to get how tired and frazzled she looked out of his mind. He also regretted being so curt about her looks—all because he was worried about hurting her feelings. How had he become such a schmuck?

Just as he would have moved out of his waiting area, Jo spun away from him and started down the crumbling sidewalk in a mad dash.

Still unsure of what he intended to do, he took off after her, staying several feet behind her, unsure whether his "coincidental" appearance would help or just upset her more.

When she'd gone two blocks to the corner of Esplanade and Royal, she slowed her pace. Her movements, however, continued to appear agitated. She ran a hand through her hair. She glanced over her shoulder, but didn't seem to notice him.

Without further thought, just knowing that he had to see what had her so distressed, he yelled out to her.

"Jo! Jo, wait."

She turned, her eyes wild with fear. Then she saw who was

calling to her, and she did turn and run. But not away from him, toward him.

"Maksim! Oh, Maksim."

He wasn't sure if should see her reaction as some sort of victory, because she was clearly distraught and desperate to see anyone she knew, but he did.

He immediately pulled her against his chest. Her breathing was ragged, shallow. She clung to him, wrapping her arms tightly around his neck.

"Jo, what's wrong? What happened?"

She didn't speak for a moment, she just clutched him as if she was afraid that if she let go he'd disappear. He held her, keeping her firmly against him. Reassuring her.

"Jo? What's going on?" he asked again when he thought she wasn't going to answer him.

Finally she broke her stranglehold, but only enough so she could look up at him. Her skin was pale, drained of all color to an almost grayish tone. Purple circles stood out under her eyes. She looked awful.

And Maksim felt . . . scared. Not *of* what she was scared of, but *for* her.

"I'm so glad it's you," she said, which wasn't the response he'd expected. Even after the violent hug.

"What happened, Jo?"

Jo pulled in several breaths, clearly trying to calm and gather herself.

"I was just leaving work," she finally said, not answering his question in the least. She looked over his shoulder as if she expected to see someone behind him.

He glanced, too. No one was there.

"Jo?" He waved a hand in front of her face to regain her attention—although he wasn't really sure he ever had it. "What happened?" Repeat, repeat and maybe he'd get an answer.

She blinked up at him, her expression dazed, fear lingering. "I . . ." She shook her head as if she could keep her train of thought. She glanced over his shoulder again in the direction of the center.

Finally she met his eyes again. "I'm fine."

She was lying, still evading the truth but he didn't call her on it.

Instead, he checked his wristwatch, pretending that he had no idea what time it was because he hadn't been sitting around all afternoon waiting for her. Also pretending like she didn't just run down the street like the hounds of hell were after her.

"Wow, you stayed late tonight," he said, keeping his voice normal and calm, deciding that would do the most toward helping her at the moment. "Did you get the grant proposal done?"

Jo's posture relaxed a little, and Maksim could tell he'd done the right thing to stick to safe, ordinary topics. She wasn't ready to discuss what had her looking like she'd seen a ghost.

"I did finish," she said. "Two actually."

"Wow. That's great," he said, then paused. What were other innocuous subjects he could bring up?

"It seemed to take forever," she added, taking some of the burden off him. "But I will get it in just in time. And with any luck, we'll see some new computers, too."

"Well, that will be good. The center really needs them." Okay, this conversation couldn't sound any more mechanical. But he could see it was helping her.

"Where were you headed?" she asked.

"I was headed to get something to eat." Given that Maksim wasn't acting the least bit like the clever, devious, manipulative demon he was, he was pretty pleased with that response. "Want to join me?"

He was already planning the best way to coax her, when she said, "Sure. I could eat."

He blinked, surprised. Then he grinned. "Excellent."

Jo may have convinced herself that she was better off without Maksim, but that didn't matter now. She'd never been happier to see a person in her whole life. She didn't even feel embarrassed for jumping into his arms.

She glanced back up the sidewalk toward the community center. But she couldn't be alone. She was terrified. And no matter how illogical it was, or how dangerous in its own right, Maksim made her feel safe. And right now, she refused to contemplate that. She just needed his presence to steady her.

He held out a hand, inviting her to start walking, then he fell into step beside her.

"So you just happened to be walking by the center now?" she asked, finding it a rather strange coincidence, but then it wasn't terribly strange compared to what had been happening to her of late.

"I don't live far from here," he answered, and she had no reason to doubt that. "And I'm heading to the Quarter."

"Really? Where is your place?"

"On Ursulines." He realized his explanation made no sense. So did Jo. "So you walked back to Esplanade only to head back into the Quarter?"

"I had an errand to do." He didn't volunteer more than that, and Jo got the feeling asking him anything more wouldn't get any answers. And what did it matter anyway? She was just infinitely glad she wasn't alone.

"Where were you headed?" he asked casually, and she wondered if he really didn't notice that she was running like a madwoman away from the center.

"Home," she said automatically, then bit the inside of her lip. She could have said anything that would have made less sense than that, and she almost groaned with relief when all he said was, "See, you were taking the roundabout route, just like me."

He smiled at her, and she got the feeling that he knew she was lying, but he wasn't going to question her about it. And she appreciated that. How was she supposed to tell anyone that she thought she was seeing her dead sister?

They walked silently for several moments until Maksim stopped in front of a restaurant, Laforesterie.

Jo hesitated. The historical building with its large windows, gas lights, and flower-decorated balcony looked very posh, and very expensive.

"I don't think I'm dressed for this place," she said, gesturing to her wrinkled skirt.

Maksim glanced down at his own black T-shirt and jeans, which he was still wearing from this morning. Probably dirt stains on his ass from the concrete stoop. "You look great. Besides, my clothes are very likely covered in paste and fruit juice and other viscous liquids that are best not contemplated."

Jo raised an eyebrow. "Like you couldn't make paste look good." She blushed as soon as the words were out of her mouth.

What was she saying?

Maksim studied her, feeling assured for the first time in a long time. So she thought he looked good in paste. Not the best compliment he'd ever received, but he'd take it. It was the first time she'd said definitively that she found him attractive.

He moved forward to open the door for her, ushering her in.

She thanked him with a small smile, and he marveled at the way that slight curve of her lips made his spirits soar. Of course, every sign of her growing more comfortable with him brought him closer to getting the sex he wanted.

And he could keep telling himself that was all that mattered.

Jean-Pierre, the maître d', came forward as they entered, straightening his bow tie. He bowed to Maksim.

"Good evening, Mr. Kostova. Your usual table?"

"Yes, thank you, Jean-Pierre." Maksim placed his hand on

Jo's lower back as he escorted her into the restaurant, and was very pleased when she didn't move away from the touch.

All good signs.

Jean-Pierre led them straight through the main dining room with its dusky blue walls, crystal chandeliers, and heavy, gold brocade curtains adorning the floor-to-ceiling windows.

The smaller, more private room off the main room was decorated in burgundy and gold with more extravagant chandeliers and velvet.

"Here we are," Jean-Pierre said, waiting at the side of the table as Jo took a seat. Maksim pushed her chair in. Then he took the chair across from her, the table in a small alcove that made it private and quiet enough to talk easily.

"Enjoy," the maître d' said, handing first Jo, then Maksim a menu.

Jo looked around, then fidgeted with her shirt, tugging at the button front.

"You look lovely," Maksim assured her, his voice low and full of sincerity. He told himself that was just part of his usual shtick, his way of getting what he wanted. Manipulation—as natural to him as breathing. And that was the only reason why he was thrilled by the rosy blush that colored her cheeks. Certainly *not* because that frightening paleness had disappeared.

Jo busied herself with her menu. He did the same, not wanting to push too hard. This was a game of moving forward, then retreating. Giving the one you wanted the chance to become comfortable with the situation—the inevitable situation.

Of course, he didn't know which one of them he was trying to let get comfortable.

"So you eat here often?" she asked, still scanning the fare.

He looked up from the menu. "Yes."

"I have to admit, this is a little out of my price range."

"Well, tonight is my treat. I don't like eating alone. And I do all too often." Maksim wondered why he'd admitted that.

He'd like to think it was because he was angling for her sympathy. Sympathy that would again lead to her trust, then more intimacy. But he wasn't really sure why it had popped out of his mouth.

"I find that hard to believe." There was no sympathy in her voice. She thought he was fishing. "I'm sure there are plenty of ladies who would love to join you."

"But you're not really one of them, are you?" This time he was angling. For an admission. And the answer was more important than he wanted to admit.

"Tonight, I am," she said, and he thought there was much more to that answer than she was admitting.

What had she been running from?

"But I can't let you pay," she added. "I already owe you for a lunch."

"No, you don't."

Jo gave him a reprimanding look that she'd seen her use on the children at the center when they weren't listening.

"I'm paying. So just enjoy it. Or else I will think you are rude." He raised an eyebrow, daring her to challenge him.

She held his gaze for a few more moments, then relented. "Okay. But you have to let me pay you back."

He raised an eyebrow and grinned slowly, suggestively.

"With a lunch," she added firmly, but then smiled, too. For the first time, she seemed to let go of whatever happened back at the center.

"Lunch on me?" she said, waiting for him to agree.

The image of a buffet set up on her bare body flashed in his mind. His body reacted instantly. Mmm, his two favorite things. Food and a naked woman.

He looked across the table. Especially this woman. Her hair had been pulled back in a haphazard knot, tendrils framing her face. Pink still colored her high cheekbones and her dark eyes watched him in return. Her seashell-pink lips parted just slightly.

"I'm a great cook," she blurted, clearly uncomfortable with his attention. Then she blushed again, as if she knew that was a leading comment.

And he didn't miss the chance to take the lead. "Well, that's how you can pay me back. I don't often get a home-cooked meal."

Jo didn't answer, and Maksim wondered if that was because she didn't want to cook for him and didn't know how to tell him so. Or if she did want to, and wasn't pleased with that desire.

"So where is home?" she asked, obviously trying to steer the conversation back to safer ground. "I realized I've never asked, and I haven't been able to pinpoint your accent."

"I'm from Russia, a little village called восьмой круг." His limited Russian sounded fluent since it was his pat response, and because the accent in the eighth circle of Hell was remarkably similar to that of Russia. Which was just a coincidence, not a commentary on Russia and its inhabitants.

"I've never heard of it," Jo said. "Although, I must admit, I'm not that familiar with Russian towns."

Maksim shrugged. "It is very small. I wouldn't expect you to have heard of it." Plus it was fictional place literally meaning, "eighth circle."

"Is your family still there?"

"No, my family is a bunch of vagabonds."

"Really. How many are there in your family?"

"I come from a very large family. But the ones I'm close to are my father, who, while I don't see him much, plays a big role in who I am. I occasionally see my twin brothers, Pasha and Andrey. And I was . . . am very close to my half-sister, Ellina."

Maksim's phrasing about his sister instantly caught Jo's notice, tugging at her. "You said *was*? Did something happen to your sister?"

Maksim waited to answer as the waiter in crisp white and black came to the table to take drink orders. Jo stuck with just ice water, while Maksim ordered wine.

When the waiter left, Maksim continued, "My sister disappeared about six months ago. I don't believe she's dead. I don't want to believe that—but all leads have gone nowhere. It's like she just vanished."

Jo's heart went out to him, understanding the quiet despair in his voice better than most. But along with her sympathy was the apprehension she'd been feeling, seeing, for the past two days.

"Have the police offered you any suggestions? Are they still looking?"

Maksim's lips thinned, making his beautiful features appear grim even a little harsh. "They haven't been any help."

"So what are you doing now?"

He shook his head. "Following any lead I can find. Waiting."

Jo nodded, understanding that feeling, too. Waiting, and waiting. Before she realized what she was going to say, it was out. "I had a sister, too. She died when she was ten. I was thirteen."

Maksim met her eyes, his own darkening to a verdant green. "I'm sorry. That must have been hard."

"It was."

The waiter reappeared with a bottle of wine and two glasses. He placed one in front of each of them, then turned to Maksim and uncorked the bottle. The waiter made a big show of pouring the red wine for Maksim's approval.

Maksim nearly grabbed the wineglass from his hand, his impatience not hidden. He took a sip.

"Fine."

The waiter filled his glass, then turned to Jo. "For you?"

Jo held up a hand. "No, thank you."

The waiter set the bottle on the table and hurried away, finally sense—from Maksim stern glare, no doubt—when he wasn't wanted.

"How did your sister die?" Maksim asked, finally getting to continue this conversation.

Jo hesitated, momentarily wishing for the waiter to return. "She drowned."

Maksim shook his head. "That must have been awful."

"It was. It was really awful." And all those horrible feelings were back in full force. The strange hallucinations, last night's dream, they had brought all that terror and all the pain of the event right back to the foreground. And she'd spent a lifetime trying to forget, trying to stay ahead of her memories.

"Were you there?"

Jo knew Maksim was just asking out of concern, but she heard censure that wasn't there. Not from him. But she still heard it, felt it. Just as she did every time she thought about Kara. Every time someone mentioned her. She had been there. She should have saved Kara.

"Yes." That was all she could manage.

"That must have been frightening and traumatic."

Jo nodded. It still was. The events of her childhood were never far from her—and closer than ever of late.

"Yes, I always blamed myself for her death. For not saving her."

"But how could you? You were just a kid yourself."

Jo nodded, having heard and told herself that very thing dozens and dozens of times.

"It's just . . ." She couldn't believe she was even thinking about going there. She'd never told anyone what she'd nearly admitted to this man. Why? Maybe because he'd lost a sister and understood helplessness. Or maybe because of the strange events of the past few days.

Maybe because she was just cracking up.

"It's just what?"

Jo started to shake her head, to keep her secret where she always had. Close to her chest. Unknown by anyone else. Even Maggie and Erika didn't know. But then the words just blurted out as if she couldn't contain them any longer. Her guilt, her shame, her confusion had finally, after all these years, boiled over.

"I knew she was going to die."

Chapter 13

Maksim stared at her. He hadn't expected that. "You knew? How?"

She shook her head, and he didn't think she was going to continue.

The waiter, who looked more than a little tentative, edged up to the table. Maksim almost sent him away, but Jo informed him she was ready to order.

She asked for the salmon. Maksim ordered the filet mignon. The waiter scurried away, obviously uncomfortable with Maksim and his impatience. Maksim didn't care.

"How did you know?" Maksim asked Jo softly, not willing to let this get brushed aside. She'd started to tell him, and he got the feeling she needed to talk about it.

Jo shook her head again, fixing her attention on straightening and restraightening the cloth napkin on her lap.

Finally when he thought he was just going to have to drop the subject totally—and struggle to find something innocuous to get her to interact, period, she met his eyes.

"I saw it happen. I—I had a premonition."

Her eyes looked pained, as if she was already preparing for his disbelief, his ridicule.

"That must have scared you."

She studied him, her gaze roaming his face, still trying to decide if he was being sincere.

"Yes."

"How did you see it?"

She frowned. "I just saw it. Like a vision, I guess."

"Well, I get that, but was it like you were seeing it, and you were there, too, and you could have stopped it. Or was it like you just watching it like a show on television? Removed from it."

"Is there really a difference? I saw it. I could have stopped it."

Maksim shook his head, even before she finished speaking. "No. That isn't true. Some premonitions are designed to prepare us for the inevitable. While there are few premonitions that are shown to us so we can stop the events before they unfold."

Jo frowned, puzzled. "I still don't see the difference."

"Well there is. Like I said, if you saw the event with you in it, then maybe, and only maybe," he added, because premonitions were always dicey at best, and she had to know that for her own piece of mind, "you could have helped."

She was silent for a moment. "I don't know. But I know that I didn't tell anyone. I didn't tell my parents. I didn't tell Kara. And that might have saved her."

"Maybe. But there could have been a reason you didn't tell anyone."

Jo laughed at that, the sound sharp and bitter. "Yeah. Because I didn't take it seriously. I didn't believe it."

"Or you were just a kid and it scared the crap out of you."

Jo stared at him, then shrugged. "I don't know. But I should have done something."

"And who's to say anyone would have believed you, anyway?"

Jo nodded, but still looked as if she didn't believe him. She straightened her napkin again.

"Just like no one would believe me now," she muttered.

"What?"

She shook her head and waved her hand as if to brush the murmured words away. "I shouldn't have said anything."

A strange sense of disappointment filled his chest. He wanted her to tell him things that worried her. Things that made her happy. Things that just needed to be said.

Then he promptly told himself those feelings were ridiculous, and not what he was actually feeling. He was horny and mistaking a major case of lust for something more. He had been the whole time.

But he couldn't help himself from asking again, "What are you talking about, Jo?"

She shook her head again, waving off what she'd said as if the words had never passed her lips. Instead she asked him, "How do you know so much about premonitions?"

He considered pressuring her further, but then decided against it. Pushing didn't seem to work well with Jo, and he could understand that.

So he let the line of questioning go, setting his attention back to the food the waiter placed before him. He cut into his filet, noting how juicy and tender the meat was. He took a bite, fully preparing to enjoy the expensive cut of meat, but the flavor didn't satisfy as it should.

He glanced at Jo. She toyed with her salmon, flaking bits off with her fork. Not eating any of it.

Determined not to care—she was a big girl after all—he cut another piece of his steak. But still, even though the seasoning and preparation was perfect, the taste didn't appease him. Didn't distract him from his feelings of concern and helplessness.

He put down his fork and regarded Jo.

Again her skin was pallid, making the dark circles under her eyes stand out.

"You've got to eat," he said softly.

She glanced up, seeming almost startled that he was there. For a brief moment, he wanted to jump in her head and see what was happening behind those sad eyes. What was scaring her? What was the secret she was hiding?

But he couldn't do that. She was clearly having enough problems, and just because he hadn't seen her thoughts last time, it didn't mean he wasn't part of what was going on with her now. He could have affected her somehow.

And she'd affected him somehow, too.

Jo didn't respond to his gently stated recommendation. She just continued to pick at her food, so he leaned forward and speared a piece of her salmon. Then while she watched him with surprised eyes, he popped the fish in his mouth.

"What are you doing?" she finally managed to sputter, her astonished look causing him to smile.

He reached over and stabbed another piece. He ate it with great relish before answering.

"Well, that's a pricey meal you've got there," he said, holding back his smile. "So I'm not going to let you just shred it into pieces."

He started to lance another piece, when she trapped his fork with her own against the plate. He raised an eyebrow, giving her a questioning look.

She cocked her own eyebrow in response, then released his utensil, tapping it away a few times, the metal clinking.

"I get your point," she muttered grumpily, but Maksim saw a hint of a smile before she dug into her fish.

Maksim watched her for a moment, then began eating his own meal again, the filet suddenly tasting absolutely delicious.

"Thank you for a great dinner," Jo said as they exited Laforesterie.

Maksim smiled over at her as they walked, and despite herself, her body reacted. He was so handsome, utterly and breathtakingly handsome. His dark hair was sexily disheveled, a slight, wonderful breeze ruffling it. His green eyes twinkling with a naughty little spark. His smile crooked and charming.

And while her body was definitely reacting to his looks, she was also reacting to his behavior tonight. He'd been there when she'd been truly panicked. He'd talked to her, made her laugh. He listened to her talk about her sister. He'd listened to her admission of the premonition—and he hadn't mocked her, doubted her, or judged her.

And he'd made her eat. Which she had to admit had made her feel so much better. Much less fragile and strung out. It was very, very stupid for her to not eat. She had to remember that. Her blood sugar was touchy at the best of times, but now . . .

Well, she just appreciated him being there tonight. Against her better judgment. But maybe she could let judgment go, better or otherwise. Just for tonight.

They strolled quietly back toward Esplanade. The streets were pretty quiet as they opted to travel down Royal Street rather than heading toward the busier and wilder Bourbon Street.

"Are you still working at the bar?"

He shook his head. "Once in a while. It's really not my thing."

"What, were the scads of adoring women too much for you?" she teased.

"Jealous much?" He winked at her, buffering his teasing.

She pulled a face at him, enjoying that she could be relaxed and playful with this man. Which she hadn't expected. Again she wondered if she'd been too quick to judge him, just because of Jackson and his failings.

Still lost in her thoughts, it took her a few moments to realize she was back in Esplanade and only a few houses from her rental.

"It's right up this way," she said, then realized it was unnecessary. She also thought of something she hadn't last night in her surprise at finding him at her door. "But you know that. How did you know where I lived last night?"

"I have my ways," he said with a wiggle of his eyebrows. Then he asked, "Why didn't you move into Ren's apartment building? He has some vacant apartments, doesn't he?"

Jo nodded. "I didn't want to invade the little love nest they have going on over there."

"Ah, yeah, I can see that."

"Don't get me wrong," Jo said as she rifled around in her oversized purse for her keys. "I'm very happy for them. I think they are wonderful matches. But well, it's just—"

"A bit much?"

"Yes," she said with a pained smile. "Does that make me an awful friend?"

"Not in my book. Love is often an overrated emotion."

"Hear, hear." Jo found her keys and unlocked the front door. She paused, the key still in the door.

"Would you like to come up?" She wasn't sure what had prompted the question. She'd like to blame it on her nerves still getting the better of her. But she knew that wasn't the case. Not at the moment, anyway. Her mind was too occupied with Maksim.

"I'd *love* to," he said, emphasizing the word "love," which made her laugh.

She opened the door and he followed her up the stairs to her second-floor apartment. Once inside, she asked him if he'd like something to drink.

"I have coffee—it's decaf, though. And tea—also decaf," she told him.

He grimaced. "You actually like decaffeinated tea?"

She smiled, not surprised that he had no use for anything that supported moderation—even with caffeine.

"You'd be surprised. It grows on you." She went to her cupboard, stretching up on her tiptoes to get down a new box of decaf English Breakfast.

Warmth encompassed her as she felt rather than saw Maksim come up behind her. Then his chest pressed against her back as he reached over her to get the tea. He set the box on the counter, then he braced his hands on the worn Formica, caging her in.

She remained still, her breath growing shallow, as her body reacted instantly to his large, powerful body surrounding her.

"Am I growing on you, too?" he murmured, his mouth right beside her ear.

Chapter 14

She closed her eyes as a shiver of pure need vibrated through her limbs at the rough velvety reverberation of his voice. Her nipples tightened, the lace of her bra abrading the swollen points.

He nuzzled her, his cheek against hers, his spicy, earthy scent filling her nose, his lips pressing moist fire along the sensitive column of her neck. With a shuddering breath, her head fell back against his shoulder, offering him better access. He kissed down her neck to her collarbone, while her fingers dug into the counter just beside his.

"What are you doing?" But the question was lost before she could even wonder at the answer. Before she could even care if there was an answer.

The hands beside hers left the counter, moving to hold her waist, sliding around her, until she was enfolded in his strong arms, her body still trapped between the counter and his large body. She gave into his prison, to his delicious torture as he nipped the skin of her neck, of her shoulder.

His hands slid up her from her waist, up over her ribcage, to the swell of her breasts. He skimmed over them, his thumbs, his fingers just grazing her hardened nipples.

She groaned, arching into his touch. He cupped her fully, squeezing, shaping the sensitive flesh in her broad palms.

"I've thought about this," he whispered to her. "Imagined touching you. Everywhere."

She whimpered, because whether she wanted to admit it or not, she'd imagined it, too. She had.

"Will you let me do that? Touch you, everywhere?"

She turned in his arms, her response to wrap her arms around his neck and kiss him.

It was his turn to groan, a low, guttural sound that reverberated deep in his chest, sending a hungry tremble through her body.

He lifted his head, his eyes roaming over her face. "I'm taking your response as a yes."

She nodded, even as a lucid, practical part of her brain tried to reason with her. But that portion of her brain might as well be trying to reach her by using two cans and some string. Because she could barely hear it. And she didn't want to hear it. She just wanted to feel.

"I want this," she whispered.

Maksim smiled, and then she found herself scooped up against his broad chest.

She laughed, surprised by the sudden shift of her world.

"Where is your room?"

She pointed toward the hallway, and he strode in that direction. Once there, he eased her down on her bed, following her down. But he just leaned over her, studying her, his handsome face cast in shadows.

"You're sure?"

She gazed back up at him, understanding his hesitation. She knew this was a huge change in attitude. But she needed to let go, even if just for this one night. She needed to feel safe, and as unlikely as it seemed, Maksim did make her feel safe.

Maksim could make her forget. She wanted that.

"You don't want this to be anything more than fun, right?" she asked, reaching up to touch his face, the sharp cut of his jawline, the hint of stubble on his cheeks.

"Just fun," he agreed.

"No commitments. No strings. No 'L-word.'"

He regarded her for a moment, and she couldn't quite read his expression. Then he nodded.

"That's what I want, too."

He leaned down and kissed her, the touch gentle and sweet and filled with a tenderness that seemed strangely at odds with the idea of just using each other for physical release.

He pulled back, his body over hers. Her hand knotted in his hair. "You are a mystery to me, Josephine Burke."

She smiled. "Well that makes us even, Maksim Kostova."

Maksim didn't know what to make of Jo's words. The mortal women he'd been with just didn't go into a relationship with these kind of arrangements laid out on the table. Even if they did, there was always a tone under their words that said, while they might be agreeing to just sex, they were expecting that to change.

Maksim studied Jo's eyes. And he didn't see any longing there, or hope, or determination like she intended to sway his opinion on the subject. He just saw lust. And he knew lust when he saw it. He'd seen it in his own eyes many, many times.

Jo just wanted good sex. Damn.

Damn.

He shook his head, taking in her smoldering, dark eyes. Her pink lips parted, glistening in the dim light.

"What?" she asked, smiling.

"Just thanking my lucky stars."

Her smiled widened, and he had to taste her.

His mouth caught hers. She opened for him instantly, while her arms circled his neck, pulling him down onto her. Their tongues touched, then darted away, only to return to savor each other's again.

But apparently now that Jo had made up her mind that sex

was what she wanted, she wasn't satisfied to go slowly. With her mouth still locked with his, she pushed at his shoulders, pressing him back into the mattress.

"Like taking control, huh?" he murmured against her lips.

"Oh yeah. I'm a bit of a control freak." She nipped his bottom lip, then rose up and straddled him. The weight of her slight body was wonderful on his. Her soft, warm ass nestled over his already granite-hard erection.

"Hmm," he ran his hands up her legs, now bared by her position and her hiked-up skirt. Her skin was smooth and hot, her thighs firm. He groaned again. He couldn't wait to feel her riding him.

"I'm a control freak, too," he told her. "But I think tonight I'm more than willing to relinquish control."

"Good," she said, her fingers going to the hem of his shirt. She slipped her hands underneath, shaping her open palms over his stomach and slowly up over his chest.

"Off," she ordered, and he obeyed, levering himself up enough to tug the shirt over his head. He flung it onto the floor.

Jo made a low sound of appreciation, then leaned forward to press open-mouthed kisses over his chest, her teeth finding his puckered nipples. She nipped in hard.

His body convulsed, his erection pulsing wildly against her.

"Damn, woman," he growled. His hands tangled in her hair, making a mess of the twisted knot she wore as part of her usual "community center director" look. That wasn't what she looked like now.

She looked like a wanton nymph draped over him, her hair mussed, her eyes dark. She was so damned sexy. He pulled her down to him, his mouth ravishing hers. His hunger, which he already considered over the top, was quickly spiraling into something huge. Something all-encompassing.

But he knew how to get this feeling under control. He needed to be inside this woman, buried deep.

He rotated his hips, mindlessly seeking where he had to be. The place that would make him feel whole, complete.

Jo kissed him back with the same ferocity he was feeling, her body writhing on his, seeking the same release he did.

He rose up, easily lifting her with him, wanting to pin her under his weight. Wanting to strip her naked and drive himself into her, hard and deep.

But to his surprise, Jo strained against him, not allowing him to change their position. She broke their kiss and placed her hands on his shoulders, using all her strength to press him back to the mattress.

"Uh-uh," she told him with a slow, wicked smile. Her skin was flushed, her breath coming in soft little puffs. She sat back, wiggling her hips, teasing him.

"I thought you understood that I like control?" she said softly, grinding her hips against him.

He gritted his teeth, imagining that movement without their clothing between them. With his cock inside her.

"Mmm," he moaned. "I forgot. I'll lie here like a good boy if we can just lose the clothes."

Jo arched an eyebrow, skepticism flashing in her dark brown eyes. A smile unfurled on her lips. "Is that so?"

He nodded, for a moment even her expression so arousing, so breathtakingly lovely, he couldn't answer.

She pretended to consider the idea. The occasional wayward wriggle of her hips was the only sign that she was as turned on as he was.

"Okay." Her fingers fingered the buttons on her sensible white cotton shirt. She flicked open one, then another, then another, each loose button revealing glimpses of more creamy white skin.

Maksim watched, transfixed as if she were a practiced, very talented, exotic dancer doing a performance solely for him. He swallowed as she slipped the material off her shoulders. She sat astride him, her small, perfect breasts encased in pale peach lace. The shadow of her rosy nipples teased him from behind the delicate fabric.

He cupped the soft swells, his thumbs brushing the hardened tips, circling them.

She gasped as he squeezed small points, her hands coming up to cover his, her head falling back, her long hair falling in unruly waves over her shoulders.

His hands slipped out from under hers, slowly shaping down over her side, feeling each gentle ridge of her ribs, the smooth skin of her stomach, stopping at the waistband of her skirt. His thumb toyed with the edge, slipping just under, then sliding out.

She watched him, her eyes heavy-lidded, but when he reached around the back to unzip the garment, she caught his hand. She shook her head.

"No, no," she scolded, her voice low, sexy. She shifted, crawling off of him, her movements fluid, sinuous. A deep, desperate noise rumbled in his throat.

She stood, giving him an almost impish smile. "I'll be right back." She then reached behind her and undid the skirt. It puddled to the floor.

He was greeted by panties that matched her bra. The scraps of lace emphasizing her long limbs, the pale perfection of her skin, her sleek, subtle curves.

She reached behind her again. She unhooked her bra and slipped it off. Her fingers then hooked the edge of her panties. She shimmied her hips and that bit of lace disappeared, too.

If he thought she'd been stunning in her underwear, he wasn't prepared for her standing in front of him nude. Her small breasts were pert and firm with raspberry tips. Her mons was plump and shadowed with a tiny triangle of dark curls.

He swallowed, his body aching so intensely for her that he almost cried out. Damn, she was beautiful. He couldn't recall any woman as beautiful as he found this one.

He sat up, snagging her wrist, tugging her back down onto the bed.

She laughed, the sound making every cell in his body throb, pulse.

"You are very bad at letting me take control," she said. She touched his face, her palm hot against his cheek. Her fingertips traced his jawline, his cheekbone, his lips.

He nipped her, and she cried out, the sound one of shocked pleasure rather than pain or dismay. He caught the back of her head and pulled her down to him. His mouth tasted her, his teeth teased her soft lips.

She moaned into his mouth, her teeth worrying his bottom lips in return. He nipped her again, and she gasped.

She pulled away from him, and for a second he worried he'd been too rough. Her lips were red and swollen, and alarm dampened his desire a little.

"Jo?" he asked, his voice raspy with warring desire and concern.

She smiled to reassure him, the curve of her lips almost painfully sweet. Then her hand moved to his chest, her small, fiery fingertips gliding down his chest, his stomach. She reached the button of his jeans, pulling at it, and for the first time, he realized her fingers were trembling.

Good, he thought. He hated to think he was the only one overwhelmed with desire. And he was practically insane with need.

She tugged again and the button came loose. A rasp of metal on metal joined their uneven breathing, and he felt cool air on his burning flesh.

Her fingers curled around his waistband, and she worked the denim down his legs. His boxers followed. Then she was still.

He rose up on his elbows to look at her. She stared at him, or rather one part of him.

Then she looked at him, her heavy-lidded expression replaced by astonishment.

"Wow," was all she said. Then, as if his cock were a lodestone, her attention returned to the rock-hard erection. She blinked, but then her hand come out to touch him.

His hips jerked off the mattress at the light touch. He bit his lip, fighting to stay in control. And let her have the control.

Her slender fingers curled around his girth, testing the weight and the texture of him.

"It's beautiful," she murmured, and Maksim couldn't recall anyone ever saying anything nicer to him. A compliment for his dick, and he was putty. Damn.

He watched, almost as if her descent were happening in delicious slow motion as her head lowered and her mouth pressed to the sensitive underside. Her small, pink tongue darted out to lick the length of the sensitive ridge. His hips jerked again, a shuddering breath escaping him.

Then her hot, wet mouth was surrounding him. He fell back onto the bed.

Okay, now he was putty.

Jo couldn't recall ever being this excited, need sizzling through her veins like a wildfire. She took him into her mouth, sliding up and down on him, her tongue swirling. She licked his arousal, the shaft like steel covered in smooth silk.

"Do like that," she murmured, keeping her lips against him. His erection bobbed along with his head as if they both had to answer. She smiled, still keeping her mouth pressed to him so he could feel the gesture. Like some sort of erotic Braille.

She ran her tongue up the length of him, then took him back inside her mouth. He made a whimpering noise that was so sexy, a noise that revealed his pleasure and his submission, both of which turned her on almost unbearably. Her breasts felt heavy, achy. Moisture, slick and hot, dampened her inner thighs.

Part of her wondered if she should be embarrassed at how

aroused she was, but another part was just filled with wonder. She didn't know she could even feel this way.

And she loved the power she wielded right now. She loved
the raggedness of Maksim's breath. The way his hips lifted to
urge himself further into her mouth. The way he hissed when
she grazed her teeth, just barely along the vulnerable, tender
underside of his very impressive penis. The way his fingers
knotted in her hair, tugging, but not hurting her.

"Jo. Damn, woman. I have to be inside you."

She kissed the tip of his cock, tasting the saltiness there.
She lifted her head and grinned. "You were inside me."

"But not inside where I want to be."

"Oh really? Well, I can change your mind about that."

Her mouth returned to him. She took him deep, his huge
cock touching the back of her throat as she bobbed up and
down on him. Taking him whole, tasting every inch of him.

She sped up her pace, taking him deep, then nearly releasing him, her tongue circling the tip with each near withdrawal.
And with each lap over the soft, cushiony head, he groaned,
his hips bucking.

"Jo," he pleaded, his voice rough, raw with need.

In response, she took him entirely again, then kept her motions smooth and swift, her fingers curling around the base of
his shaft, joining the fluid, fast strokes.

Then she felt him tighten, his muscles locking, his hips arching up. Warm liquid hit the back of her throat, salty, musky
and a little sweet.

She swallowed, savoring the quivering of his body under
her. Savoring the taste of him.

"Damn," he said, his voice weak, trembling.

She looked up at him then, smiling smugly. He was sprawled
on the bed, panting.

"Like that, huh?"

"Oh, yeah." He remained still for a moment, then lifted
his head, his eyes clouded with satisfaction like opaque green
sea glass.

Her grin widened, the power she felt making her giddy.

"Don't you look pleased with yourself?" he said.

"Mmm-hmm." She didn't even bother to look repentant. As if she hadn't seen that same look on his face many times. "Why? Are you pleased?"

She knew the answer to that.

"Oh yeah. Very much so." He fell back onto the bedding.

She laughed. She liked having the ability to make this gorgeous man dissolve into a big puddle of contentment.

She idly caressed the solid muscle of his thigh.

He elbowed himself up again. "Come here."

Even though she liked her control, she didn't even hesitate, raising up on her knees to lean over him.

She made a small noise of surprise as he kissed her fiercely, all his lazy fulfillment gone.

She pulled back to study him. Now he looked like a cat, wild and ready to pounce. Amazing. No man she'd been with could recharge that quickly.

She glanced down at his penis. It was thick and hard again.

"Holy cow," she said aloud this time.

Now, he smiled with smug satisfaction. "I can go all night."

And she didn't even consider thinking that was just an arrogant boast.

"But you haven't even gone once," he murmured as if it was a terrible shame. "Let me take care of that."

He touched her thigh, and she slid her knees apart, desperate for his touch. His fingers skimmed between her legs, teasing her, then parting her.

"Mmm, you are nice and wet, baby."

Without preamble he slipped a long finger into her, entering her roughly, wonderfully.

She gasped, and it was his turn to smile.

He kept his finger inside and inserted another. She cried out as his thumb found her taut, hypersensitive clitoris, and he swirled.

"So wet," he said, stroking her, inside and out.

She couldn't control her hips; they ground against his hand.

A moan filled the air, and she wasn't sure if it came from him or her. She was too caught up in the feeling of him, and his amazing touch. He shifted his fingers inside her, and suddenly everything got more intense, too intense.

She caught his wrist to stop him, to control the extreme sensation ripping through her.

"Just let go, baby."

Just let go. She shook her head. Danger always came with just letting go. But as he continued to massage that spot deep inside her, she realized he wasn't going to allow her to do anything else.

The hand that pulled at his wrist now just gripped him, using him as an anchor in the wild, reckless release that threatened to suck her in completely.

"That's it," he said, his other hand coming around to hold her waist. "That's it, darling. Come for me."

She gritted her teeth, shaking her head. "I can't. I can't."

"Yes, you can. For me, you can."

He pressed the pad of his finger hard against her, and she exploded. A violent scream tore from her throat as pleasure so intense, so consuming it bordered on pain, rushed through her body.

Jo had no idea how much time lapsed as breaker after breaker of astonishing release washed over her, through her.

When the orgasm calmed to ripples, she realized Maksim held her limp weight. He sat up, one arm around her back, the other still inside her, stroking her easily, gently.

Warmth burned her cheeks at her unrestrained abandon. She'd never had anything like that happen. Ever.

He smiled at her, the curl of his lips lopsided, sweet. "Good?"

She blushed further, but nodded her head.

"Good," he said and he leaned forward and kissed her.

To her complete shock, the touch of his firm, smooth lips rekindled reaction in her. After that, after the most intense orgasm of her life, she was becoming aroused again.

But this time, he didn't rush her toward ecstasy, he eased her. Kissing her slowly, sweetly. Sucking and teasing her breasts, stroking her like a treasured pet. His hand cupping her mons, circling the hard nub at the top of her sex unhurriedly. Each caress arousing in its leisurely enjoyment of her body.

She touched him, too. The hard muscles of his shoulders, his back. His taut, perfect stomach. His straining erection.

"You feel so good," she murmured against his mouth as she ran her hand up and down his imposing length.

"Thank you. You too. You too," he said. He nipped her beaded nipple.

She gasped, feeling the bite throughout her body, until it pulsed where his thumb rubbed her clitoris.

He eased her back on the mattress then, parting her legs. She let them fall open, easily, willingly. Wanting him inside her. That thick, hard length filling her, stretching her.

But instead of coming down on top of her, he remained sitting between her spread thighs.

"You are so beautiful."

She gasped as one of his large fingers entered her. Then he bent forward and his tongue replaced his swirling thumb. And immediately the gradual, steady build to complete arousal was catapulted into powerful, overwhelming passion.

He licked her, teased her, suckled her until she was mindless with need.

"Please, Maksim," she begged, tugging at his short hair, yanking him up her body in her desperation to have him inside her.

He slid up her, skin to skin, a glorious friction. She arched and moaned, cradling him between her thighs.

The touch of their body seemed to ignite his passion, too. He positioned himself and entered her in one swift thrust. She writhed under him, the heavy feeling of him deep inside her more thrilling than she could have imagined.

Then he started to move, and time lapsed. All she could do was follow his rhythm, and feel. His muscles undulating over her, his magnificent weight pinning her to the bed, his large cock filling her completely.

"You feel so good," he breathed, plunging over and over into her.

She curled her legs around his back, straining against him. Taking all of him over and over. Then his movements became faster, harder, more demanding.

And she gave into him, shouting out her climax. He followed her, his own yell of release filling her ears.

Then she fell into blissful oblivion.

Chapter 15

Sometime during the night, Jo was aware of Maksim lifting her up to the pillows and tucking the covers over her. But she didn't rouse enough to speak or even know what he did after that.

When she woke in the morning, she found the other side of the bed empty, and she realized he must have left. She sat up, still disoriented from her deep sleep. His clothes were gone and she heard no sound of him in the apartment. The destroyed bedding and her scattered clothing were the only signs that last night had ever happened.

Disappointment filled her, then she pushed the feeling away. They hadn't agreed to anything more than sex. So she couldn't very well expect him to be cuddled in beside her in the morning. And in truth, she didn't want their arrangement to be different. Anything more would be too complicated.

Complicated was something she already had plenty of in her life.

Telling herself everything was good, she fell back against her pillows and stretched. She glanced at her alarm clock. It was 7:00 A.M. She smiled slightly and sighed.

She couldn't recall a time in the past two months when she'd slept that soundly. Or for that long. She'd been functioning on two-hour intervals of sleep every night, usually never making it more than six hours before giving up and getting out of bed to wander around in a dazed exhaustion.

Who knew that the perfect treatment for her insomnia was good sex? She stretched again, her muscles aching, but in a very satisfying way. Good? Okay, she'd give Maksim credit where credit was due. Great sex. Stupendous sex. The best sex she'd ever had.

She lounged amid her fluffy bedding for a few moments longer, then groaned, forcing herself to get out of bed. Enough basking in the fond memories of last night. She padded to the kitchen and forced herself to drink a glass of milk.

She shuddered and grimaced as she set the glass in the sink. *Yuck.* She really hated milk.

But a shower. Now that she could really enjoy. She stretched again; muscles she didn't even know she had were protesting.

She stopped in the hallway to open a small cupboard that she used as a linen closet. She grabbed a towel and a washcloth, then continued to the bathroom. The small room, which was only big enough for the shower/tub, toilet, and pedestal sink, was dim. The one small window was covered with a curtain decorated in big colorful daisies.

She walked into the room, not bothering with the light. She set her towels down on the closed toilet seat, then turned back to flip the light switch. But as she took a step forward, her foot landed on something.

Quickly stepping away from the unknown object, she flicked on the light and looked down to see what felt both hard and squishy at the same time under the ball of her foot.

There in the middle of her daisy-covered bath mat, which matched the curtain was . . .

She leaned forward to pick the item up, certain she was seeing things. As her fingers curled around it, feeling the rubbery texture, an icy chill stole over her still bed-warmed skin.

She stared at the object, telling herself there was nothing to get nervous about. She shouldn't make a big deal over this. It wasn't that weird. But even as she told herself that, she knew she didn't have one of these. Even though she'd seen the object before. In fact the last time she'd seen one of these up close was burned indelibly into her mind.

A shiver racked her body as she continued to stare at it.

A swimmer's nose plug, the kind with a clip that fit over the nose with a band that wrapped around the swimmer's head. Made out of pale blue rubber.

Like the one that had been around Kara's neck when they'd pulled her out of the water.

How had it gotten there?

Maksim wasn't surprised to see Jo walk into the daycare room, clearly looking for him. After all, she'd been a very satisfied lady last night, and he knew she'd be back for more.

Of course, he wasn't going to analyze why he'd been checking the door every five minutes since he arrived here an hour ago. He also wouldn't analyze why he'd shown up so early this morning. He avoided the topic when Cherise asked him about his premature arrival.

But now that Jo beelined straight to him, he waited with a wide, contented smile on his face, showing no signs that he'd been waiting.

"Hey," he said easily, walking over to meet her.

"Hello. Did you drop this?"

Maksim blinked as something swung back and forth inches from his face. Well, that wasn't the greeting he expected.

"What?" He frowned, not able to make out the item, because it dangled so close to him.

"Did you drop this?" she asked again impatiently. She shook the swinging thing closer to him. He stepped back and took the item from her hand. He stared at it.

"I don't even know that the hell it is."

She studied him, her eyes narrowing. "Are you sure?"

He looked at the blue rubber strap with a clip at one end. Then he smiled. "Is this a sex toy?"

Jo glanced around them, clearly concerned the kids or Cherise had heard him.

Not likely. Nothing could be heard over the constant jabbering.

Jo glared at him. "No, it is not a sex toy." Her voice dropped to a whisper on the last two words.

Maksim shrugged. "Well, I've never seen it. Why?"

He held it back out to her, and for a second, he got the feeling she didn't want it back. She eventually took the odd little strap and tucked it into the pocket of her black capris.

Clearly, whatever that thing was, she found it upsetting in some way.

He studied her, wanting to understand. He also wanted to know how she felt about last night, but her gaze wasn't on him anymore. She was distant, her thoughts clearly not on him or last night.

"Are you okay?" he asked. What was that innocuous little thing and what did it mean to her? Aside from her agitation about that, she looked better than she had in days.

Of course, he knew when he left her, she'd been sleeping soundly. Which he knew she needed. He'd been tempted to stay, but decided waking up together might imply more than he was willing to give.

Jo frowned now, her mind miles away from this room, from the kids chattering around her. From him.

"Jo?"

Her attention didn't return to him immediately, but after a moment, she shook her head as if physically casting off whatever was plaguing her.

"What?" She blinked, clearly confused by his question.

"What's going on? Are you okay?"

"Yes. I—yes."

He couldn't help himself. He touched her, his hand coming in contact with the warm skin of her bare arm. A charge of electricity shot through him. Just from that innocent touch. She met his gaze, and he could tell she felt the energy, too.

"I'm fine," she assured him, offering him a tentative smile. Then, surprisingly, she touched him back, moving her arm out from under his hand to catch his fingers, squeezing them.

For a moment, their eyes locked. More energy passed between them.

He smiled. "Good."

She stared at him for a moment longer, as if she wanted to say something more. He wanted to say more as well, to question her about her obvious anxiety, but he didn't. In part because he didn't quite know what he wanted to say, and in part because he was afraid if he did know what to say, it wouldn't be the words she needed or wanted.

"I should go to work," she finally said.

He nodded. "Okay."

She walked back toward the hallway, and he remained in the center of the room, watching her go. That was until a tug came on the back of his shirt.

He turned to see Damon regarding him with those wide dark eyes.

"Mr. Maksim, is you a player?"

Maksim frowned, wondering where a kid that age even learned such a word, much less the proper usage of it. And apparently, the kid hadn't missed the interaction between him and Jo.

"Is you?" he asked again when Maksim didn't answer.

Maksim glanced back at the doorway to the hall, now empty. Jo shut away, out of sight, in her office. And again, he wondered what he'd wanted to say to her.

Something too personal. Something that he normally wouldn't even think of saying. Which was ludicrous. The ground rules of "just sex" were perfect. Exactly what he wanted. He couldn't ask for a better arrangement.

He looked down at the four-year-old who was an odd combination of innocence and savvy.

"Yeah, Damon, I'm a player."

The boy nodded, his reaction holding no disappointment,

no approval. No judgment at all. Then he scampered back to the table to work on his coloring.

And Maksim looked back to the empty doorway.

Jo closed her office door and moved around her desk to her chair. Sitting carefully, she leaned back a little, rooted around in her pocket, and pulled out the nose plug. She dropped it on the desk and it naturally coiled like a pale blue snake ready to strike. At least that's how she stared at it.

It was just a strange coincidence. Not anything scary. Not anything paranormal. Just a weird . . .

She shook her head, unable to find any legitimate, plausible explanation for that nose clip being in her bathroom. And unlike the glimpses she'd had of the girl in the rainbow bathing suit, she couldn't write this off to her imagination. If it was her imagination, then Maksim had just held the figment in his hand and denied knowing anything about it. He didn't even know what it was.

She opened her desk drawer and brushed the clip inside, closing the touchable figment out of sight, praying it went back to wherever it came from.

To Jo's surprise, she managed to push the strange discovery on her bathroom floor out of her mind. She'd like to say it was because she was so busy working, but that would have been a lie. Instead she'd spent the morning alternating between trying to work and fixating on Maksim. Another typical day.

Last night had been . . .

Well, it had been wonderful. And that was so very dangerous. It was especially precarious, because not only did what happened between them make her skin tingle—along with other parts of her body—but also she found herself wanting to confide in him.

She'd actually considered telling him what she thought

she'd seen over the past few days. But she couldn't do that. She couldn't get close to him in that way. That reaction was, in many ways, more risky for her than just straight lust.

And frankly, he was more likely to accept that she thought she was seeing her dead sister than the other truths she was hiding about herself.

She had to play it cool. But several times, when she heard the kids' laughter, or the rumble of a male voice, which she knew could be no one else's but Maksim, she had to fight the urge to go see him.

Dangerous. Dangerous. Maybe she should just call off the physical thing with him, too. It was too risky.

Just then her cell phone rang, forcing her to focus on business. A woman wanted to set up a course teaching quilting. Jo leapt at more chance to get people into the center.

After she agreed to meet with the woman later that afternoon, she flipped her phone shut, only to realize she had a voice mail.

"Hey girl," Erika's voice greeted her, "I've been trying to call you all evening. I hope you are okay. I wanted to see if you'd like to come over tonight. Maggie's taking the night off from playing with The Impalers, and we thought we could have a little impromptu get-together. Hope you are okay, and you feel up to coming over. Call even if you can't come, I'm worried about you. Talk to you soon. Bye."

Jo erased the message. She dialed Erika back, knowing she'd get her voice mail, too, and left a quick message telling her that she was fine and that she'd be there.

Then she hung up, feeling better. If she kept busy, she wouldn't be tempted to go there again with Maksim.

Great. Another thing in her life that made her feel like she had to keep busy. To keep ahead of her thoughts, her worries, her truths.

A rap on the door snapped her out of those thoughts. Saved again.

"Come in," she called.

But she was only saved for a brief moment as the door opened, and the main topic she shouldn't be thinking about stuck his head in the door.

"Hey there," he said, the simple sound of his voice sending ripples of desire through her.

"Hi," she said, keeping her calm. This man was too much for her. She had to put things back onto a . . .

Well, she didn't know what kind of footing they'd had before last night. It had always been precarious at best. But she needed to take it to a safer level. And she supposed any level was safer than where they were last night.

"I was wondering if you'd like to join me for lunch." He smiled, tilting his head slightly with inquiry.

God, he was so cute—cute, of course being the most understated description she could have given him. He was cute, to be sure, but he was so much more than that. Sexy, charming, breathtakingly handsome.

She actually had to suppress a sigh.

See, she told herself, that was why she needed to let last night stay what it was—a great time with no strings. And if she was smart, leave it at a one-time event.

"I can't," she said, keeping her voice level, feeling like even lunch would be too tempting for her. "I have a meeting."

So what if the meeting with the quilt lady wasn't until three this afternoon?

He frowned, his eyes narrowing as he tried to read her reaction. She gave him a brief regretful smile.

He finally nodded. "Okay. Well, I guess I will head out for the day."

"Okay," she said readily, trying to stay as cool as she could.

He nodded, his smile disappearing behind a composed look of his own, but he did ask, "I'll see you later?"

She couldn't miss the longing in his tone. She also couldn't ignore the yearning that rose up in her instantly in response. She squashed the feeling down.

"I'm actually going over the Erika and Maggie's tonight."

His expression grew almost grim, his beautiful sculpted lips compressing into a line.

"Okay, then." He lifted a hand in salute, then left.

She watched the door being pulled closed behind him and fought the urge to call out to him. To stop him.

This was for the best, she told herself. What was the point of going forward with this relationship—even on a purely physical level? It would have to end sooner rather than later anyway.

As soon as the door clicked shut and she was alone again, she dropped her head to her desk. What the hell was she doing now? Hadn't she learned her lesson yet?

This was for the best.

It was.

Chapter 16

Is you a player?

Maksim sure as hell didn't feel like a player at this very moment. He felt—rejected.

He made a face. Rejected. Him. Unheard of.

He refused to think that. But one thing was for certain, he wasn't acting like a player. Flying without a net. That was the better description of what he was doing. And it was pissing him off. A lot.

He was used to not being able to read preternatural creatures' minds. He knew how to accept that, and most of the time paranormal beings were easy to understand. Jo, however, was a total mystery to him. And he was not pleased that he couldn't read her mind.

Not that he knew that for sure.

He'd debated jumping into Jo's head again just now. As soon as that damned unreadable mask had fallen back into place, he'd been irritated beyond belief. But still he didn't jump in.

And that pissed him off, too. What was stopping him? Was it the fear that he'd discover he couldn't read her mind again? Or was it the fact that he didn't want to hurt her?

Which idea bothered him more?

He was ruthless in getting what he wanted. And he wanted to keep having sex with Josephine Burke. After last night, he definitely wanted to have sex again. Yet, here he was walking away.

He should have just jumped in her head and mucked around. He wanted to know what she was thinking. About him. About her sister. About everything.

But he'd held back. He'd walked away.

Maksim Kostova, a demon known as Malebolgia, ruler of the eighth circle of Hell, didn't walk away from anything he wanted. He was known as a seducer, a flatterer, a deceiver. He always got what he wanted by using these abilities. These sins, as some saw them.

But instead of walking back to the center and taking what he wanted, he found himself wandering into a bar on Bourbon Street. He sat at a table in the corner and ordered a double whiskey on the rocks—how dreadfully human of him. Drowning his rejection in drink.

He was pathetic.

"Maksim is what?" Erika stopped slicing cheese and gaped at Jo.

Jo didn't look at Maggie, but she heard her wineglass hit the kitchen table with a loud clink.

Jo drew in the condensation from her glass of ice water, making wet swirls on Erika's sunshine yellow kitchen table. "He's been volunteering at the center." She tried to sound blasé.

"Jo," Erika said, her voice full of warning. "Do you think that's wise?"

Jo stopped water-doodling and glanced back and forth between her friends. Both women stared at her, and for some reason their shocked expressions irritated her. Even though she knew this was the reaction she would get.

"I had my doubts, too. But he's doing surprisingly well."

"I don't know," Maggie said, shaking her head.

"He's not a good person, Jo," Erika added, leaving the counter to sit at the table with Maggie and Jo.

Jo was surprised at the bluntness of her friend's statement. It wasn't like Erika, but instead of increasing her concern, it made her oddly protective—in Maksim's defense.

"You two are acting like the man is Satan himself."

Maggie coughed, choking on the sip of wine she'd just taken. But Jo's attention was distracted by a brushing around her ankles. Erika's cat mewed at her as she looked down.

"That was wrong of me to say," Erika said, once Maggie's coughing fit calmed. "We don't mean to pry or make you feel uncomfortable." She reached down and picked up her cat, who yowled in protest.

"Silly Boris," she murmured to the cranky black cat, stroking his fur.

The cat looked sullenly at Jo.

I hear ya, cat.

Her friends' reaction wasn't a surprise, but it still rubbed her the wrong way. She wanted to share with her friends. Her best friends. But she got the feeling they would be somehow disappointed in her. She was disappointed in herself.

She began drawing with the water again, getting lost in her thoughts about, well, everything.

Maggie reached out and placed her hand over Jo's, stopping her drawing.

"What is he helping with?" Maggie asked quietly as if she knew Jo was conflicted, the she needed her friends to understand.

Jo sighed. "He's helping with the daycare."

"The daycare?" Erika and Maggie said in unison.

So much for the understanding.

Jo laughed, although it was sounded flat even to her ears. "Yes. He's been up to his designer-clad neck in paste and finger paints and sticky fingerprints."

Neither of her friends said anything for a moment, so Jo added, "And surprisingly, he's good at it. The kids love him."

"Really?" Maggie said. Her brows drew in over her eyes as if Jo's assertion was the most puzzling thing she'd ever heard.

"Yes. He actually has pretty amazing past work experience with children. Better than mine as far as the community center goes."

"He does?" Erika also looked as if she'd never heard such a strange thing.

Jo nodded. She took a sip of her water, then she got up to grab a piece of cheese and a cracker from the platter Erika had been preparing, before Jo dropped the Maksim bomb.

She leaned on the counter. "He's been a Big Brother and worked with mentally challenged children." She took a bite of her cracker, chewing thoughtfully. "He's worked with terminally ill kids."

Erika and Maggie exchanged looks again, but for once, Jo didn't find the shared glance suspect or confusing. She knew exactly what they were thinking.

"Believe me," she said, "I didn't expect that about him, either. In fact, I didn't believe it to the point I thought he must have manufactured his résumé. But I was wrong. His recommendations were wonderful. I checked them all."

Maggie and Erika looked at each other again, clearly dumbfounded.

"I find that hard to believe," Erika finally said.

Boris picked that moment to meow, jump out of Erika's arms, and begin twining through Jo's legs again.

"I did, too," Jo told them, looking down at the persistent feline. Then she shrugged, irritation rising up in her, but she refused to show it. Instead she busied herself with eating her cheese and cracker, debating why their reactions were bothering her so much. Just a week ago, she'd have agreed with them completely.

Just a week ago.

God, a week ago she wouldn't have contemplated sleeping with him, either. Okay, she might have contemplated, but she wouldn't have done it.

She was a mess, and she was taking her own issues with herself out on the wrong people. Erika and Maggie loved her, and they just worried. Of course, there was no sharing the fact that she had slept with him. Her friends were pretty accepting, but that would do them in.

She did consider telling them about Jackson. Who would have thought bringing up her married ex-lover would be a welcome change of topic?

But Maggie spoke before she mustered the courage of opening that can of worms. "You look good. Are you feeling okay?"

Jo finished chewing the cheese she'd just popped in her mouth and nodded. "I'm feeling good. Not as tired." Not after the satisfied sleep of last night.

"I've heard the tiredness passes pretty quickly," Maggie said with a smile.

But Jo frowned. "What?"

Maggie blinked. "I—I thought you might have had a touch of a flu that has been going around."

Jo studied her friend for a moment, trying to tell if that was really what she'd meant.

"Maybe that's what had me so tired," she agreed. "But I have to admit having Maksim around has really helped me out. And I've been able to sleep better." Boy, was that an understatement.

"Well, if he's a help," Erika said without finishing the sentence as if the idea was so unlikely it didn't even merit completion.

Jo didn't add to it, either. Instead she changed the topic to Erika's work, a commissioned sculpture for the New Orleans Library. Then they talked about what Jo planned to do at the community center. They talked about the new furniture Maggie and Ren had bought, and about the trip to Italy they were planning in the summer.

By the end of the visit, things had gotten back to an easier, more pleasant place. Jo still hadn't told them anything about Jackson, or everything that had gone on between Maksim and herself. She was still holding back, but at least Erika and Maggie had let go of the fact that Maksim was working at the center, and that Jo wasn't going to get rid of him right away.

"I should head home," she finally said, after suppressing the third yawn in as many minutes.

"Are you sure?" Erika asked. "You could spend the night here."

Jo laughed. "I only live a few blocks away."

"We will walk you home," Maggie said, rising from her chair.

"No. I'm fine. It's not even late."

"New Orleans can be dangerous," Maggie said, still not returning to her seat.

"I know, and I will be fine. It's only ten o'clock. And I'll stay on Royal all the way. It will be fine."

Both of her friends looked as if they wanted to argue, but they didn't, perhaps worrying they'd disagreed with her enough for one night.

"And I have my cell. I will call you if I get the least bit nervous," Jo promised.

"Okay," Erika agreed. "But call Maggie's phone if you need us. You know my phone has a mind of its own. I really need to get a new one."

Jo laughed. Erika had been saying that for years.

"I will." Jo gathered her purse and headed for the door. "Okay. I'll talk to you both soon."

Maggie came forward and hugged her. "You do know we'll support anything you do, don't you?"

Jo studied her friend, getting that weird sensation again that she somehow knew more than she was telling. More than she possibly could.

"I know," Jo said—and she did. Jo just couldn't deal with talking yet.

"We are here for you," Erika said, joining them in their hug. Jo laughed, although tears suddenly threatened to choke her.

Man, she was a mess.

"Okay," she said, blinking to hide her reaction. "I think I'm hitting the wall. Off to bed with me."

She opened the door and Boris darted past her as she did.

"That cat," Erika said. "He's been acting so weird for days now."

"Cats are always weird," Jo said, watching the animal in question pace back and forth in front of the porch door, waiting to get out into the courtyard.

"Call when you get home," Maggie said, clearly still not pleased with the idea of Jo walking home alone.

"I will. 'Night."

She waved to her friends and headed out into the courtyard. The air was still balmy and if Jo listened carefully she could hear the revelry from Bourbon Street. The nice weather and nearness of so many people made her feel at ease taking her evening stroll home.

Boris scampered through the courtyard, his dark fur making him appear as nothing more than a shadow before he disappeared totally in the lush greenery.

Jo dug around in her purse looking for her key ring. She found it and unlocked the large doors that led to the street. Once outside on St. Ann Street, she could really hear the music and partiers on Bourbon.

She hummed a little, recognizing the strains of an eighties rock classic as she relocked the doors. She tossed the keys back in her satchellike purse and turned in the direction of Royal.

It was then that she saw her. The woman Jo had seen in Maggie and Erika's courtyard a few days ago. The woman whom she'd now written off as one of the bizarre lucid dreams she'd been experiencing of late. She'd even convinced herself that she had dozed in the lawn chair and dreamed the whole event.

But there she stood as clear as day by one of the posts supporting the gallery balcony on the front of Ren's building. Her black hair fell down her back in waves; her eyes were pale and almost seemed to glow in the lamplight. She watched Jo as if she was waiting to see if she noticed her.

Jo didn't move, and she didn't look away from the woman.

"Hello," Jo called, and again Jo was struck with the notion that the woman seemed to expect her to be talking about someone else. She didn't look behind her like she had the first time, but she seemed a little startled by Jo's attention.

The woman didn't move, so Jo took a step toward her.

"Can I help you?" Jo asked.

The woman frowned, the wrinkling of her forehead doing nothing to mar her ethereal beauty. Then she nodded.

"Are you in trouble?" Jo got the feeling she was. Not that she looked frightened or panicked. More like sadness wrapped around her.

She hesitated, then nodded.

"Do you need me to call someone?"

Again she nodded.

"Can you give me a name?"

Another nod.

Then the woman mouthed something. Jo shook her head, unable to make out what she'd said. She stepped closer, trying to get a better look at her face. Shadows from the balcony above played across her lovely face, making it hard for Jo to see her clearly.

"Say it again."

The woman mouthed the words again, and when Jo shook her head, still not making out what she said.

"I'm sorry. I can't see you well. Can you step into the light?"

The woman shook her head, and Jo wondered why not. Why did she have to cling to the shadows?

Loud laughter and voices drew Jo's attention away from the woman. A group of drunken revelers weaved down the sidewalk toward them. Jo moved out of the way, giving them plenty of space to pass as their impaired motor skills were making it hard for them to navigate.

When they finally weaved and cackled their way to the next block, Jo turned back to the woman.

She was gone.

"Hello?" Jo called, searching the shadows for her. "Hello?"

She looked, seeing nothing. No hint the woman had ever been there. Just as before.

She walked to the corner of St. Ann and Royal, which was the only direction she could have gone in. Otherwise she would have had to pass Jo. But Jo saw no one who looked like the woman on the streets.

She debated, then paced back to Ren's. No sign of her at all.

Then Jo heard a noise and looked up. Erika's cat sat up on the courtyard wall, peering down at her with pale eyes that flashed iridescently in the streetlight.

Jo stared at the cat. The cat stared back, those glittering eyes familiar, and the strangest notion entered her mind.

No. She was being crazy. Yet again. How could she even consider something so outlandish?

She tugged her purse up higher on her shoulder and started walking briskly in the direction of Royal.

She laughed out loud at her train of thought, realizing she probably looked and sounded like a madwoman. Not that her behavior would even merit a second glance in the Quarter.

But she felt like she might be going mad. In fact, given the events of the whole week, the chances were pretty high.

Was she really entertaining the idea that the strange mute woman and Erika's cat were one and the same?

She hastened her steps as if she could outrun the preposterous and frankly disturbing idea.

Chapter 17

Jo was relieved when she made it home without any more sightings of disappearing mute women—who could potentially be cats. Or little dead girls in rainbow-striped bathing suits. Or anything else that might be perceived as disturbingly weird. And that signified her fall into the abyss of insanity.

She bolted her door, then rooted around in her purse for her cell. She dialed Maggie's number, waiting only two rings before her friend answered.

"You made it?"

"Yes," Jo said, trying to sound normal. God, she was feeling anything but.

"Good. Listen, Jo, I'm sorry if we sounded critical about Maksim. I think it's great that he's been a help."

Jo nodded, then realized Maggie couldn't tell that over the phone. "Thank you, Maggie."

"And I want you to know you can tell me anything. Erika, too."

"I know," Jo said, believing her friend. But still none of the truths of her life in the past few months came to her lips. Why? What held her back?

Maggie would understand her pain over Jackson's betrayal. Maggie had been badly hurt by a man before meeting Ren. If anyone would know how Jo felt, it would be her.

And Erika always believed in the ability to tell the future. She loved going to psychics. She'd believe Jo's story about her sister and the long-ago-experienced premonition. She'd probably even believe her about what she'd thought she'd seen.

Yet, no words came. Why? Why?

Despite her questioning, she knew the answer. If she told her dear friends, then everything would be real. She couldn't deny it any longer. And she wasn't ready for the truth. About anything. She wanted to hide—to let all those things stay in her past.

But they can't. Not now. Not with what was happening.

"You'll talk to us when you are ready, right?"

Jo blinked, almost forgetting Maggie was still on the end of the line. How long had she been silent?

"Yes," Jo said. "Thanks."

Jo said good-bye and hung up. She set her phone on the kitchen counter, then looked around, not quite certain what to do next.

She glanced at her phone, tempted to call Maksim. But instead, she shook her head. As if she didn't have enough going on. She didn't need to add him to the mix.

Sighing, she headed to her bedroom. Tonight, she would crawl into bed early. Maybe read. Do something calm and normal and relaxing.

She changed into a pair of baggy men's-style pajamas, then crawled into her bed. She grabbed a novel from the top of a pile she had on her nightstand. Books she'd been meaning to read, but hadn't had time.

Dead By Dawn. That didn't sound like a story that would calm her overactive imagination. She grabbed another one. *Mansfield Park* by Jane Austen. One of the few Austen books she hadn't read yet. Getting lost in the social webs of the Regency era seemed like a good fit for her mood.

She'd let herself get involved in other people's deceptions and missteps in propriety. Flipping open the book, she read the first line . . .

Oh, yeah, this would work. She was immediately drawn into someone else's drama. Good.

A crash woke Jo. She sat up in her bed. The lamp still cast warm yellow light around her room. Blackness still colored her windows.

She must have fallen asleep reading. She looked around the bedding, discovering the book had fallen to the floor.

She sank back against her pillows. That was all that woke her. Her eyes drifted closed again, and she told herself she would turn off her lamp. In a minute.

Sleepy. She was so sleepy.

Then she heard another noise. The sound faint, just barely seeping into her fatigue-hazed mind. But then the sound came into clear focus. A sound she knew and had heard before.

Her eyes opened as she listened. The noise hadn't come from within her room. At least she didn't think so. It seemed like it must have come from the hallway.

She didn't move, keeping absolutely still, waiting. Telling herself she wouldn't hear it again. That she'd imagined it.

But there the noise was again. Faint, but there.

Fear rose up in her chest, burning the back of her throat. But she didn't stir, paralyzed with her own dread.

Go away. Go away.

Then she heard it again, closer this time. The sound from the restroom, the sound from the hallway at the community center. Pattering feet. Small feet. But more than that, she now knew what made the sound so distinct.

They weren't just small, bare feet on hard wood. They were wet feet. The watery pattering echoing from in the hallway. The sound made more distinct by that slap of wetness on a hard surface.

Jo swallowed, only her eyes shifting toward her doorway. From her angle on the bed, she could only make out the dim light from the kitchen. But the hint of light didn't make the situation less frightening.

Jo didn't want to see the moving shadows of what was coming in her direction on small wet feet. She didn't want to see it. Her.

She closed her eyes, digging her fingers into her comforter, tugging the material up to her chin. She was acting like a terrified child, but she didn't care. She was terrified.

The steps stopped.

Jo remained quiet, except for the occasional shaky, shallow release of her own breath. Minutes ticked by, or at least it felt that way. Still no sound.

Finally, Jo peeked an eye open. Her room was quiet, empty. She loosened her grip on her bedding and opened her eyes fully. Nothing appeared out of the ordinary. Her dresser stood against the far wall. A chintz chair in pale yellow sat in the corner, its matching pillow angled against the back.

A picture of cows grazing in a wildflower-filled field hung on the wall by her bed. Everything was just as it should be.

Except for the creepy coldness that prickled her skin. The chill she now realized had surrounded her as soon as she'd heard the first steps. Eerie chilliness draining away all the warmth of the room.

She eased upright, leaning forward a little to try and see out into the hallway. She could make out one small corner, the start of the built-ins that lined the length.

This is crazy. She couldn't hide here, huddling under the covers like a little kid.

She needed to prove to herself for once and all that this was just some strange waking dream. Some crazy hallucination brought on by the changes around her.

Even as she came up with these justifications, she doubted them. Had a waking dream created the nose clip she'd found this morning? No, but there had to be a rational explanation for that, too. She hadn't thought of one, but it had to be there. Just like there were answers to all of these odd events.

Carefully, she swung her legs over the edge of the bed. She fought the urge to scurry away from her bed as the image of something shaking out from under the dust ruffle and grabbing her ankle flashed in her mind.

Stay calm. Stay calm. If she didn't expect to find anything, then she wouldn't. And there was nothing there. Just the noises of an old house. The odd quirks of aging air conditioning.

"It's nothing. It's nothing," she chanted softly to herself as she took tentative steps toward her bedroom door. She paused, just as she reached it, suddenly terrified to take the final stride and see what was there.

"What *isn't* there," she corrected, her voice barely above a whisper. "There's nothing there."

With a forced movement, she made herself step into the doorway.

Pent-up breath rushed from her as she was greeted by an empty, dimly lit hallway.

She laughed slightly at her own ridiculousness.

"See. Nothing."

But the laughter died on her lips as she noticed something. She shook her head, not wanting to believe what she was seeing, but closing her eyes, looking away, then looking back, but nothing made the sight go away.

Down the length of her hallway puddles glistened in the faint light. Small, wet footprints headed right toward her bedroom. Headed right toward her.

She made a panicked noise in the back of her throat, backing away from the sight. She didn't understand what was going on, but she did understand one thing. She was scared. Very, very scared.

Maksim lay on his bed, staring up at the ceiling. He gritted his teeth, irritated by the sense of melancholy that filled him. The five glasses of whiskey hadn't numbed the aching want in him, in his loins, in his chest.

He should just go back to Hell. The fiery pit with all its suffering and pain would be a welcome relief compared to what he was experiencing now.

What was the human saying? It's easier to deal with the devil you know? Something like that. And he was getting a pretty good understanding of what that meant.

He rolled over onto his side, sighing. He looked at the paintings on his sister's wall. A still life of flowers in a blue vase. A portrait of a lady with her brown hair pulled up onto the top of her head in some elaborate twist. Her pale shoulders bare.

He immediately thought of Jo—not that his thoughts were ever far from him these days. He gritted his teeth again, closing his eyes and concentrating on the dry, stark, unwelcoming environment of the Eighth Circle.

As he pictured it, the smell of brimstone encompassed him, sulfur and heat burning his nostrils, the back of his throat.

Just as he would have materialized back into his domain, his cell phone rang. The T-mobile jingle pulling him back from his astral travels.

Damn, you can't even go to the Eighth Circle of Hell without a damned cell phone interrupting you.

He reached over to the nightstand to the small ringing device. He peered at the illuminated screen, his heart jumping at the number he saw there.

He shook his head at his own ridiculousness. Despite his irritation with his eagerness, he flipped the phone open, quickly saying, "Hello?"

He was greeted by silence.

"Hello?" he repeated.

"Maksim?" Jo finally said, her voice weak and strained.

"Jo?" He sat up, pressing the phone tighter to his ear. "What's wrong?"

"Can—can you come here?" Her voice broke on the last word, but he couldn't tell if that was because she was crying or what was wrong.

"What's wrong?" he repeated, even as he was swinging his legs over the edge of the bed. He toed around for the shoes he'd kicked off as he'd fallen onto his bed.

"I—I just need you."

"Okay," he said, shoving on his shoes and already heading through his sister's apartment to the front door. "Just tell me what's going on?"

"I'm—scared."

Now he could hear that something akin to hysteria tinged her voice, making it reedy and hard to hear.

"What are you scared of?" He paused with his hand on the door, waiting for her to speak.

"My sister," she said so softly he wasn't sure if he'd heard her right.

"Your sister?"

"Please just come."

He didn't wait any longer. Without further thought, he dematerialized, there one minute, gone the next.

Jo clutched her cell phone with both hands, pressing it like a lifeline to her ear, as though as long as she had that connection to Maksim, nothing could hurt her. She huddled on the sofa, her back pressed against the back, her legs curled up to her chest. She watched the hallway, waiting for him to respond.

"Maksim?" she said, not hearing him. She listened, trying to hear over the pounding of her heart in her ears, over the panting quality of her breaths.

"Maksim?"

Oh God, she'd lost the connection with him. She lifted her phone from her ear, looking at the screen. It said they were still connected.

"Maksim? Are you there?"

Nothing but dead air.

She flipped the phone closed, then reopened it, and quickly scrolled through her saved numbers, searching for Maksim's number. But in her panic, she pressed too many times, passed it, and started dialing some other number.

"No," she said, snapping the phone closed again. She reopened it and tried again.

Just as she reached his number, a loud bang on her door made her jump. She nearly dropped her phone in her surprise.

Staring toward the kitchen and her front door, she waited. Another loud pound, then a muffled voice called, "Jo? Are you there?"

She eased up off the sofa, still feeling too shaken by all the events of the night that she was hesitant to even believe her ears.

Crossing quietly to the door, she leaned an ear toward it.

"Maksim, is that you?"

"Yes? What's going on? Let me in."

With shaky fingers, she unbolted her door. She tugged on the doorknob, practically sagging with relief when she saw it was really Maksim there. He still held his cell phone, although it was no longer pressed against his ear.

"Jo?"

She didn't answer him, she just fell into his arms, trembling and fighting back tears.

His strong arms came up to hold her, and instantly some of her fear drained away.

"What's wrong? Please tell me."

Jo shook her head. She didn't want to talk about it, she just wanted to know she was safe. And somehow she knew having him here would make her feel that way.

He shifted her away from him, so he could see her face.

"Come on, baby," he said, his voice low and coaxing. "Please tell me what's got you so upset."

She looked up into his eyes. Green eyes like sparkling chips of peridot. Except not cold, not lifeless, but filled with such concern. Such fear—for her.

Without further thought, she pressed her lips to his.

Chapter 18

Maksim didn't know what was going on, but there was no way in hell he was going to stop Jo's kiss. Instead, he pulled her closer, taking control of her frantic embrace. Gradually, her movements calmed under his, not growing any less passionate, just less frenzied, less desperate.

Her arms curled around his neck, clinging to him as if afraid he would disappear, but her lips moved more slowly, more sensually under his. She groaned, leaning into him. He pulled her up against his chest, lifting her bodily against him.

Without breaking their kiss, he picked her up completely, carrying her inside her apartment, kicking the door closed with his foot.

For a moment, they remained in the kitchen, her cradled in his arms, their lips tasting, tongues tangling, desire rising.

He moaned as she gently nipped his bottom lip.

Thinking of only one thing, he headed in the direction of her bedroom. But before he even reached the hallway, she broke the kiss and strained against him. The panic he'd seen when she'd opened her door was back, completely blotting out any hint of desire.

"I don't want to go down there," she said, not looking at "there," just staring at him.

"Down where? To your bedroom?"

"Yes. Please stay here." Her arms tightened around his neck as if she thought that would stop him from moving.

And he let that be the case. He nodded and headed to the sofa, settling on the slipcovered cushions, keeping her on his lap.

"Okay, tell me what the hell is going on," he said.

Again, he thought she was going to avoid the question. But finally, after a bit of fidgeting and toying with the buttons of his shirt, she spoke.

"I saw something in the hallway."

He waited, allowing her to gather her words.

"I saw footprints."

He frowned. Now that wasn't what he'd expected her to say. Not that he'd been sure what she'd say. Maybe a mouse? A rat? A big spider? One of those large, unnervingly fast cockroaches?

"Footprints?"

She nodded, clearly not hearing his bewilderment as she shot a glance over her shoulder at the hallway. As if she expected these footprints to come—and do what?

"Jo, what kind of footprints are we talking about? Do you think someone broke in?"

She shook her head, again casting another quick, very nervous look at the door.

Maksim waited again, really starting to wonder if Jo was losing it. He didn't think she was the type to be this frightened without cause, but what the hell had her so scared of some supposed footprints on the floor?

"Show me," he said, and for a moment she didn't move on his lap. He half-expected her to say no, but then she did move, slowly dropping her bare feet to the floor.

He rose behind her, slipping his hand in hers and squeezing her fingers, fingers that felt like cold, stiff twigs against his palms.

Whatever she was telling him, one thing was clear, she was terrified. She stared at the hallway, and he squeezed her fingers again, giving her silent encouragement.

She took a hesitant step, then another, until she was standing at the mouth of the hallway. The pale yellow walls of her bedroom glowed warmly at the far end. Otherwise, the hallway was empty, quiet, harmless looking.

She stared at the floor. He did, too, seeing nothing but slightly uneven and worn hard wood. He looked at Jo, who frowned. She took another step, actually entering the hallway proper. Then she flipped on a light switch on her left.

The light blazed on from the middle of the hallway, brightly illuminating the off-white walls, wood floors, and shelves of books and pictures.

But he did not see anything that looked like footprints.

"There's nothing," she said, confirming his opinion. "They are gone."

Maksim didn't answer her, instead tugging at her hand, walking down the length of the hallway, examining the flooring, trying to see something. Because he knew she needed someone to confirm what had her so afraid.

"Are you sure you weren't just dreaming?" he finally asked once they'd reached her bedroom.

"Yes. I know I saw them."

He nodded, not trying to rationalize away her visions any further. He knew she didn't want to hear that. She had to come to terms with what she saw, or thought she saw, on her own.

She stared back down the hallway, then turned to collapse on her bed. Maksim followed her, sitting beside her, the mattress dipping under his weight, making her tip against him.

He put an arm around her, pulling her stiff body against his side.

They were both silent for a moment.

Finally he asked, "Who do you think left the footprints?"

Jo stopped staring off into space, lost in her own thoughts, her own memories—probably her own justifications—and gaped up at him.

"You believe me?"

He nodded. He couldn't very well tell her that he'd seen much stranger things in his existence, on a regular basis. Things that would make disappearing footprints look like an average everyday happening.

"So who do you think they belonged to?"

Jo wasn't sure whether she wanted to laugh or cry. Maksim seemed to readily accept she'd seen what she'd seen. But she didn't know if she wanted that. Part of her wanted those prints to be there, because it would prove she wasn't losing her mind. But if they were there, then she was at risk of losing her mind anyway. Neither choice said good things for her mental health.

But as she stared at Maksim, who waited for her to answer, his pale green eyes holding no doubt, no judgment, all that mattered was that he was there, willing to accept whatever she told him.

Instead of speaking, she leaned up and kissed him again. Having him here, having him hold her and take her away from her thoughts, seemed far more important than her answer. At least at this moment.

And he responded to her kiss, just as easily, just as willingly, as he'd accepted what she'd seen. But this response was so much sweeter.

She shifted, turning to him, linking her arms around his neck. His arms came around her back and he pulled her down with him as he fell back onto her bed.

She followed readily, sliding more fully on top of him, her breasts pressed to his hard chest. Her legs tangling with his, her fingers slipping into his hair.

"Jo," he murmured against her lips, her name a sensual

brush against her own mouth. A hot breath, a hungry plea. She moaned and captured his mouth, her tongue mingling with his tongue, a delicious, rough rasp.

Quickly the kiss grew frenzied, ravenous as desire grew between them, around them like a rising eddying whirlwind. Maksim's large hands caught her head, taking control of the kiss. Her fingers knotted in his hair, tugging, taking a measure of control back.

Then she found herself flipped, her body pinned between the softness of her bedding and delicious hardness of his body.

"I've thought about this all day," he told her, nipping the bare skin of her shoulder. Her collarbone. The side of her neck. She arched under him, loving each bite, each teasing pinch, the hard edge of his teeth against her fragile flesh.

"Me, too," she heard herself say, even though she knew she shouldn't admit something like that. More dangerous than the admission of a dead sister wandering around her apartment. More dangerous for her mental health. But it was out and she couldn't take it back. Just like she couldn't stop what was going to happen here in this bed.

With that realization, she tugged at his T-shirt, pulling it up, baring his muscular back, his amazing flat, hard abdomen.

Maksim rose up, his legs straddling hers, his hands stroking up and down her thighs. The strength of his fingers feeling deliciously strong and masculine even through the cotton of her pajamas.

"Are you sure you don't want to tell me what had you so upset?" he said, his voice soft, as if he didn't really want to address the issue but thought he should.

She shook her head, her fingers slipping under his shirt again. His eyes drifted close as she caressed his smooth skin and hard muscles. His dark lashes looked sinfully long against his cheeks, every inch of him, even those lashes exuding sex appeal.

Maksim opened his eyes, his lids heavy with desire, but serious, too.

"Have you considered that you are doing this with me, because you are trying to avoid what happened to you tonight? To forget what you saw?"

Her fingers paused on his skin. "Yes."

Maksim stared at her for a moment as if he hadn't expected her to admit her strategy so readily. Then a slow, sexy smile spread across his beautifully sculpted lips.

"I'm good with that."

Jo smiled too. "Good."

Maksim slid back over Jo, wondering what the hell had motivated him to ask her such things. To give her a way out. To be the voice of reason.

Now that was something he tried to avoid.

He kissed her, tasting her instant response, those amazing fingers of hers stroking over his skin, around his sides, up his back. Thankfully, she wasn't looking for reason. Despite his own stupidity in offering it.

This time he broke away only long enough to strip his shirt off over his head. Jo made a noise of appreciation, the low sound as seductive as her fingers on his skin. Then her fingers moved to the button of his jeans, and he changed his mind. Nothing, absolutely nothing beat the feeling of those fingers.

She slipped the button open, then the zipper. Her fingers then disappeared inside, cupping him.

"You have a very nice penis," she said with a satisfied little smile, gently squeezing him. His cock pulsed in response through his shorts.

"He likes you, too."

She laughed. "I can tell."

She levered herself up to kiss him, her mouth soft and sweet clinging to his, showing him what she wanted from him, by the movement of her lips, of her body brushing against him.

He caught her head between his hands, taking control of the kiss.

But Jo being Jo, she wasn't about to let him have all of the power. She slipped an arm around his neck and pulled him down onto her, her hand still holding his painfully hard erection. They kissed, their passion building each caress of their lips, their hands fanning their need. A rising fire burning inside both of them.

His hands left her hair, sliding down over her shoulders, tugging down the strap of her camisole top, exposing one breast. His lips latched onto the swollen nipple, tugging deeply on the rosy tautness. She gasped, her hips grinding up against him.

"Sensitive, aren't you?"

"Ohh, yeah."

He abraded the peaked tip again between his teeth, being rewarded by another sharp gasp. So he suckled her gently, soothing the sensitive flesh with his tongue.

But that didn't seem to calm her. Instead, she captured his head and pulled his mouth back up to her.

"That makes me crazy," she muttered roughly against his lips. "They are so sensitive."

Maksim smiled against her mouth. Something about the way she said that made him think that her breasts normally weren't so tender, so responsive. Pride expanded his chest at the idea that she was reacting more to him than she had others in the past.

He pulled back, his fingers brushing her distended nipple, twirling it between his fingers, watching her closely as he did so. Her brown hair spilled around her on the cream-colored sheets. Then her fingers still in his jeans worked up and down the responsive underside of his cock.

Even through his jockey shorts, her touch was almost too much. She drove him wild. How something so tame, given the types of things he'd done in the past with creatures who were far from tame, could almost push him to ejaculation was mind-boggling.

But there was something about this mortal. This slender, stunningly lovely mortal with dark, dark eyes and a guarded heart.

His fingers paused on her breast. Where were these thoughts coming from? He had her lying under him, and he was thinking about her heart. He should be thinking about how tight she would feel around him. How good he'd feel buried deep inside her. How loud he could make her cry out as he plunged into her over and over. How he could get through that guard with every orgasm.

He groaned, frustrated with his own desperate, needy thoughts. And aroused all the same.

Pulling away from her, he stood and tugged his shirt off, then his pants, impatience in his movements. Impatience with himself and with his uncontrollable desire for this woman.

She watched him with a small, smug smile on her lips. She stretched as he watched, her movement sinuous, sensual. Then she wriggled her hips, working down her pajama bottoms, baring herself from the waist down, her legs long and perfectly shaped, the tiny triangle of hair equally perfect. Her hands moved to her top, easing it up slowly, arching her back to toss the small garment aside. Her firm breasts glowed creamy white in the mellow lamplight.

She stretched again, the movement seductive, enticing like a siren basking in the sand, luring men to her.

"Vixen," he said, his voice filled with both frustration and amusement: Frustration that he couldn't seem to check his response to her and amused because she knew it, and she loved it.

"You do realize you are about to get so fucked."

She laughed at his coarse statement.

"Oh, I'm counting on it," she said with another self-satisfied grin.

His muscles tensed, his skin prickled with painful aware-ness; he groaned, this time with surrender.

Did he care how easily she controlled him?

He crawled back over Jo's delectably stretched-out body. She moaned as his weight came down on her. Her arms pulled her tighter to him. Her legs parted to cradle him, the moist heat there making his whole body pulse with unbridled desire,

Oh, hell no, he didn't.

Chapter 19

Jo gasped as his weight pressed her down into the mattress. She loved the way he felt—all hard muscles, all velvety skin. She loved the possessiveness of his kisses, the dominance of his touch.

She kissed him, her lips clinging fiercely to his. Then her hands, which had been stroking his back, came up to brace his shoulders, curling into the latent strength there. She pushed him over, crawling onto him, straddling him.

"You just lay still," she told him.

He raised an eyebrow, but did as she asked. She grinned, even as intense passion surged through her. Passion made all the more sharply intense by being able to dominate this strong, powerful man.

She leaned down and lightly bit his nipple and he gasped, his body jerking under hers. She lapped it, soothing away an hint of pain.

A hand came up, cupping the back of her head, directing her to him. But she caught his wrist and pinned it back to the bed. Her other hand found his other wrist and pinioned it up over his head, the position bringing her breasts level with his face.

"Now, you behave," she warned.

He lifted his head and captured her nipple in his mouth, drawing on her hard.

Pleasure shot through her, puddling between her thighs. Unable to control herself, she ground herself against him, his thick hard shaft slipping between her wet lips, rubbing right where she most needed to be touched.

Both of them groaned.

She straightened slightly, still restraining his arms above him. Watching him, she moved, sliding her hips back and forth like she was riding him in a slow, delicious canter.

His eyes closed and his breath escaped him in shallow shudders. She continued, her flesh growing slicker from their mutual arousal. Her own breath grew more harsh, more broken as her desire rose, taking her over.

A small sob escaped her lips as her head fell back, her orgasm right there, right on the edge of spilling over.

Then Maksim broke her hold, his hands gripping her hips. He lifted her and set her down on him, filling her wet vagina to the hilt in one smooth thrust.

A loud cry surrounded them, and Jo was only vaguely aware that it was her own voice. She was too overwhelmed, too encompassed in her own release. Nothing existed but Maksim's strength filling her and her own pulsating bliss.

Gradually, reality came back to her and she realized she was draped over him, her body a puddle of sated release. His hands still held her hips, loosely now.

Finally, after her breath returned to some semblance of normalcy, she muttered, "You just couldn't let me have control, could you?"

He chuckled, although she was glad to hear the sound was breathy.

"You had control," he assured her. "My brain is mush."

She smiled, pressing a kiss to his chest. Then she stretched, savoring his sinew under her.

She raised her head, her eyes wide. "Well, your brain is all that's mush." She wiggled her hips. He was rock hard, still buried inside her.

She frowned. "You didn't?"

He smiled at her, raising one of his dark brows. "Didn't what?"

She sat up, widening her eyes.

He laughed. "Not yet. Believe me, I am not done with you." He jerked his hips, moving inside her.

Instantly she could feel her body coming alive, anticipating what he had in mind for her now. As if reading her mind and more than happy to show her, the hands on her hips tightened and began to guide her on him, moving her in a slow, persuasive motion.

Jo braced her hands on Maksim's chest, balancing herself as he moved inside her.

"You feel so damned good," he muttered, his voice rough with hungry need.

She made a noise in response, clearly lost in the feeling of them joined. Flesh to flesh, a tight slick joining.

Her fingers curled into his chest, her blunt, tidy nails digging into his skin. He relished the bite of them, the feeling somewhere between pleasure and pain.

Then she used her leverage to steady herself, and gradually, and magnificently, she started to take a little control. It wasn't until she'd changed the rhythm totally that he realized what she'd done. She simply felt too damned good.

First she moved a little faster, then shifted a little slower. For a moment, he tried to maintain his command, but then he gave over to her.

He moaned long and low, arcing his back, feeling ecstasy gripping his spine.

"How does that feel?" She rotated her hips slightly as she continued sliding up and down him.

He groaned, closing his eyes, doing nothing but feeling her. Feeling himself inside her.

"Damn, you feel good."

She smiled, pivoting her hips more. He groaned again. But he couldn't let her keep the pace. He was too close. Too willing to submit to her.

"Turn around?" he said, his voice a harsh demand.

"What?" She blinked at him, her eyes hazed with lust-muddled confusion.

"Turn around. On your knees."

He half-expected her to deny him. But she slid off him, cool air a jarring, not particularly pleasant shock to his wet, glistening cock.

Don't worry, buddy. You'll be home again. There was no way he was staying out of this woman a moment longer than necessary.

He turned to her, finding her on the mattress, her perfect, wonderfully rounded ass in the air, the pink lips of her sex glittery, damp, and luscious in the low lamplight.

He touched her, cupping her cheek, running his thumb down the crevice of her derriere to those hot wet lips. He brushed over them, letting her juice soak his finger. Then he leaned forward and pressed his mouth to her, his tongue entering the tight heat his cock had just left.

She cried out, her hips bucking. And he moaned. Then his tongue flicked out of her, sliding down to find her pebbled clitoris.

The small nub of flesh pulsed at his touch. He licked her, savoring each pulsating, mindless little whimper she made into her mattress.

"Jo, you taste so good."

She made another unthinking moan, her only response to indicate that she heard. Or that she might have heard.

He returned his mouth to her, licking, swirling, sucking until she cried out, that noise telling him exactly what had happened.

Then as she lay, her face against the covers, her sweet ass still raised in the air, he took her hips in his hands, positioned himself and returned his cock to the place it most wanted to be.

To his utter shock, he thrust only a half-dozen times, and she shouted out again, the walls of her vagina squeezing him in violent convulsion. He made it two more pumps, then roared out his own release.

He collapsed beside her, pulling her against him, his body curling around hers.

Neither of them spoke, the room echoing with their ragged breaths. Finally, when her breathing had evened out and he thought she must have fallen asleep, she roused herself enough to glance over her shoulder at him.

She smiled, her expression sleepy and sweet.

"Well," she said, then paused as a cute little yawn escaped her, "I guess we both got so fucked."

For a moment, Maksim didn't react. Then a burst of laughter shook his chest and filled the room. He hugged her against him, feeling . . .

Happy, content, that all was right with the world.

He tried to muster concern that none of his inherent disillusionment seemed to be present, but the disquiet didn't come.

He squeezed her and kissed the top of her head, feeling fine with his sense of well-being. He could worry about being a bitter, cynical demon tomorrow.

Unfortunately tomorrow came all too soon.

Maksim stretched, liking the cool, soft feeling of the bedding around him. He liked the smell, too, a scent of warmth and flowers like heated roses with vanilla. Jo's scent.

He rolled over and opened his eyes, expecting to find Jo sound asleep beside him. But he was greeted by tossed-aside blankets and the impression in the pillow where Jo had been.

Sitting up, he scanned the room, then listened once he discovered he was truly alone. He could hear her in the kitchen, the clatter of dishes, the opening and closing of the fridge. The faint sound of music.

Throwing his legs over the side of the bed, he stood, then stretched, his muscles feeling good and well-used. Then without bothering with clothes, he padded to the kitchen.

"Good morning," he said to Jo's back as he entered. She turned, nearly sloshing her coffee as she took in his naked state. Her eyes skimmed quickly over him, then stayed on his face.

"Good morning." Her voice was cool and distant. "Coffee?"

He frowned. "Sure."

She turned back to the counter as if she'd turn to stone if she looked at his nudeness a moment longer. She reached up into her cupboard for a mug, the mug in question clattering against wood and other ceramics in her hurry to retrieve it. Finally, she snagged it.

"Milk? Sugar?" she asked, not looking at him.

"Both."

She nodded, still not looking at him. She busied herself with preparing it. The clack of the spoon on the edge of the cup was deafeningly loud as she stirred. Her attention was conspicuously focused on her work.

Finally when there was truly nothing more she could do with the damned coffee to keep her focus off him, she turned.

Still barely looking in his direction, she placed the mug on her café-style kitchen table.

"There you go."

He stepped forward, bringing himself just inches from her, and took a sip.

"Perfect."

She nodded, her gaze darting past him toward the hallway. Toward escape.

It almost seemed like a dream now. Last night. The fear of that very same hallway. The security she found in his presence. The pleasure.

"Okay," she said with a smile that didn't reach her dark eyes. "I'm going to go get ready for work."

She brushed past him.

And just like that well-being disappeared. And he instantly remembered why he'd avoided that particular feeling. It only made the bitterness all the more intense and unbearable in its wake.

Jo rushed into her room, closing the door behind her as if a panel of wood could keep him out. Or protect her from her own thoughts.

God, last night had been wonderful. Truly wonderful.

And that scared her to death. Maybe more than her crazy delusions about her sister. But then, wasn't this just another crazy delusion of a different kind?

She stood in the middle of her bedroom, not really seeing anything, not really sure what she was doing. She just knew when she woke up this morning she'd been ridiculously pleased that Maksim was still there, one arm flung over his head, the other flung possessively over her.

She had stayed beside him, even as she told herself she should get up, she should put space between herself and her feelings for him. But she hadn't left him right away. Instead she'd touched his hair, his arm, the soft skin of his lips. And she'd let herself imagine them having a future.

She drifted in a fantasy of romance and love and a home with this man. A family.

And that was what pushed her out of bed. That she couldn't expect that kind of feeling from Maksim. She'd been with Jackson for months, and she hadn't gotten that response from him. He'd denied her all of that. He'd cheated, he'd lied, and in the end left her to handle all the mess herself. He hadn't wanted her, or what she was offering.

She wrapped her arms around her midriff and fought back tears. He hadn't wanted her and a family, and why would Maksim?

She kept her arms wrapped tightly around her as she wandered to the bed, trying to ignore the memories the rumpled bedding brought back to her.

She couldn't let herself feel anything. She couldn't. And God knew she was good at that particular defense mechanism. Control and denial. That was what kept her going, kept her safe.

So she would tell herself she wasn't feeling anything about Maksim. She'd get dressed for work, she would go to work, and she would emerge back into what made sense to her. And she'd get through this.

She tightened her arms around her stomach.

She would get through it all.

By the time Maksim knocked on her door, Jo was fully dressed in a no-nonsense blue suit, her hair up in a tight, severe bun, her glasses in place. All traces of the shaken, unsure woman were gone.

Of course, once she opened the door, she was confronted again with the fact that he'd been sitting in her kitchen all this time, naked. But she managed to keep her eyes averted as she said, "Sorry. I'll leave you to get dressed."

She slipped past him, making sure not even her sleeve brushed against him. Maksim didn't move into the room, nor did he speak.

As she hurried away, she could feel his eyes burning into the center of her back all the way down the hallway. But she refused to look back, or to let herself be shaken.

Falling for Maksim Kostova was destined to be doomed.

Chapter 20

Maksim watched Jo dart down the hallway, and he fought the urge to enter her head to understand what the hell had happened to her in the course of a few hours to make her so wary of him, so on edge, so unwilling to even look at him.

He glanced down at himself, then raised his eyebrow. He was nude, but that certainly hadn't bothered her last night. He turned and entered her bedroom. But he knew he wouldn't jump into her head. He was already afraid that he might have caused her damage.

What if her fear last night had been somehow related to what he'd done to her? He had to consider that. And while he wasn't pleased with her reaction this morning, he wasn't willing to hurt her.

He paused while pulling on his jeans. Why was he doing this again? Why was he putting his concerns for this mortal woman above his own desires? He tugged his jeans up and fastened them.

He needed to think about all of this. And he really needed to get a grip. Tugging on the rest of his clothing in abrupt, irritated movements, he decided he needed a break from this woman. She was making him crazy.

He shoved his feet into his shoes and headed directly back to the kitchen. Jo stood, leaning a hip against the kitchen counter. Her arms were folded around herself in an almost protective way. She worried her bottom lip between her teeth. Her dark eyes were distant, distracted.

Everything about her stance annoyed him. Where was the warm, open, and uninhibited woman from last night?

After a second, she looked at him. "I think we should talk."

Mmm, he didn't have to be a genius to know that wasn't a good announcement.

"About what?"

"About this situation." She turned so her whole body faced him, although her gaze moved around the room. Everywhere but on him.

"Okay. Go ahead." He didn't want to hear her words, but he didn't think she would be stopped.

"I think this needs to end. It's too complicated."

Maksim tried to remain calm, cool, which was hard given his blood had come to a slow, steady simmer. She was ending things? When they'd barely begun? After how they'd both reacted last night?

Humans were certifiable. No wonder he usually had little use for them. She was lucky to have his attention. His lust. She was lucky, and he should be the one calling the shots, deciding when things would end.

But instead of saying any of that, he asked, "Why is it too complicated?"

Jo didn't answer. She tightened her arms around herself, and stood so straight, she looked as if her spine could snap in two with just a little pressure.

Finally, she said, "I just think it's for the best."

He stared at her. That was it? That was her whole answer?

He gritted his teeth. You know what? He didn't give a shit. He got what he wanted out of her. Twice.

Sure, he'd have liked more. A lot more.

A lot more of what he got last night, he clarified to himself. He didn't want anything else from her. But he was damned if he was going to pick through a woman's mercurial moods just to get a little ass. He knew that already being damned kind of took some of the emphasis out of his declaration, but he really did mean it.

Chasing human tail was beneath him.

Not his style. Period.

"Well, I guess I should head out."

Jo came back from the faraway place where she was, tightening her arms around herself again. "Okay."

Maksim's teeth ached as he gritted harder, furious at her vague response.

What the hell had happened since last night?

No! No. He wasn't going there. It was time to cut out and focus on what mattered to him.

"See ya," he said, his voice sharp, laden with sarcasm.

He shut the door behind him with more force than necessary when no reply came, irritated with her and more so with himself that he cared.

Jo barely recalled walking to work, or answering her e-mails or anything else she'd done when she got to her office. In fact, she'd been sitting with her fingers poised on her keyboard, doing nothing but thinking, for about twenty minutes or so now.

And she likely would have continued to remain lost in her thoughts of Maksim and the disaster her life was for another twenty, if Cherise hadn't appeared in her doorway. The larger woman's telltale eyebrows were furrowed together, concern thinning her lips.

"Have you heard from Maksim?"

Jo shuffled around a few papers on her desk, trying to make it look like she'd been doing something, anything besides fixating on the man in question.

"No, I haven't."

"Well, he isn't here. And that's not normal."

Jo's heart skipped slightly at Cherise's words. What if he didn't come back? What if he was gone for good? The chances of that were almost 100 percent, if she had to guess.

But she pushed away her thoughts, trying to keep her voice cool and calm. "Maybe he had something come up."

Cherise shook her head. "He'd have called me and let me know."

"How can you be so sure? He's only been here for a week. That hardly makes you an expert on the man."

One of Cherise's eyebrows rose up. "Well, you can just tell these things."

Jo bristled, straightening in her rickety chair, aggravated that the other woman was so willing to defend the man's work ethic. Which wasn't rational. After all, he had been working hard for the center. But she didn't want to worry about whether he'd be back again. And she didn't want to think about what drove him away.

Her.

"I think you should try to call him," Cherise said. "Just to make sure he's okay."

No. Jo wasn't going to do that. Not with the way things ended this morning. No way.

"Actually, you know," she said, turned to her computer and clicked on the calendar icon. "I think he did tell me he had something going on today."

Jo even went to the extent of looking at her entries as if there would really be something written there. Another explanation aside from the real one as to why Maksim was absent. All that stared back at her was . . . Maksim, 8 A.M. to noon, in bright red letters.

But she managed to keep her voice steady and convincing as she said, "Oh yep, it does say that he had an appointment today. He wasn't sure if he'd be in or not."

Jo looked back at Cherise, forcing herself to meet the woman's dark gaze directly. "Sorry. I forgot."

Cherise's eyebrows indicated that she didn't believe her, but then she nodded and left the doorway, heading back to the ruckus in the daycare room.

Jo closed the calendar, unable to look again at the day labeled with Maksim's times.

And here was another bad effect of her decision with the man—she was going to lose her only decent volunteer.

And someone who she had to admit she really liked.

"Great," she muttered, dropping her head into her hands.

"Jo." Erika grinned as soon as she saw Jo on the other side of her door. "What are you doing here?"

Jo laughed, the sound even a little brassy to her own ears. "Well, it is Friday night. I thought you'd be up for hitting Bourbon Street."

"Really?"

Jo frowned at her friend. "I know I've been a bit of a homebody since I got here, but is it really that shocking I'd want to go out?"

Erika studied her for a moment, then shook her head. "No, I . . . no, of course not."

Jo smiled, but the smile dissolved as Erika added, "Are you feeling okay, though?"

Jo attempted to suppress her annoyance, though she knew that she probably wasn't doing a great job.

"You and Maggie are giving me a complex. I feel fine."

Which was a lie. She was tired, frazzled, sick of thinking about Maksim and her future. Sick of wondering if things could be different. Sick of worrying about the fact that she was apparently seeing things that weren't really there.

She forced a smile at Erika. "I really do feel fine. Just not wanting to be alone tonight."

Well, at least she could say that in all truth. She'd stayed late at the center, determined to do some work, the work she hadn't managed to do all day. But when the center emptied and grew quiet, and the sun sank low, casting long shadows in the hallway, she'd had to leave. Her nerves got the better of her.

And heading home didn't seem any more appealing. So she'd gone for a decaf latte at a coffee shop on Chartres. She'd lounged in an overstuffed wingback chair, sipped her coffee and read about the trials and tribulations of Hollywood's A List. And while that helped calm her nerves, it didn't keep her mind from returning again and again to Maksim.

Even the announcement of Brad and Angelina's twentieth pregnancy couldn't keep her mind from wandering. So she'd given up on the showbiz mags and went in search of human distraction.

She needed to be with her friends.

"Come in," Erika said, realizing she'd been blocking the doorway and leaving Jo standing on the porch. She ushered her in, and for the first time, Jo realized that her friend was getting ready to work.

Her dropcloth was spread on the dining room floor. And one of her sculptures, just a barebones metal frame, sat on top of it. Once Erika started working with polymer and other sculpting mediums, it would take become something completely different, something lifelike and breathtaking.

"I'm sorry. I'm interrupting you."

Erika waved a hand. "I'm thrilled to be able to avoid working for a while. And I'd love to get the chance to hang out with you. I know we just saw each other a couple days ago, but I feel like we haven't gotten a chance to really talk."

Jo nodded, although she wasn't sure she wanted to *really* talk. She wanted company and a distraction, but she didn't want to think anymore—not about what was real in her life, although, honestly, she was starting to wonder what was real. Everything seemed to be a weird fantasy.

And she wasn't about to tell Erika that she felt like she was losing her mind. That would open a line of conversation she could do without. She'd just keep her insanity to herself. Thanks.

"Is this piece commissioned or for a show?" Jo asked before Erika could ask her anything that might be difficult to discuss.

Erika walked over and touched the metal framework fondly. She loved her work, every creation one of her babies.

Jo breathed in slowly through her nose, wrapping her arms around herself, watching, trying not to think.

"It's for a gallery on Royal. The owner asked me for two new pieces." Erika stopped regarding her art and turned her full attention to Jo. Her gray-blue eyes dropped to Jo's stance, focusing on the arms folded over her stomach.

"Are you okay?"

Again with the "are you okays." Jo forced a smile, dropping her arms to her side. "I told you I'm fine."

"Okay."

"Listen, let's go see Maggie and the guys play."

Erika pursed her lips, and for a moment, Jo thought she was going to say no. Then she smiled, the curve of her lips transforming from worry to impish delight.

"Okay, let me change."

Jo smiled as her friend scampered down the hallway to get gussied up. Jo glanced down at her own black jumper with a white T-shirt underneath. Hardly Bourbon Street attire, but she thought the short length and the Empire waist made the style younger and sort of hip.

Beggars couldn't be choosers, and this style was cooler and more comfortable than the type of thing she would have normally worn out for a night on the town. She supposed the lack of her usual style was a minor concession preferable to being hideously uncomfortable.

She wandered over the sofa, sinking onto the blue velvet cushions and letting her eyes close. She was tired, but suffering a little sleepiness and a few yawns at a bar was much more appealing than sitting home alone. Not sleeping, anyway, because her mind wouldn't let her.

She stretched and willed her eyes open.

A noise rumbled beside her, startling her. She turned on her sofa cushion to see Erika's cat sitting on the arm of the sofa. Golden eyes watched, then disappeared behind a face of black fur. Then they slowly opened and Jo seemed to be held captive by their ochre yellow depths.

They stayed that way, feline and human locked in an unwavering stare.

"What do you think?"

Jo started, actually jerking at the sound of Erika's voice, the connection between herself and the black cat with the hypnotic eyes broken.

"Oh," Jo forced herself to smile at her friend. She managed to focus on Erika's outfit. "Oh, you look great."

Which Erika did. Her legs were encased in a pair of skinny jeans, which showed off their length and lithe shape to perfection. A graphic tee clung to her subtle curves, making her torso look long and feminine. The ensemble was topped off with a chunky belt and high-heel boots. Plain silver hoops adorned her ears.

"You look great," Jo said again, this time with less preoccupation in her tone. "The quintessential rocker chick."

Erika laughed. "I gotta keep up with all the other groupies."

Jo smiled, knowing that Erika could wear a burlap sack and Vittorio would find her the loveliest woman in the bar. Or anywhere. Vittorio and Ren were nothing if not devoted to their wives.

Would Maksim ever be that devoted to a woman?

Jo rolled her eyes, thoroughly annoyed with the ridiculous train of thought. Who cared what Maksim did?

But even as she said that to herself, she knew she did. She hated it, but she did care.

But she would get over it. She'd gotten over Jackson, she'd get over Maksim, too. Although she didn't doubt, despite the short amount of time she'd actually had with Maksim, he'd be harder to get beyond

Just then, Erika's cat leapt off the arm of the sofa, disappearing around behind the back. Jo couldn't say she'd miss the strange animal with its eerie eyes. But the animal's departure didn't calm her uneasiness. Instead the hair on the back of Jo's neck rose, a chill snaking slowly down her back.

Something was not right. The air seemed to hold a strange thickness. Electricity prickled her skin.

She tried to ignore the sensation, attempting to focus on Erika, who said something about The Impalers playing at a different bar.

Jo nodded in an absent effort to appear attentive. But the strange heaviness in the air seemed to intensify, crowding in around her.

Then out of the counter of her eye, she caught a movement. A shadowy shift, something, or someone, standing at the end of the sofa.

Jo didn't move, not wanting to see or feel what was happening. It was just her crazy imagination. Everything had been her overactive, overwrought imagination.

And it had to be her imagination, because Erika wasn't reacting as if anything was amiss. Erika talked about God knows what, while all Jo could focus on was that hint of something to her left.

"What do you think?"

Jo straightened, realizing Erika was addressing her directly. "I'm sorry?"

Erika smiled indulgently, seeing that Jo hadn't been listening. "I was saying that the band is considering changing bars permanently. And I wondered whether you thought it was a good idea."

Since Jo hadn't heard any of the pros or cons her friend had said, she really had no idea. So she just gave her a vague nod. "Sure."

Erika nodded, too, began to dig through her purse. "I think so, too."

Well, at least she answered that right, Jo thought. But her dubious feeling of relief was blotted out by another movement at her left, this time closer.

And there was a form now, solid—not just shadow. The hint of black hair, of pale skin. Just flashes like watching a person on a subway platform as the train rushes by.

Jo concentrated on Erika, willing her friend to see this person, thing, whatever it was. But Erika merrily searched through her purse, glancing in Jo's direction every now and then. Talking animatedly. And certainly not aware of an unexplained vision near Jo.

Jo opened her mouth, ready to ask her outright if she could see something there. But then closed her mouth. Did she really want further validation she was insane?

So instead Jo sat perfectly still, willing the image away. Willing herself to stay calm.

But both of those goals were quickly abandoned when the image beside her reached for her. A pale hand with long fingers and blunt nails stretched toward her arm, coming into clear, crisp view, even as the rest of the apparition remained indistinct in her peripheral vision.

Jo jumped up, blind panic taking over. She headed for the door.

"Hey," Erika called, confused by her sudden departure.

But Jo didn't stop. She had to get out of there, her only thought to escape the visions and the oppressive feelings surrounding her. She needed air. *Breathe. Just breathe.*

Erika didn't catch up with her until she was already out on the sidewalk. "What's the rush?"

"Sorry," Jo said, fighting the urge to brace her hands on her knees and lean forward to push away the rush of dizziness making it hard to focus.

Erika touched her arm, and Jo jumped.

"Sorry," Jo said that her own overreaction, laughing, the sound brittle and tinged with hysteria.

"Jo, what's going on?"

Jo supposed it was impossible to convince her friend she was fine now. But she wasn't admitting what she thought she'd just seen. Erika might believe her, being a big fan of all things occult, but telling Erika wouldn't make her feel better.

Jo just wanted to feel normal. Sane.

"I just felt a little dizzy. I need some fresh air."

Erika studied her for a moment, her blue-gray eyes roaming over Jo's face.

"Do you need some water or anything?"

Jo shook her head, relieved Erika wasn't going to grill her further. "I'm fine. Just need air."

Erika regarded her a moment longer, then nodded. "Okay. I'm going to get my purse. Do you need yours, too?"

"Yes. I think it's on the sofa." And she didn't want to go back near that sofa at the moment.

"I'll be right back," Erika said as if she expected Jo to do something rash in her absence. Which probably did seem likely. She clearly wasn't acting normal.

"All right. I'll be right back," Erika repeated, then hurried back toward her apartment.

Jo remained on the street, her arms wrapped around her middle. She paced, keeping her attention on the cracks in the sidewalk.

Then she heard a noise. Against her will, she looked up, following the direction of the noise. On the upper balcony stood the woman from her other trips to Erika and Maggie's. Her pale hands curled around the railing as she watched Jo.

From this distance, Jo couldn't feel the crushing weight of the apparition's presence. No tingle of electricity ran over her skin, but Jo now realized this was who had reached out to her.

The woman watched her with those pale eyes, her sadness

and despair stretching out to her, even if her otherworldly vibe couldn't. The tenseness and fear faded a little. This woman needed help.

That didn't make Jo feel better about the fact that she was seeing ghosts. But at least she realized she didn't need to feel threatened by her.

The woman waved at her, as if testing the theory that Jo could really see her. Jo waved back.

Great, seeing ghosts wasn't bad enough. Now you know you've been interacting with them.

"Who are you waving to?" Erika said, reappearing by Jo's side.

Jo glanced at Erika, then back at the balcony. When she looked back, the woman was gone. All she could see was a pair of golden eyes blinking down like a lazy owl halfheartedly regarding a mouse.

"That cat," Erika said, assuming now that was what held Jo's attention. "He is the strangest pet I've ever had."

Jo couldn't disagree with that, especially if her thoughts about the creature were true. Good Lord, was she really debating the idea? That the woman and the cat, a male cat at that, were one and the same?

She supposed once you got into ghosts and shape-shifting, gender juxtaposition was really the least unbelievable part, wasn't it?

"Boris, what are you doing up here?" Erika called to the cat as if the animal might answer.

Then again, he might. Again, that would hardly be the weirdest thing Jo had had happen.

The cat didn't, though, and Jo was admittedly relieved.

"I swear that cat doesn't even like any of us, yet he stays." Erika handed Jo her purse.

Jo nodded, glancing up there again before falling into step with her friend.

"Yeah," Jo agreed, her voice dry, which was better than hysterical, "that cat is weird."

Chapter 21

Maksim remained in the doorway across the street, watching. He'd considered approaching Jo when she'd been alone on the sidewalk. She'd been pacing, her movements agitated, nervous.

But he'd remained hidden, distracted by her behavior. She'd stopped pacing and stared up at the balcony on the front of Ren's apartment building.

He followed her gaze, trying to see what held her so rapt, but the balcony appeared empty to him. Nothing there out of the ordinary. Nothing at all.

Then, to his further confusion, she waved. The gesture was oddly tentative, as if someone waved to her first, and she wasn't quite sure whether she should respond in kind.

But then, Erika came out to join her, and when they all looked back to the balcony, it appeared that they were watching Erika's strange cat. Maksim wasn't a cat person to begin with—although he liked them better than dogs. Needy little creatures, dogs were. But to wave at a cat? But then, that cat was weird, he had to admit. More than once he could have sworn that same cat had shown up at his place—well, his sister's place.

And like just now, he would have bet money that cat hadn't been on that balcony moments before?

Something wasn't right. And given Jo's behavior last night, with the whatever in the hallway, he wondered if he should be questioning the woman's mental state.

Maybe that's why he couldn't read her mind. She was just too crazy.

But he immediately dismissed that idea. Maksim had met insane—hell, his last tryst had been with Vittorio and Ren's mother and she'd been certifiable. No—that made Orabella sound just normally nuts—the woman had been batshit crazy.

Jo wasn't. Something was going on with her. And whatever it was, he'd like it to explain her hot/cold behavior with him, too, but he wasn't sure about that.

And because of his confusion, he'd resorted to being a stalker. But he didn't have much time to think about the depths to which he'd fallen—which again for a person whose home base was Hell was really saying something—because Jo was on the move.

Maksim waited a little before following the twosome. He couldn't get too close, because Erika might sense him. Lampirs weren't quite as attune to other preternaturals as the regular bloodsucking vampires. Unless they were older, which made him glad that neither Vittorio or Ren were with the women. They'd sense him, he was sure.

But as it was, he only had to stay about a block behind. Not that it mattered; he had a good idea where they were headed.

Sure enough, the two friends headed directly to the bar where The Impalers were playing.

Maksim waited outside, watching them as they wove their way through the crowd. It was still early, so the bar wasn't terribly crowded. The band played on a stage at the far end of the room. Jo and Erika went up to the stage, waving to the others. Vittorio did a hair toss, clearly for Erika's benefit.

Ah, the vanity of vampires. Right up there with demons, to be sure.

Jo greeted everyone, too, but she didn't look like a woman

out for a wild Friday night. Instead, she seemed tense and tired and he wanted to just go up to her and suggest they go back to her place. His place. He didn't care, he just wanted to be with her.

And that didn't please him. Not when he was getting the brush-off. But he didn't leave. He came into the bar, staying near the front, finding a bar stool and ordering a whiskey on the rocks.

Jo and Erika stayed up on the dance floor, near the stage for a couple songs, swaying more than really dancing. Then Jo gestured toward the upstairs, and Erika nodded. Both women waved at the band again, then headed to a staircase that was almost unnoticeable if a person wasn't really looking.

Maksim picked up his drink and trailed along behind. He didn't even bother to be surreptitious as he passed the stage. Vittorio nodded at him from his spot playing bass. Ren waved as he belted out the lyrics to a Journey song. That man loved his Journey covers.

Even the other guys in the band, Drake, Wyatt, and Elton, their new drummer, acknowledged Maksim, used to seeing him when he bartended. Maggie was the only member to address him with anything less than affability. And even her reaction wasn't rude exactly, but more one of circumspection.

Her eyes narrowed and she gave him only a slight nod. Then she looked at the stairs as if she wanted to give Jo a heads-up that he was there.

He entered the doorway and climbed the steps. She'd know soon enough.

Jo sat on the bar stool, telling herself this was good, calming. Being with Erika, the music pulsing down below them, the warm glossy wood of the upper bar.

Nothing would happen here. Of course, her visions happened right in front of Erika. So Jo couldn't say what would and wouldn't happen. But she hoped, prayed, she could just have an uneventful night.

"This is good," she said to Erika as if saying something affirming aloud would make her feel even more definite about the whole plan.

"Yeah, it's nice up here, isn't it? Not so loud or crowded."

Jo did like that. Sometimes that kind of massive sensory overload was as lonely and overwhelming as being by oneself. It still forced a person to be stuck inside their own head, unable to really talk or hear, and she didn't want that. She also didn't feel like dancing. Fatigue weighed heavily on her.

Then she saw him, and all thoughts of exhaustion and stress left her. Well, the stress was replaced by a different kind of nervous tension. And all hopes of an uneventful evening were gone.

Maksim didn't notice them at the other end of the bar as he took a seat and held up his glass to the bartender, indicating he wanted another.

Jo stared at him, eating up the sight of him as if she hadn't just seen him this morning. All of him.

That particular thought didn't help her already aware body. It was amazing. The man could walk into a room, and she wanted him.

"Maksim is here," Erika said, the announcement striking Jo as rather funny. The classic after-the-fact sort of comment.

But all she said was, "Oh yeah?" She pretended to follow Erika's glance to locate him. Then she took a sip of her club soda and lime.

"Aren't you going to go say hello?"

"No."

"But you want to."

Jo frowned. "How do you know that?"

Erika shifted on her bar stool. "Well I just assumed you would want to. Since he works with you."

"Not anymore." Jo took another sip of her drink, trying to remain casual and not stir any suspicion in her already too perceptive friend.

"Really?"

Jo nodded, even though she wasn't totally sure about that fact. She was assuming after her blatant cold shoulder this morning, he'd want very little to do with her. If the slammed door and not showing up to volunteer were any indication, he definitely wanted nothing to do with her.

Yet he was here. Not that he had an idea that she was. Just a coincidence, obviously.

"Oh, listen," Erika said. "This is my favorite song." A look of longing came over her face.

Jo smiled, knowing where Erika wanted to be. "Go down and watch him if you want. I'm fine here."

"Are you sure?"

"Absolutely." She wasn't fine, but she didn't want to let her friend on to that anymore than necessary.

"Come with me."

Jo shook her head, a little more adamantly than she needed. She did not want to walk past Maksim. She wanted to stay right here. Invisible.

"Go on. I'm enjoying listening from up here. Plus I need to sit for awhile."

A flash of concern darkened her friend's eyes to stormy gray. But then she nodded. "Okay. I'll be back in a bit."

"Have fun. Don't worry about me."

Erika rose, and for a second Jo doubted her agreement to let her go. She was going to pass Maksim, too, and then he might know she was there as well.

But he didn't notice Erika, because he was interacting with the bartender, a young thing with pert breasts and her midriff bared.

So what, Jo told herself. She was the one who'd put the distance between them this morning. Who cares what or who he did?

She shook her head, knowing that answer wasn't the one she wanted it to be.

She shifted back on her stool, so that the few people between them would shield her from view. And him from her, too. All she needed was for him to see her ogling him at the end of the bar. With any luck, he'd have no idea she was here.

Maksim knew the exact moment when Jo spotted him. Her eyes widened and she shrank back in her seat, trying to hide behind Erika. The reaction irritated him a lot.

The bartender, a girl in her early twenties in a pair of skintight, low-rise jeans and an equally tight black camisole placed a whiskey on the rocks in front him.

She leaned forward, offering him a hint of her cleavage. "Can I get you anything else?"

She smiled invitingly.

Maksim lifted the drink to his lips, downing the amber liquid in one swallow.

"Yeah. Another," he said, sliding the empty glass back to her.

She looked slightly disappointed by his blatant disinterest, and while he wasn't particularly worried about her feelings, he could relate to her displeasure. He'd love to have his attention drawn to another woman. Hell, little Miss Bartender would do. But that didn't seem like a possibility while Jo Burke filled his every thought.

Taking no more notice of the bartender, he shifted forward to sneak a look at Jo. He could only make out part of her face and her shoulder.

Sadly, the partial glimpse of her did more to his libido than the obvious and provocatively clad bartender. He closed his eyes, blocking out the limited image of her.

He was losing it. That was the only explanation. Going completely mad. The cut of a cheekbone, the corner of a mouth, the curl of brown hair around the pink shell of an ear, the curve of a shoulder. None of those features should be enough to drive him to utter distraction.

But they did. She made him nuts. Lust pulsed through his body as much a part of him as his blood. Just from having her in the same room with him. But something else mixed with the lust, making it more powerful, more intense. He didn't want to consider what they thing could be.

Crazy. That's what he was.

He opened his eyes, needing just another glimpse. But this time broad shoulders blocked his view of her.

A man in faded jeans and a T-shirt stood between Maksim and her, his elbow leaning on the bar, his body swaying toward Jo.

Maksim could see her hand reach for her drink. The curl of her fingers around the glass, the leisurely lift of it out of sight. Maksim could visualize those pretty lips of hers, as she took a small sip. The movement casual, not agitated. Maybe she smiled at the guy afterward, her lips wet and glistening from the liquid she'd just sampled.

The glass returned back to sight, but she didn't take her hand away. One of her elegant fingers circled the rim, the swirling hypnotic, a little flirty.

She liked this guy's attention.

Fuck that.

"So what's your name?"

Jo debated whether she should tell this guy, or just be straight up and advise him he was wasting his time. She decided that while she was in no mood to make small talk with a stranger, much less flirt with one, it wouldn't hurt to answer.

"Jo."

"Jo. I like that. Is that short for Josie?"

Jo shook her head. Did people have nicknames for Josie?

"Jolene?"

She supposed the guy was getting closer. Sort of. And she'd have to give him a little leeway, he was clearly a few drinks into the night.

"Josephine," she supplied for him, a little afraid of what his next guess might be. Joanie? Jody?

"Oh, Josephine. That's a pretty name." He swayed toward her, his gaze on her lips.

She took a sip of her drink, not wanting to risk him moving in for a kiss, although he was likely swaying because of the alcohol and focusing on her lips because the room was spinning.

"What's your name?" she asked, not that she particularly cared, but it seemed the polite thing to do. And actually, he was doing a terrific job of hiding her from Maksim. He wasn't necessarily keeping her mind off him, but he was a distraction of some sort.

The guy rocked forward again, this time enough to make Jo lean back in response. Okay, a pretty poor distraction, but she'd take it right now.

"My name is Cameron." He squinted, looking like he didn't know why he was telling her that. Clearly her question had become a distant memory in a matter of seconds.

She wished she could drink. Maybe then Maksim could become a distant recollection to her.

"So, are you from here?" Cameron asked.

"Just moved here."

"Me, too!" Cameron raised his huge plastic tumbler filled with some sort of orangey-pink liquid that looked pretty noxious. It seemed to be doing a number on him.

"To us. And our move to the best city in the world."

Cameron clearly had been toasting many things over the course of the evening. But she lifted her glass, again to be polite, tapping the rim to the side of his cup.

He sloshed a little of the toxic mixture on his oxford shirt on his way to his mouth, supporting her theory this might be one toast too many.

He just chuckled as he wiped the liquid off with his hand, which made her laugh, too. He wasn't an obnoxious drunk, just a jovial one, and she decided maybe she was enjoying the distraction.

She set down her drink, her hand lingering on the coolness of the glass. She absently circled her finger around the rim, her thoughts skipping back to Maksim. He was so close, but a lot of good that did her.

Okay, maybe good ole drunk Cameron wasn't much of a diversion after all.

"What do you do for work?" Cameron asked as if he'd read her mind and was trying to do a better job for her.

Sorry Cameron, but there's fat chance of that.

"I'm the director of a community center," she said.

"No way! I work at the Micro Center. It's a computer store."

Jo stared at him for a moment, trying to decide if he was making a joke. She concluded he wasn't, but laughed anyway. Because he was so sincere in their almost eerie kinship that what else could she do.

"Wow, that's so spooky," she managed to say once she stopped laughing.

"I know," he agreed wholeheartedly, his eyes widening at the very thought.

Jo laughed again, but the laughter died on her lips as Maksim walked past them. His green eyes sought hers, leaving no doubt that he was aware she was here. Without even turning to follow his path, she knew he stopped and took the stool on the other side of her.

To confirm her thoughts, she heard him call out to the bartender.

"Hey sweetheart, mind bringing me another down here?"

The bartender smiled at him, clearly pleased with his endearment. She nodded and bounced off, happy with his attention.

As most woman would be, Jo supposed. And the idea rankled her.

Jo didn't turn around, but she could feel him right behind her. His presence was like a physical touch across her back.

*   *   *

Maksim didn't bother to slide the stool next to Jo away from her. He wanted to be in her space. He wanted her aware of him. But if she was, he couldn't tell.

"Do you like being a director?" the guy who was standing far too close to Jo's other side asked. He swayed slightly, and Maksim could see he was pretty well wasted.

Jo's voice was muffled slightly, because she wasn't facing him, but Maksim could still make out her words.

"Umm, yeah, I do."

"Do you have pottery classes?"

Maksim raised an eyebrow and fought the urge to roll his eyes. Jo had given him the deep freeze just to go out and talk to this winner. He didn't know whether to be insulted or amused.

"No," Jo said slowly, clearly finding the guy's question a little strange too. "No, we don't."

"Ah, that's too bad. People like to do pottery."

Maksim shook his head, unable to suppress his disdainful amusement.

"I guess that's true," Jo said.

"You know, you have really pretty eyes."

Any hint of amusement evaporated, and Maksim couldn't help looking at the guy.

The schmuck touched Jo's hand, which had stopped swirling seductively around the edge of her glass. Maksim gritted his teeth as he watched the man's thumb brush over the soft skin of her fingers. Jo didn't pull away.

Before Maksim thought better of it, he shifted, his arm grazing Jo's back. She straightened like an elastic snapping into place, aligning her spine, but she still didn't look at him.

The guy rocked toward her. "You smell nice, too."

Maksim scowled at the man, but the stupid, leery drunk was too lost in his interest in Jo to notice.

"Thank you," Jo said, and still didn't move her hand out from under his. Maksim fought the urge to pull her away. Pull her away and kiss her senseless.

"Do you have a boyfriend?"

Maksim couldn't stop himself from turning on the stool to face the two of them. Now this he wanted to hear.

"No. I don't."

Technically that was true, Maksim supposed, but that didn't matter at the moment. Her words still made him see red.

He hooked a hand under her elbow and tugged. She slid around on the stool like the seat spun on its own. Her dark eyes snapped open wide and her lips rounded into a perfect "o."

"The hell you don't."

Maksim pulled her against him, so she was only half on her stool and mostly leaning against him.

And he kissed her soundly.

Chapter 22

Jo froze for half a second, then melted into Maksim's embrace. His lips moved possessively against hers, his teeth tugging at her lower lip, his tongue mingling with hers in an intimate way that made her whole body tingle.

Then she realized that someone was tapping on her shoulder.

"Um, excuse me."

She jerked away from Maksim, looking over her shoulder at who was interrupting her. Interrupting one of the most sensual moments of her life. She frowned, not immediately recognizing who was speaking to her.

Finally her brain kicked in. "Cameron?"

Her new friend nodded, looking decidedly more sober than he had before. "Is this really your boyfriend?"

Jo opened her mouth to deny it, but Maksim reached around her and extended his hand.

"Yes, I am. I'm Maksim Kostova." His voice was civil, but there was no mistaking the possessiveness, the resolve.

Cameron frowned at Maksim's hand, but did accept, giving a quick shake.

"I'm sorry, man," Cameron said, stepping back from Jo, establishing the appropriate amount of space between them. Clearly he didn't want to upset Maksim further.

Jo glanced at Maksim. A smile curved his lips, but there was coolness there, a hard cast to his green eyes.

"Not a problem. I know what a stunning woman she is. I'd be chatting her up, too, if she didn't already belong to me."

Jo shook her head slightly, feeling as if she had to be having some weird dream. Or she was on a reality show where the host jumped out and told her the whole thing was a joke. A spoof.

Maksim caught her hand, tugging at it.

"Come here," he muttered roughly, right beside her ear, his voice causing ripples of arousal to shimmy down her spine. His broad chest brushed against her back. Another shiver made her vibrate with need.

He pulled her again, and she found herself sliding off her seat and between his legs. Then he situated her so her bottom was nestled against him, his arms wrapped around her waist. She held herself stiff, trying to comprehend what was happening, trying to decide how she should react, and definitely trying to ignore the very aroused, very hard penis prodding her rear end.

"Okay, well, umm," Cameron looked around as if he too wasn't really sure what he should be doing. After a few more befuddled looks around the bar, he raised his cup.

"Good to meet you."

Jo wasn't sure if that was directed at her or Maksim. Or maybe both. Despite his obviously impaired equilibrium, Cameron managed to stride away at fairly impressive speed.

Before Jo could turn to confront Maksim, Erika returned, her pacing slowing as she spotted them. Her dark brows were drawn together in puzzlement.

"Hey there," she said once she reached them, clearly not sure what to say. Not unlike Jo—it was bewildering to say the least.

"Hi Erika," Maksim answered tucking Jo closer to him. Not that he could get much closer without being inside her.

The idea of that made her shiver despite her confusion, which was starting to transform into irritation.

"Am—am I interrupting something?"

"No," Jo said, trying to wriggle away from Maksim, but his hold didn't loosen.

"Not at all," Maksim agreed, his voice smooth and sexy and slightly amused, which made Jo's ire flare even more.

"Okay," Erika said, her gaze flickered between the two of them and she clearly didn't believe their protests.

To prove that, she gestured over her shoulder. "I think I'll head back downstairs to listen to the band."

"No!" Jo reached out and caught her friend's wrist. She didn't want Erika to leave. Jo didn't know what she intended to say to Maksim, and having her friend there as a buffer seemed like a good choice.

Erika looked down at where Jo's fingers locked around her arm. But she smiled, giving her a reassuring nod. "Sure."

Jo released her and Erika slid onto the empty stool she'd left before she'd gone downstairs again. Before more weirdness started in Jo's life.

This might not be potentially paranormal, but it was just as strange as everything else in her life these days.

The arms around Jo tightened just slightly, adding to her confusion. Okay, maybe she could see him being jealous about another man's attention, but what was he doing now? They'd had an arrangement of just sex. And even that had ended this morning. And she'd wanted it to end.

She'd thought he had, too, from his reaction to her coldness. And she hadn't pegged him as the type to grovel.

But this wasn't groveling, exactly. It was staking his claim. But she hadn't expected that at all—ever.

"So, how are you enjoying working at the Community Center?" Erika asked in an obvious attempt to get the situation somewhere normal.

"I like it," Maksim said, his face right beside Jo's. His

voice reverberating through her. Making her react. "And I think I'm good with the kids. What do you think, darling?"

Jo gritted her teeth. Why was he doing this? What was the point? She knew he was mad at her. Was he trying to make her look like a fool?

She couldn't understand his plan.

He rested his chin on her shoulder, leaning his head against hers. "The kids seem pretty fond of me, don't they?"

Well, no matter what the reason, he was manipulating her, and Jo did not like it.

"Well, these children are starved for attention," Jo said, keeping her gaze directed at Erika and her voice even and pragmatic, "so they readily attach to anyone who is kind to them."

"She doesn't like to give me too many compliments, does she?" He chuckled and then pressed a kiss on Jo's cheek.

Jo jerked away. "Don't do that."

"What? Are you embarrassed to show our affection in front of Erika?"

Jo didn't answer. What was he doing? Why?

"You don't mind, do you, Erika?"

Erika regarded Jo for a moment, then shook her head. "Of course not."

Jo started to make a face at her friend, but Maksim's fingers caught her chin and turned her face toward him.

"See, she doesn't mind. So you shouldn't, either."

He leaned forward and kissed her. The kiss wasn't aggressive or possessive, just a sweet clinging of his velvety soft lips with hers.

It unnerved her more than his first kiss of the evening had. And her body instantly hummed with intense need.

To Jo's dismay it was Maksim who pulled away, and it took her a moment to realize that Erika was feigning a coughing fit to get their attention.

It worked for Maksim, while Jo had noticed nothing but

him. She could feel her cheeks burning at how easily he got her to respond. But then, she wasn't denying that she was attracted to him. She just knew they wouldn't last. Not with the bombshell she was hiding.

"I think I will head downstairs. It sounds like the band is on break," Erika said. She smiled, although the stiff curve of her lips revealed she was uncomfortable.

"No," Jo said, her voice breathless, but still insistent, "please stay."

"I really think you two have some things you need to discuss."

"No, we don't," Jo said quickly.

"No, sweetheart, Erika's right," Maksim said, leaning forward so he could see Jo's face. "We do have a lot to discuss."

Jo opened her mouth to argue, because her gut told her she didn't want to be alone with this man. Not in the strange mood he was in. But then she realized she had to talk about it. She needed to understand why the hell he was doing this.

"Yeah, you're right."

Jo nodded, letting Erika know silently that she would be fine. Whatever Maksim was, he wasn't dangerous. Well, not to anything but her heart. Which just seemed so crazy, given her initial opinion of him and the short time she'd known him.

"Okay," Erika said, "I'll be right downstairs near the stage, if you need me."

"Thanks," Jo said.

Erika gave her one more searching look, then headed down the length of the bar to the stairs.

As soon as she was gone, Jo tried to pull away from Maksim, but he kept her firmly positioned between his legs.

"Let me go," she gritted out.

"In a minute." Maksim's lips nibbled the side of her neck. His lips were warm and wonderful, just the right amount of pressure, the right amount of nips and suction.

Her knees threatened to give out as she lost herself to the sensation.

But it was his fingers brushing gently over her belly that managed to snap her thoughts back to what was she had to do. And it wasn't leaning back against his solid, broad chest, letting him make love to her.

She yanked away, turning to face him, making sure their bodies weren't touching in any way.

"Maksim, why are you doing this?"

Chapter 23

"**D**oing what?" Not his snappiest of comebacks, but the taste and scent of Jo had him more unnerved, more aroused than he'd like to admit.

"Why are you acting like we are a couple?"

Maksim might be a little mush-brained at the moment, but not enough so that he was going to answer that one honestly. He'd been acting the way he was because he'd been blind, raging jealous.

He hadn't initially recognized the emotion, because frankly he hadn't ever felt it before, and really he didn't understand what he was feeling until he was already heading down the bar toward Jo and the drunk, dullard college boy.

And when the dumbass had asked her if she had a boyfriend, he just knew he couldn't hear her say no. He just couldn't.

Boyfriend? Were demons ever anyone's boyfriend? That seemed oddly incongruent. But in that moment, Maksim was damned well going to be her boyfriend.

"Maksim, didn't this morning make things pretty clear?"

Hell, no. Nothing had been clear this morning. Her words, her stance, her reaction had all been as confusing as hell. And believe you me, he knew how confusing Hell was.

"I don't think we really agreed on anything," he said.

Jo stared at him as if he'd lost his mind.

"We agreed that things were too complicated. That the idea of just—" she dropped her voice, "having sex is not going to work out."

"I don't recall agreeing to any of that. I remember you saying that you thought things were too complicated, and when I asked why, you didn't answer."

She didn't answer for a moment again, and he had no doubt she was replaying the events of the morning in her mind.

Finally she sighed. "Well, that's the reason. Having sex isn't going to work out for me."

"Why?"

Jo shook her head, then fiddled with a nick in the bar's glossily shellacked wood. "It just isn't."

"Because the sex isn't working for you, physically?"

She didn't answer, but just continued to finger the deep scratch.

"Because it sure seemed to be working for you last night."

Jo eyes snapped back to him. "That isn't the point."

"What is the point?" Maksim really did want to understand. He wanted her to say something, though he couldn't say exactly what the something was.

"I just think it's going to become too difficult. These things never really work out. Someone ends up getting hurt."

"Are you afraid I'm going to get hurt? Or you?" Maksim's first thought was to tell her that he'd never hurt her, but he held his tongue. Why would he tell her that? He couldn't keep a promise like that. He wasn't exactly a gallant knight who'd swoop in on his white charger and carry her off to safety and love.

He didn't know how to love. Demons weren't created with that particular ability. Coveting, lust, desire, craving, even obsession—those were all things that demons could disguise as love. But they never, *never* cared for some other soul more than their own damned ones.

Jo didn't answer, and he wasn't surprised. She didn't easily let down her guard.

"Josephine, I won't ever hurt you."

He heard the words as if someone else had control of his body, as if he hadn't just told himself that he couldn't promise her anything akin to security or devotion.

Jo didn't react. She clearly didn't recognize what a huge pledge that was. Maybe if she knew what he was, she'd understand. But that was the trick, wasn't it?

Telling someone you care about you're a demon was bound to hurt them.

"You know," Jo smoothed her hands down the skirt of her jumper, "I have to go."

He frowned. He had just told this woman more than he'd ever told anyone, and she was leaving.

"We haven't resolved this," he said.

"I've told you already, I can't do this."

"Jo." He started to reach out for her, but she shifted out of his grasp.

"No," she said to him. "No."

She was clearly upset, but he didn't know why. Out of instinct, he poised on the edge of her brain, ready to jump in, tired of not having a clue what motivated this woman. But he stopped.

He told her he wouldn't hurt her.

He rose from his stool and followed her, catching her arm in just a few steps.

"Jo, I think you are making a mistake. I think we have something pretty special starting here."

Jo stared at him, the heartbroken look she'd seen so many times darkening her eyes to nearly black in the dimly lit room.

"Maksim, I just can't."

She extricated her arm from his hold and turned to walk down the length of the room. Maksim watched her, having no idea what to do or say to make her stop. To change her mind.

He didn't want to hurt her. But letting this all go wasn't an option. Without further thought, he jumped. He jumped right inside her mind.

Jo hesitated at the doorway into the stairwell. She gripped for the doorframe, overcome by a fullness in her head, like her brain was chock-full. She remained still unwilling to move, not because her head ached. It didn't hurt, exactly—it just felt heavy and she couldn't seem to think clearly. Thoughts came, but not in any consistent order.

She blinked. Then blinked again. Gradually the feeling dissipated. She had no idea how long it had taken for the strange episode to pass, but she was relieved that her thoughts seemed to be coming back to order. Her head felt normal, no longer crowded.

Using the wall for balance, even though she didn't think she wasn't going to pass out or anything, she entered the stairwell and started down the stairs.

Green neon light bathed the concrete steps, bright enough to make it easy to see, green enough to make it just a little disorienting.

She clutched the handrail, keeping her gaze focused on the steps. Three steps down, something ahead of her shifted, moving into her downcast line of sight.

She moved closer to the wall, offering the approaching person room to pass her. But the person stopped a few steps below hers.

When she looked up to politely acknowledge the person, she didn't get out a smile or a courteous comment. Instead her mind blanked, her eyes fastened on the individual in front of her. Her mouth gaping wide in shock. No sound, no breath escaping her seized lungs.

No, it couldn't be. Not here. But it was her. Long dark hair, wet and clumped together. Large eyes that Jo knew were was dark as her own. Thin, pale arms and legs bare and glistening with a faint sheen of water. This wasn't just a flashing impression, a snapshot of an image. She was there—right in front of Jo.

"Kara?"

The name escaped Jo's lips as her vision narrowed, rapidly fading to black. Only the faint sound of someone crying out her name reached her, before all light, all comprehension disappeared.

Maksim stood at the top of the stairs, when he saw Jo come to a sudden halt. Her hand clutched the railing, her knuckles gleaming white even in the pale green light of the neon beer signs.

He started down the stairs, realizing something was wrong and just as he would have grabbed her, she crumpled.

"Jo!"

He tried to catch her, his fingers brushing the back of her dress as she lurched forward, escaping his hold. Maksim watched helpless, sick, as if in slow motion she rolled down the stairs and hit the wall below, ending up in a crumpled heap at the base of the stairwell. She didn't move.

Taking the stairs two at a time, he reached her side, kneeling. He started to scoop his arms under her, his first instinct to pick her up, to protect her. But some logic surfaced through his panic.

What if she'd broken her neck, her back? He rose, shoving a hand into his pocket, finding his phone. He dialed 911.

"There's been an accident," he said as calmly as he could to the voice on the other end of the phone.

He answered the subsequent question as he returned to her side, gently touching her face, her hair. She was warm. She was breathing. That had to be good, right?

Once he was certain the medics were on the way, he rose again and stood in the doorway, scanning the bar until he spotted Erika swaying by the stage, watching Vittorio.

Maksim waved. He made several attempts before he caught her attention, but once she saw him, deep concern marred her features and she hurried toward him.

"Jo fell," he said simply when she got to him. He moved aside to reveal Jo's prone body to her friend.

Erika cried out, shocked and clearly scared.

Damn, he was scared, Maksim realized. Terrified.

Erika dropped down beside her, touched her face and hair in the same searching way he'd just done. She turned to glare up at him.

"What did you do to her?"

He gaped at Erika, stunned that she was blaming him, then his breath left him as he realized she was right. This was his fault. He didn't physically push her down the stairs, but he'd created the reaction that did.

He'd jumped in her head, and whatever had happened to Jo was a direct result of his selfish action.

Erika didn't wait for him to answer. She jumped up. "We need to call an ambulance."

"I called 911."

"Okay." She looked back at Jo, clearly debating something. "You wait here," she finally said, although leaving him alone with her definitely wasn't her first choice. "I'm going to get the others."

She narrowed a warning glance at him, and he nearly told her he would never do anything to hurt this woman, but stopped himself. He'd just made that vow to Jo directly, and look at her now.

Oh, God, look at her.

So he only nodded.

Erika dashed away, and soon Maggie, Vittorio, and Ren were all there, all checking Jo. All talking in low, concerned voices.

All looking at him accusingly.

And he couldn't say anything in his own defense. So he left them with her and walked outside the bar to see if the paramedics had arrived.

In the distance, Maksim heard a siren and within minutes, even with the pedestrian-laden streets, an ambulance managed to weave its way through the crowds.

"She's this way," Maksim said, approaching the EMTs before they could even jump out of the vehicle.

Sprinting back to the stairwell, Maksim called out for the friends to step aside. They did so, only resenting his order for a moment.

Maksim then watched helplessly as the EMTs did their jobs, immobilizing Jo's neck, checking her briefly for broken bones, then carefully sliding her onto an AZ backboard—stabilizing her neck.

Two of the men lifted her, their movements fast but steady. Maksim followed right behind as they wheeled her out to the street.

"I'm riding with her," Maksim said as they lifted her into the ambulance.

"No," Erika appeared at his side, addressing the medics, "we're going to ride with her." She gestured to Maggie, who looked even paler than a lampir normally did.

"I only have room for one of you," a medic with tree-trunk-sized arms and a barrel chest said, giving them an impatient look.

Maksim turned to the two friends. "Please. Let me go with her. Please."

Erika looked as if she was going to argue, then Maggie touched her arm. "Let him. Jo needs to get to the hospital now. We'll meet them there."

Erika still looked like she wanted to disagree, but she nodded, knowing Jo might not have time to wait while they bickered.

Maksim hopped up into the ambulance taking a seat beside Jo. Another EMT, a woman, who now took Jo's blood pressure and other vitals.

Carefully, Maksim took Jo's hand, again pleased that her fingers were warm, but amazed at how fragile they felt against his palm.

"You are going to be okay," he murmured to her, pressing those delicate fingers against the side of his face.

God, he prayed she would be okay.

Chapter 24

The hospital was a complete whirlwind when they finally arrived. Jo was wheeled away as soon as they entered the ER, even though Maksim asked everyone he encountered if he could go with her.

A doctor in a white coat with a pair of scrubs underneath that were pink with heads of a little white cats with bows on their heads, was the final person to tell him no.

"Just wait here," she told him firmly, pointing to some vacant plastic chairs lined against a peach painted cinderblock wall. "Someone will be out as soon as we can to tell you what's going on."

Maksim didn't sit. Nor did he follow the doctor as she disappeared through gray swinging double doors.

He gritted his teeth, hating every minute of the helpless feeling coursing painfully through is body. And he didn't know if he trusted Jo's well-being to a woman in cartoon-covered clothing.

But he knew causing a disturbance wasn't going to help Jo, so he began to pace.

Very soon, Jo's friends appeared in the waiting room.

"Is there any word?" Erika asked.

"They just took her back." That was the problem with

preternaturals. They expected everything to happen instantaneously. Waiting was hell.

The four lampirs sat down. Maggie leaned against Ren. Vittorio held Erika's hand. Maksim continued to pace. And no one spoke.

Finally Maggie said, "Maksim, you didn't hurt her, did you?"

Maksim paused, looking at her, warring for what to say.

"Not on purpose. No."

Maggie nodded as if that was good enough for her. Erika didn't look as convinced, and Maksim couldn't blame her.

Because the truth was, his greed had gotten the better of him as always. He might not have wanted to hurt her, but he'd done something he'd know wouldn't help her in any way, just because of his selfish need to know.

He dropped into a chair several over from the others and dropped his head into his hands. What was he going to do if she wasn't all right?

Just then, the swinging door swished open and the doctor in the pink and cats appeared.

She gestured for Maksim to follow her.

Erika and Maggie rose, but the doctor held up a hand to stop them.

"She will be fine," the doctor said. "No major damage. A good-sized knot on her head, some nasty bruises, and a pretty tender shoulder, but nothing that won't heal in a few days."

"Can we see her?" Maggie asked.

The doctor nodded. "But let's let the father have a moment with her first."

Maksim frowned, confused, but allowed the doctor to usher him out of the waiting room. Once they reached a closed door past several others lining one wall, the doctor stopped and faced him.

"First of all, let me say, she was very lucky."

Maksim nodded. He'd seen the fall, every horrible moment of it, and he had no doubt about that fact.

"The baby is fine, and . . ."

The rest of the doctor's words faded away as he tried to wrap his mind around what she'd already said.

The baby. The baby?

An overwhelming, breath-stealing, knee-weakening rush of joy filled him. Jo was pregnant? She was having a baby. His baby. He suddenly felt buoyant, estatic.

Then the feeling faded, his feet quickly returning to the ground. Even if she was pregnant with his child, it would be far too soon for her to know. Far, far too soon.

". . . she is going to have to remain off her feet for a few days. I'd be pleased if she could do a whole week. She does have a concussion, so we are going to admit her for tonight."

Maksim found himself nodding even though nothing was really making sense to him.

"You can go see her, now."

The doctor pushed open the door, waiting for him to enter. He hesitated, still unable to wrap his mind around this news, unsure of what to say to Jo.

But he couldn't very well just continue to stand there like an idiot. He stepped over the threshold and the door closed behind him.

Jo lay on the bed, looking pale and drawn and frightened. She didn't move as she saw Maksim. He lingered by the door for a moment, then couldn't stay away. She so desperately looked as if she needed someone to protect her.

"How are you feeling?" he asked, irritated that his voice sounded thick with emotion.

"Okay," she managed to say, her own voice strained.

"Does your head hurt?"

She nodded slightly, clearly not able to jar it any more than necessary.

They were silent for a few moments, then Maksim had to touch her. He caught her hand, gently squeezing her fingers reassuringly.

"The doctor told me the baby is fine."

Jo pulled in a shuddering breath as if she'd been waiting for those words, then tears began to roll down her cheeks.

"I'm sorry." Her voice quavered painfully.

"Sorry? Why?"

"I should have told you, before . . . well, before all of this."

Maksim shrugged. "Why didn't you?"

Jo laughed, the sound broken and watery. "I was in denial. Very, very deep denial."

That shouldn't have surprised him, but it did. "Why?"

She laughed again, though there wasn't an ounce of humor in the sound. "That's a long, pretty pathetic story."

He squeezed her hand and leaned forward. "Tell me anyway."

She looked at him for a moment, her teary gaze roaming his face, her eyes so large and dark and wary.

"Who is the father?" he asked, when she didn't speak, surprised at the emptiness in his chest now that his brief moment of fatherhood was over.

"A man I had a relationship with in D.C."

That was hardly a revelation, since she'd just moved down here, what? A month ago.

"How far along are you?"

"About thirteen weeks."

He nodded, realizing that he'd seen her naked, quite extensively, twice, and hadn't noticed any signs of pregnancy on her body. But why would he? He'd never seen her unpregnant, and he didn't have much pregnant sex to compare it to. Any, really.

"So did you decide you didn't want the father to be a part of the baby's life?"

She laughed again, and he was beginning to hate that broken, pained sound.

"Oh, I wanted him to be a part of our lives. He was the one who wanted nothing to do with us. Turns out he was married, which I didn't know. Fool that I was, he duped me completely. And when I told him my news, he made it very clear that I was never anything but a fling. And I was welcome to keep the baby, but he wasn't going to be any part of it. Seems he really, really loves his wife."

She laughed again, more pain and this time so much self-derision he ached for her.

They were quiet again, then Maksim realized that silent tears rolled down her cheeks again.

"What is it?" he asked.

"What the hell kind of mother am I going to make? I have an affair with a complete ass without even realizing it until I'm pregnant with his baby. I move to start a new life, but can't even manage to tell my very best friends why I'm here. I can't even bring myself to deal with my impending motherhood. Then I sleep with a man who I know is utterly unsuitable."

Maksim raised an eyebrow at that, but she didn't notice.

"Not once, but twice. And then a fall downstairs in a bar, because I'm nuts and seeing . . ." She stopped and just shook her head. Fresh tears trailed down her cheeks.

"I'm a mess."

Maksim sighed, then rose to go in search of a tissue. He found some on a counter by the door. He returned and dabbed at her cheeks.

"You will be fine. No one can know everything about a person. Believe me, I know." He had no idea what she was thinking most of the time. "You can only know what he told you. And he lied."

He finished wiping her cheeks, then handed her a second one, just in case.

"And you will be a great mother. You are just scared. It's a lot to take on by yourself."

She nodded, sniffing. Then she met his eyes. "I'm so glad I didn't lose this baby. I was terrified I had when I regained consciousness."

He nodded. "I'm glad you didn't, either."

And he realized that was true, and not just because of the

role he would have played in the loss. But because she would have been devastated. And he couldn't watch her go through that. Her pain now was hard to bear.

He smiled then, trying to lighten the mood, because he couldn't manage all these foreign emotions roiling through him.

"You do realize that the doctor thinks I'm the father?"

Jo returned his smile albeit weakly. "If only." Then she immediately blushed, the pinkness making her look much healthier, even if it was brought on by embarrassment rather than wellness.

His own chest tightened with that weird need from earlier. Before either could say anything further, a knock sounded on the door.

"Come in," Maksim called, relieved that they were getting an interruption.

Maggie, Erika, Ren, and Vittorio came into the small room, their presence taking up most of the space and pushing out some of the strangeness of their last words.

"How are you feeling?" Maggie asked, going over to the other side of the bed. Her eyes paused momentarily on Maksim's hand holding Jo's, but he didn't release it, and Jo didn't try to pull away.

"I've definitely felt better. But I'll be okay."

"What did the doctor say?"

"That I'm here for the night." Maksim noticed that Jo didn't tell them about the baby's welfare. Clearly she still wasn't ready to take on that conversation, and he couldn't really blame her. Today had been emotional enough for her.

"And everything is okay?" Erika asked, emphasizing there was more she wasn't saying.

Then he remembered her friends were lampirs. They could likely sense or smell or something Jo's pregnancy. From the very concerned looks on all their faces, it was pretty clear they knew something.

And here he was a demon, and he didn't have a clue. But maybe that was the explanation, he couldn't read pregnant humans' minds. Not that there should be any reason for that.

"I'm going to be fine," Jo assured her friends, her voice more resolute than he'd heard it since stepping inside this room.

Her determination calmed him a little. Jo was tough; he knew that without seeing inside her head. And she would be fine. She would be a great mother. She would survive.

And her resolution seemed to solidify something within him. He would be there for her. He would take care of her.

It was the least he could do, given the pain he'd just caused her. Even as he told himself that, he knew that wasn't his motivation.

Whether he wanted to accept it or not, Josephine Burke had been on his radar from the moment he met her, and she wasn't about to leave it. He'd do what he had to do to make sure she was okay.

"So what do they recommend for you to do?" Ren asked, his gaze interestingly enough going from Jo to Maksim and back to Jo.

Apparently all her friends were trying to figure out what was going on between the two of them.

"They said one night here, just for observation. Then if all goes well, I'm going to be sent home. But they want me on bed rest for a few days," Jo said.

"A week," Maksim corrected.

Jo rolled her eyes, but she did concede. "A week."

"You will stay with us," Erika said.

Jo started to shake her head, but Maksim interrupted. "No. She'll stay with me."

All eyes in the room turned to him.

Jo opened her mouth to protest, but he pressed a finger over her lips.

"No arguing. You are staying with me."

She stared at him for a moment, then nodded.

He turned and gave the others in the room a hard look, silently warning them not to challenge her decision.

Ren narrowed his eyes, suspicion clear on his face. Vittorio looked mildly annoyed. Erika looked wary and Maggie worried. But none of them said a word.

"Okay, folks," said a nurse from the doorway. "We need to let Ms. Burke get some rest."

Her friends said their good-byes, telling her they would check on her tomorrow. Only Maksim lingered behind, and again because the nurse assumed he was the father of her child and thus her significant other, she left, allowing him to stay.

"Are you sure?" she asked, not needing to explain what she was asking any more than that.

He nodded. "I want you with me."

She nodded again, although she looked unsure.

He couldn't help himself, and leaned down to kiss her. Her lips clung to his, sweetly vulnerable, yet hungry for him.

Maksim rested his forehead against hers, his chest swelling and filling with such strong, confusing emotions.

"I'm going to take care of you," he vowed, knowing he'd finally found someone he had to put before himself.

And that knowledge scared him.

Chapter 25

Even as Maksim opened the door to the cab to help her inside, Jo wasn't sure she was doing the right thing. Maksim had arrived first thing that morning, staying with her while they waited for the doctor to arrive, and give her the okay to check out.

She'd slept very little, her mind abuzz with everything that had happened in the past twenty-four hours. She'd been very lucky. She knew that. She also knew that little life growing inside her had become so very, very precious, and she felt sickened that it had taken something so horrific to make her understand that.

She kept telling herself that maybe that was why she was seeing images of her sister. Somehow it was her subconscious trying to reach out to her, to make her realize what she needed to do now. Jo always felt she'd failed Kara. That if she'd said something to someone, maybe she would have survived.

She couldn't save Kara, but she could protect her baby. Her sister's image was just a reminder that she couldn't fail another person in her care.

She winced as she settled onto the vinyl seat of the car.

"Are you okay?" Maksim asked.

She nodded. Her right shoulder was painfully stiff, her

back and legs bruised, and she would be sore for several days, but she would be okay.

Maksim studied her for a moment, then closed the door to go around to the other side of the car.

He slid in beside her, giving the driver her address. She leaned her head back against the hot vinyl of the backseat. Just leaving the hospital had her exhausted. She would need a little extra rest.

"I have to call Cherise," she said, realizing no one had contacted the woman. It was Saturday, so things would be okay. This would the one and only time the lack of programming at the center was a relief to Jo.

"I can call her," Maksim said.

"Thank you," Jo said wearily, the lack of sleep from last night and her injuries exhausting her.

She felt Maksim's arm loop around her, gently pulling her against his side. She didn't resist, curling against him.

In the brief ride, she must have fallen asleep, because when she came to, Maksim was carefully lifting her out of the cab.

"Oh," she said a little confused and surprised, peering up at him like a sleepy child. "I can walk."

"I know." He smiled, and continued to carry her. He set her down and waited while she rummaged through her purse for her keys. Then when it was clear between the pain in her shoulder and her grogginess that the lock was going to get the better of her, Maksim gently took them from her and opened the door. He scooped her up again, and she marveled at how gentle he could be.

"I really can walk," she told him again.

"I feel better holding you."

Jo thought to ask him why that was so, but her sleepy, muddled brain couldn't seem to manage the words. Instead she rested her head against his shoulder, allowing herself to revel in his strength.

He must have contended with both her and her keys, because the next thing she was aware of was Maksim placing her in her bed.

She groaned slightly as he released her.

"Can I get you anything?" he asked, concern furrowing his perfect brow. "The doctor said you can have some Tylenol for the pain."

She shook her head. "Just sore, nothing that won't go away eventually."

"Okay. Well, please let me know if I can get you anything."

"What are you going to do?" She imagined he'd be pretty bored in her place.

"You have lots of books. I'll read or something."

Jo smiled, letting her eyes close. "I don't see you as a big reader."

"Why not?" There was umbrage in his tone.

Her smile widened, even though she didn't bother to open her eyes. Her lids were simply too heavy. "You seem like someone who's too active. Someone who couldn't sit still long enough to read."

"Mmm," was his response and Jo couldn't decide if the noise was agreement or just acknowledgment.

She heard his steps on the hardwood floor, then a blanket covered her. She sighed. The warmth felt wonderful.

"Can you read here?" she asked him, peeping one eye open. He stood by the bed, the strangest look on his handsome features. Something so like adoration, it stole her breath away.

"Please stay in here with me," she said softly. She reached out to catch his hand.

He nodded.

He eased onto the bed beside her, keeping his movements slow and stable, trying not to jar her. Once he was settled with the pillow propped behind his head, he took her hand in his, rubbing his thumb back and forth over the back of hers. The steady motion was nice and calming.

"I like that," she said, sighing. Her eyes drifted closed again.

* * *

Maksim watched her, the constant state of concern still not leaving him. Even though her color looked much better today and the doctor had told him she would be fine, he couldn't seem to relax.

"Are you going to read?" she asked suddenly, her words slow and sleepy. "There are some books on the nightstand."

"Okay," he said, not moving. Not releasing her hand.

She was quiet, except for her breathing, which was low and even, and he was sure she'd drifted off when she said, "What are we doing?"

He was surprised, thinking she was far too tired to be analyzing their relationship, but he should have known Jo's brain wouldn't shut off until sleep truly claimed her. And even then he was willing to bet she had dreams still analyzing everything. Very symbolically, of course.

"I'm not really sure," he answered honestly.

Her head bobbed just slightly as if she agreed, and Maksim couldn't help asking, "Did you love the baby's father?"

"Jackson? I thought I did."

"Jackson? That's his name?" Maksim asked, wanting to know more about this dickwad who'd cheated, lied, and left Jo expecting a baby alone.

"Yes." She laughed slightly, even that sound sleepy. "Jackson Johnson, the man with two last names."

Maksim smiled, even though Jo had her eyes closed and couldn't see.

"Would you have married him?" he asked, even as he wished he could just drop the subject. But he had to know.

"Yes," she said without hesitation, and the answer hurt more than he would have thought it could.

"So you had to have loved him."

Jo shrugged, then nestled her head deeper into the fluffy down pillow. "I did love him. I just didn't know who I was loving."

Her words again like a sucker punch to the gut. She didn't

know Maksim either, and how would she feel about the truth about him? Did "demon" trump "married"? He suspected it did.

"I've had a hard time getting over him," she murmured, then yawned.

Maksim looked at her, realizing that explained a lot about her past behavior. She wasn't sure about how she felt, which explained her hot-and-cold shifts. She wasn't sure she wanted to move on, that much was clear.

"Are you still in love with him?" Maksim carefully rolled onto his side, trying not to move her overly. But the only answer he received was a soft snore.

Maksim sighed, remaining still, continuing to watch her. She was still in love with him. That was a perfect explanation for her reaction to Maksim. She wasn't sure what she wanted from Maksim or from Jackson.

He hooked a stray strand of her hair that clung to her cheek with his finger, tucking it behind her ear.

"Would you go back to him if he wanted you?" he asked in a whisper, expecting and receiving no response.

"Has he realized that he made a mistake?" he wondered aloud to himself. He lounged there for a few moments, thinking about that possibility.

Regretting his decision, but knowing he couldn't be stopped from this course, he gently nudged Jo.

Jo blinked her eyes open, looking around, uncertain where she was. When she got her bearings, she offered him the cutest, drowsy smile.

Maksim smiled back, hating that he'd woken her, but loving her sleepy genialness.

"Jo, where does Jackson live?"

"Right in D.C. On Capitol Hill. He's a lobbyist." Lingering sleepiness as good as a truth serum.

A lobbyist on Capitol Hill. Named Jackson Johnson. How hard could he be to find?

Maksim leaned forward and pressed a kiss to Jo's mouth. She responded, her lips instinctively moving against his. But when he pulled back she didn't speak. Sleep had claimed her again.

He eased out of bed, deciding right then that he was going to see this Jackson and find out why the hell he'd let this woman go.

Maksim stood on the sidewalk outside an office building in the nation's capital. It was moments like this that being a demon was really so convenient. Dematerialize here, materialize there.

Unfortunately this little venture wasn't for his own enjoyment. He needed to know what this Jackson guy was thinking. Maksim needed to give Jo the opportunity to be with the twit, if the guy had come to his senses during their separation from each other.

He walked up the steps and into the main lobby of the building. A directory greeted him, listing floors and office numbers of the different businesses in the large building. Jackson Johnson worked on the first floor in Suite 1A.

Maksim glanced around, easily finding the hallway and door he needed.

He entered a small outer office. A pretty receptionist with a chin-length blond bob and pale blue eyes smiled immediately when she saw him.

"Hello. Can I help you?" Her smile deepened in a subtle way that Maksim knew meant she liked what she saw. At one time, he would have reveled at that, eating up the attention. But now he was only aware of it in a very cursory way.

"I'm here to see Mr. Johnson."

"Okay," she said glancing at her computer. "Let me see. I don't seem to have anyone down at this time. Are you sure your appointment was for today?"

Maksim smiled. "I don't actually have an appointment, but

I'm sure he'll want to speak with me." He kept his voice congenial, even though he was feeling anything but about the man.

The receptionist nibbled her bottom lip, considering what she should do. Clearly she was new—or just not that bright. Finally, she stood.

"Let me check with him, Mr . . ."

"Mr. Kostova. We haven't actually met, but tell him I'm here in regards to the Burke initiative." He smiled again, this time pouring on the charm, although for once the act didn't give him any satisfaction when she quickly nodded, knocked, then disappeared into the office to the left of her desk to do his bidding.

Not in the way it once would have.

As he had hoped, his request was met with immediate response.

The office door reopened right away and the blonde gestured for him to enter.

"Mr. Johnson will see you." She beamed at him as he passed her.

Maksim nodded in response, dismissing her now that he had what he wanted.

When he entered the Johnson office, he got the impression of gray walls and black furniture with a modern flair, but it was the man standing behind the desk who held his attention.

As much as he hated to admit it, Jackson Johnson, despite his unfortunate name, was a good-looking man. Tall, leanly muscular with a haircut that Maksim suspected cost a pretty penny to look that carelessly tousled. He was in his early forties maybe, but had the kind of face that made it hard to be sure. Wire-rim glasses gave him an intellectual quality, but his smile gave him a slight used-car salesman vibe.

"Mr. Kostova," he moved forward offering his hand, "nice to meet you."

Maksim didn't say anything, but shook his hand, unable to

stop himself from squeezing a little too tightly. Johnson only reacted by letting his smile slip a little.

"So how can I help you?"

It was Maksim's turn to smile. "Well, as I had your lovely receptionist mention, I'm here about Jo Burke. You do remember her? The woman you lied to and left pregnant."

Johnson stopped smiling totally. He returned behind his desk and sat down. Clearly the man didn't expect Maksim to be that forward and that blunt.

"I know Jo Burke," he said. "But I think you have your story wrong."

"Really?" Maksim raised a disbelieving eyebrow. "So you didn't have an affair with her?" He didn't keep his voice hushed as Johnson had.

Johnson opened his mouth, then snapped it shut. He was considering his words like any good lobbyist or political figure would. And Maksim suspected he was going to believe this guy about as much as he believed any politician.

"We did have an affair. It was nothing more than that. An affair. She was the one who kept making it seem like it was something more. I'm actually a happily married man."

Maksim nodded slowly as if he was considering his words. Not likely. They didn't merit consideration.

"Do happily married men usually cheat?" Maksim asked with indignation.

"Listen, I don't really see what the point of this is. We are over. And I'm moving on now."

"To your secretary?"

Johnson rose again. "I think you should go, and tell Jo that I don't appreciate her sending over her newest lover to bully me. I made it clear that things were over between us."

Maksim stood too. "Jo didn't send me over. I had to come see you for myself. Where I come from, we don't have spineless creatures like you. Even my kind take responsibility for their actions."

"Where you are from? Russia?"

Maksim didn't bother to answer. He had already said more than he should have.

"I came here to see if you had any feelings for her," he said instead. "To see if you had any feelings for the child she's carrying, and it's clear you don't."

Jackson Johnson just looked at Maksim as if he didn't even comprehend what he'd just said.

Maksim stared back at him, barely restraining the urge to do the man bodily harm. The truth was, the scum wasn't worth it.

Maksim headed toward the door.

"I'm surprised she didn't try to pawn that brat off on you."

Maksim stopped in his tracks and turned slowly back to the ass. Oh, what the hell. Maksim raised his hand, mimicking the action of grabbing Johnson by the throat, even though he was several feet away from the man. His favorite Darth Vader trick.

Instantly Johnson's hands went to his neck, clawing at a hand that wasn't there. Then Maksim raised his hand higher in the air, and Johnson's feet lifted off the gray Berber carpeting, flailing in the air.

Maksim then gestured with his hand, imitated nothing more than a negligent casting of something aside, and Johnson flew across the room, his back hitting the wall. He crumpled to the floor in a heap, still grasping his throat and gasping for breath.

Maksim sauntered over to him, standing over him. Johnson tried to back away, huddling against the wall like a frightened, helpless rat.

"Don't think about ever contacting Jo. Because you'll have to deal with me. And, as you can see, that isn't pleasant."

Maksim left feeling more satisfied than he could remember.

Being a demon wasn't all bad.

Chapter 26

Maksim could believe that until he was with Jo. Then he wondered how he was ever truly going to have a relationship with a human woman. A normal relationship.

Dear God, he wanted to be normal. *Never* had he wanted that. And when had he started to refer questions to God? That went against the whole demon/Hell creed.

He stood at the end of Jo's bed, where she still slept like the dead. She hadn't even appeared to have moved in the hours that he'd been gone.

Quietly he shucked off his pants and shirt, leaving on only his jockey shorts. Carefully, he crawled into bed beside her.

She immediately shifted, curling up against him, her skin silky and warm from sleep.

"Hi," she murmured.

"Hi," he replied, placing a kiss on her forehead.

"Where did you go?"

So she had woken enough to notice he was gone.

"I just had to talk to someone."

"Mmm," she said. "Was it a good talk?" Her voice was already slurred as sleep tried to reclaim her.

"Yeah, it was very satisfying." He pulled her closer as one of those overpowering waves of protectiveness she brought out in him washed through him.

Her hand curled on his chest, and he could feel her even breathing on his skin. To his surprise, the closeness and contentment of being with her, snug in her bed, lulled him and soon he slept, too.

When he woke again, the sun had set, casting the room in murky shadows, but it wasn't the change in lighting that roused him. It was the hand with delicate fingers slipping under the waistband of his jockeys.

He snagged the hand before it reached its goal, which was already pulsing against his stomach in the hopes she'd reach the goal, too.

"Hey there," he said, his voice gravelly with sleep. "What do you think you are doing?"

He felt Jo smile against his shoulder. "Nothing."

Maksim kept hold of her hand as he rolled onto his side, his face inches from hers. "Nothing is what you should be doing."

Jo groaned with disappointment. "I don't want to do nothing. I want to touch you."

Her other hand, which Jo didn't have restrained, slid up between them and stroked over his stomach, then lower, shaping over his erection through his boxers.

He groaned. "Jo. The doctor said you need to stay in bed and rest."

"I am in bed," she pointed out reasonably. "And the rest is really more about my bruises. Not about the baby."

The baby. The idea that she was carrying a life inside her was staggering and humbling. His hand released hers and moved to her stomach. He slipped his hand under her shirt and slid his palm low on her abdomen, cupping the slight swell there.

She placed a hand over his and the moment, just lying there, like that, was as intimate as Maksim could recall.

"The baby will be fine," she said with certainty. She wiggled closer to him and pressed a kiss to his mouth. "She managed to be fine after a fall downstairs, I think she'll be fine if we make love."

Make love. He'd never thought of the act in that term before. But he found he wanted to now.

"How do you know it's a girl? Did they tell you that when they did the ultrasound yesterday?" He was directing the subject away from amorous ones, because he still wasn't sure she should be doing something like that so soon.

"No. I just have a feeling."

She hooked a leg over his, pulling herself closer to him still. The hand still over his erection moved, just slow, persuasive caresses. She kissed him, her lips as leisurely and coaxing as her fingers.

"You are relentless," he murmured against her mouth.

"Mmm-hmm." Her hand left him just long enough to tug his boxers down, freeing his arousal, which was more than happy to be set loose.

Then she wriggled her own hips, working off her panties. They came back together, bare legs intertwining. Her arms came around his neck, although he did freeze when he heard a small gasp.

"Are you okay?"

He felt her nod rather than saw it. "The shoulder is just a little sore."

"Jo," he said again. "This is too soon."

"Shut up and kiss me."

Even though he still wasn't sure, he obeyed her. For a long time they just kissed, their lips exploring, their bodies staying pressed tight, skin against skin. Every movement pushing them a little further into their desire. Her breast brushing against him, her nipples hard, a delicious friction.

His hands stroked over the sleek skin of her back, down lower still, shaping over the soft cushion of her ass. His mouth left her peppering kisses down her neck over her chest finding the nipple closest to him. He drew the taut point into his mouth, swirling his tongue around it until she cried out.

"I love how sensitive your breasts are."

"Mmm, a pleasant side effect of pregnancy."

He touched her stomach then, also savoring the gentle swell of her belly. Something about knowing she carried life aroused him. It wasn't even life he'd put there, but that didn't seem to matter—he still felt possessive and protective of it.

Then his hand moved lower, finding the narrow strip of curls that protected her sex. He slipped his finger into the slit, discovering her dripping wet and so ready for him.

He groaned at the feeling of her slick and hot.

One finger slid deep inside her, while his thumb stroked her clitoris. Her hips moved, riding his hand in the way he knew she wanted to ride him.

He reveled in her movements, in the sexy noises she made. She strained and pulsed around his finger. Until she shattered, a low cry escaping from her into him as he kissed her as she came.

Then while she was still limp from her release, he positioned her legs around him, keeping them on their sides but spreading her wide so he could enter her. Her soaked warmth made it easy for him to thrust into her core, rocking her slowly and gently toward another orgasm.

She cried out again, but even then he didn't stop, still moving in her until she pushed him onto his back and straddled him.

He watched her moving above him. His cock deep, deep inside her, her hips setting the rhythm. He closed his eyes and let her take total control, sliding up and down on him until he didn't know where she stopped and he began.

Then her motions grew faster, her body riding his, steering their release.

When his orgasm hit him, he ceased breathing. He did nothing but feel. Her body milking his, her hands braced on his chest, her lips on his face.

He gave himself over to her and the second orgasm that hit

him drove all logical thought from his mind. If he could go to paradise, this was what it was like.

Then he fell into sated oblivion.

Jo woke to Maksim stroking her tangled hair away from her cheeks, the touch so tender, so breath-stealing.

He leaned in and kissed her sweetly, leisurely, and she suddenly knew she had to take the risk. She had to allow herself to trust this man. He wasn't Jackson. Not even close, and in truth, she felt more for him in this short time than she'd ever felt for Jackson. She'd believed Jackson was the real thing when she'd been living it, but now . . .

She couldn't let this slip away. Maksim *was* the real thing. She could love him. God, she already did.

"Maksim?" she said.

His hand paused rubbing up and down her back in an easy, delicious massage. "Mmm?"

"Are we . . ." The question sounded so stupid given where they were, lying naked in each other's arms, basking in the aftermath of amazing, perfect sex, but she needed to know. ". . . are we a couple? Is that what we're doing here?"

Maksim was quiet for a few moments, but it felt like minutes, hours, and Jo started to think of ways to backpedal, to get back the peacefulness they'd just had.

"Yes."

She remained utterly still, even holding her breath, hoping he'd say more than that. Thank God, he did.

"Jo, I've never felt like this before. And I will be dead honest with you, I have no idea whatsoever what I'm doing. I just know I don't want any of this to end. I want to be with you."

Jo's heart swelled in her chest. It wasn't poetry, but it was the most beautiful thing anyone had ever said to her.

She kissed him, joy filling her. He caught the back of her head and kissed her back more intensely. Maksim's usual possessiveness was returning with gusto.

And she loved every moment of it.

Chapter 27

"You look so good," Maggie said, as Jo set a cup of tea in front of her.

"I feel better than I have in months," Jo admitted, knowing for the first time she looked like the fabled glowing pregnant woman. "It's amazing what some rest will do for a person."

"Oh, I think it's a bit more than that," Erika said with a smile.

Jo grinned, unable to temper her joy. "Oh, I think you could be right."

She knew Erika and Maggie were in part talking about her pregnancy, which she'd finally told them about days ago and didn't seem to shock them too much. Jo must not have been hiding it terribly well. But most of Erika's comment alluded to Maksim.

Her two best friends had been over every night since the fall, and very time they visited, Maksim was there. He'd make himself scarce so the friends could talk, but Jo knew Maggie and Erika were impressed with how solicitous he was to her.

"I didn't think Maksim had it in him to be so caring. It's really not in their nature," Erika said, then snapped her mouth closed.

"In their nature?" Jo sat down, frowning at her friend, puzzled.

Erika glanced at Maggie, who laughed and said, "You know, good-looking men. They are usually so self-involved."

Jo laughed. "That is true enough. And believe me, I originally thought that was totally true about Maksim, but I couldn't have been more wrong. He's been going to the center to help out. He's been taking care of me—even though I really don't need it. He's been wonderful."

"You are so smitten," Maggie said, smiling fondly, enjoying Jo's behavior.

"I am," Jo admitted.

"I've never heard you say that about anyone," Erika said with genuine surprise.

"That's because I've never felt this way." Jo sighed, then took a sip of her tea.

"Not even the baby's father?" Maggie asked, her voice sad. Jo reached over and patted her friend's hand. Maggie was always the sentimental one.

"No. Not even him, although I thought I did, or could. It's funny how things happen. Maksim came along right when I didn't trust or even particularly like men and showed me I could feel real love."

Maggie sighed, too. "It is funny how that works. Ren did exactly the same thing for me."

"And we all know Vittorio is my dark-eyed prince."

Jo laughed, surprised at her giddiness. But she just felt happy these days.

"Speaking of which, I need to go," Maggie said. "The band goes on in about half an hour."

Erika nodded. "And I need to work on my sculpture."

Jo hated to see her friends leave, but in truth, she had plans for this evening, too.

Maggie took a sip of her tea—the first, and last of the cup—then stood. Erika rose, too.

"Where is Maksim tonight?" Maggie asked.

"He's at his place. We have a date tonight."

"Oow," Erika said, wiggling her eyebrows. "I'm jealous."

Jo laughed. "Yeah, you two both married real thoughtless, unromantic men."

They laughed, too.

"Yeah," Erika said, "I can't complain."

"No complaining here." Maggie grinned.

Jo said her good-byes and then immediately headed to her bedroom. She opened her closet, rummaging through her clothes, trying to find something that would still fit. It was as if the baby now knew she was accepted and loved, she'd started to make her presence more obvious. Just a little belly, but enough to make Jo's usual clothes fit oddly.

And then there was the enlarging breast issue, which she rather liked. Mainly because Maksim liked them.

With that thought, she remembered a sundress she'd bought last summer, which she'd never worn because it required a pretty impressive padded bra to fit right, which she knew when she bought it, but still did.

She found the dress toward the back of the rack, pulling it out and inspecting it. The style and floral pattern in oranges and greens and browns were very retro. Very fun. And the Empire waist should be perfect to accommodate the slight baby bump.

Ha, and who says you should never impulse shop?

Humming, excited for the evening, and feeling good in general, she headed to the bathroom. Maksim said he had reservation for nine. He wouldn't say where—that was a surprise—but she did have the time, and because of Erika and Maggie's visit, she was running a little behind. Not bad, but she was going to have to get moving. She didn't want to be late.

She hung the dress on the door, then turned to the tub. Once the shower was running, she went the medicine cabinet over her sink to grab a razor. As she was closing the cabinet, a movement caught her eye in the mirror. She paused, her heart skipping at the sight. Slowly she spun around, facing the open bathroom door.

There was nothing there. No movement, no sound. She stayed still for a moment, but nothing out of the ordinary happened.

It must have been the dress hanging that caught her eye. Just to make herself feel better, she moved the dress to the back of the door and closed herself in. She nearly twisted the lock, but stopped herself. She had no reason to be nervous.

Things had been fine for days. No sightings of dead sisters, ghost cat ladies. Nothing. Of course, she hadn't been over to Erika's since the last weird sighting, but she'd convinced herself that it really was stress and lack of sleep getting to her. That and the overwhelming tension of keeping her pregnancy a secret. Her subconscious was just wreaking havoc on her.

She returned to the shower and tested the water. Nice and warm. She undressed, tossing the clothes carelessly onto the floor. She groaned when she stepped into the warm spray, amazed that some of her muscles still ached from the fall. Luck really had been with her that night. Things could have so easily been worse.

Then she heard a sound. She paused, her fingers resting on the slippery bar of soap. She listened again, then picked up the soap. She still listened as she rubbed a lather between her hands. All she could hear was the hum of her air-conditioner. That old thing was enough to wake the dead when it kicked on.

"Perhaps not the best analogy," she said, then started to hum again and washing her limbs.

Where would they go tonight? Maksim had said to wear a dress. Of course that could just be for his own benefit. This made her wonder what *he'd* wear. The man had great taste in clothes, she had to admit.

Setting down the soap, she picked up the bottle of shampoo sitting on the corner of the tub. Squeezing a dollop in her hand, she set the bottle back. As rubbed her hands together, she again got the impression of a movement in her peripheral vision, this time through the opaque shower curtain. A definite image of something moving downward, quickly.

With the shampoo still on her hands, she caught the curtain with the tips of her least soapy fingers and pulled back the edge to look out into the bathroom.

Her dress lay in a crumpled pile on the tile floor. She smiled, telling herself she knew she was being silly for even looking. And for holding her breath, which she hadn't realized she'd been doing until she laughed.

She debated getting out and hanging it again, but decided against it. Her hands were slick with shampoo, she was nearly done with her shower. Just a quick shampoo and leg shave and she'd be finished.

Plus that dress wasn't likely to wrinkle. Hallelujah for poly-cotton blends.

She scrubbed her hair, then stepped totally under the spray, letting the suds and water run down her body. While under the rush of the shower, she again heard something. This time whatever it was sounded much closer than before, but it could just be the distortion from the water in her ears.

She finished rinsing quickly and looked back toward the curtain. This time she saw something on the other side of the curtain. A shape she was certain hadn't been there before.

Her heart skipped, thumping up into her throat. She tried to breath in slowly, but her breathe couldn't seem to get through her tightened throat.

It had to be the shadow of something she hadn't noticed earlier. It had to be. But she wasn't sure. Then the shadow seemed to shift.

"Maksim?" she said, her voice barely reaching above a whisper.

The thing didn't respond, but it did move, seeming to get closer to the curtain.

"Hello?" Jo said, hating the panic she was hearing fill her voice. There was an explanation. There was.

The form moved again, and this time she could see it was short. Shorter than herself, and she could make out some colors.

Colors. Dread swelled in her, and she backed away from the curtain, her back making contact with the cold tiles walls.

Slowly the curtain moved toward her, pushing in toward her.

"Maksim," she managed to say again, although even weaker than before.

The thing on the other side of the curtain advanced still, and Jo could see a repeating pattern, the colors muted and blurred because of the opacity of the plastic, but she could see them as much as she didn't want to see, to know who it was.

Then the curtain pushed in even farther, and Jo saw a hand, a small hand reaching for her, only the flimsy shower curtain keeping the hand from touching her.

Jo screamed.

Maksim tried to tell himself that any self-respecting demon did not go to these lengths, but he couldn't bring himself to care. He juggled an enormous bouquet of flowers, flowers of all kinds, roses, tulips, gerbera daisies—lots of those because Jo had made the offhanded comment one night in bed that she loved them—asters, and who knew what else. He also carried a bottle of sparkling cider, and a stuffed giraffe. That last item was more for the baby than Jo, but he knew she'd like it, too.

Damn, he was so whipped, but again, he just didn't care. He loved being with Jo. She was funny and sexy and did things that just made him smile. And that was good.

Bitter could only be entertaining for so long.

He shifted all the items into one arm as he fumbled with Jo's key. He considered just materializing inside her apartment, but thought better of the idea. After all, what if she was in the kitchen? Materializing. Yeah, that was hard to explain.

For just a moment, his spirits dampened. There was a lot about him that would be hard to explain, but he wasn't thinking about that tonight. Tonight, he was a pussy-whipped demon with a hot date.

He finally got the key in the lock, not easy with several sprigs of greenery and a gerbera daisy poking him in the face. He opened the door and dropped the items on the table.

"Jo?" he called, then realized he could hear the shower running.

He frowned. He'd told her to ready by nine, and he was fifteen minutes late. Jo was a punctual person, and she was excited about the evening. He'd expected to see her waiting in the living room, demanding to know where they were going.

Ah, well. Something must have come up and delayed her. And this was good for him; he could get the flowers in water and open the sparkling cider.

He went to her cupboards and got down two wineglasses, then he searched the other cupboards, finally finding a plastic iced-tea pitcher with colorful sun umbrellas and sunglasses all over the sides.

Not his first choice, but it would do.

He turned on the water, then walked back to the kitchen table to get the flowers. He found a knife in one of the drawers and cut away the plastic sleeve keeping the giant bouquet together.

Reaching for the pitcher, he noticed he'd turned on the hot water rather than the cold. He started to switch the faucet the other direction, when he realized the water was ice cold.

Frowning, he flipped the handle in the other direction. He waited, then tested the water again. It was freezing, too.

Could she really be in the shower still? He walked down the hall. Yes, the shower was definitely running, and instantly alarm filled him.

He knocked. "Jo?"

No sound greeted him.

He knocked again. "Jo? Are you in there?"

This time he thought he heard a sound, but the faint sound didn't ease his feeling of dread. He checked the knob; it turned easily in his hand.

He stepped in the room, finding the air inside freezing. Jo wasn't outside the bathtub getting ready. So he strode over and whipped the curtain back.

Jo huddled in the far end of the tub, her legs pulled up to her chin, her eyes wide, staring, terrified.

"Jo!" He reached into the tub, bodily lifting her out. She seemed to snap out of her horrified trance as soon as she was secure in his arms, her body pressed full to his chest.

"Maksim," she said her voice panicked, reedy. "It's you. Oh God, it's you."

"Yes, I'm here. What's wrong?"

She didn't answer. She just buried her head into his chest, clinging to him like a frightened child.

He balanced her against him as he snagged a towel from the rack. He held her away from him long enough to wrap her frozen, wet body in the soft terrycloth, then he scooped her up.

Heading to the bedroom, he asked her again, "Jo, what happened? Are you okay? Is it the baby?"

She shook her head, her wet hair brushing his chin. "The baby is fine."

Relief filled him, even though he hadn't believed that was the issue. She didn't seem in pain—she was clearly terrified of something.

Setting her down on the bed, he pulled the comforter up to cover her. Still she shivered.

"What happened?" he asked again, sitting beside her, taking one of her hands in his. Her fingers felt like icicles against his palm.

She breathed in slowly through her nose. Then she met his eyes, fear and dread and worry all vivid in their dark depths.

"I just saw my sister. My dead sister."

Chapter 28

"Your sister?"

Jo expected Maksim to look at her as if she was mad. Clearly she was. She'd had hopes that wasn't the case, but apparently that was not to be. She was nuts.

She nodded.

She waited for him to tell her she must be mistaken. That she had to be imagining things, which she still wanted desperately to believe, but knew she couldn't. This time, like the last on the stairs, had just been too vivid.

"Has she appeared to you before?"

She gaped at him for a moment. Did he believe her? The phrasing of his sentence implied that. Not, has this happened before? Or could it just be a hallucination?

"Yes. I've seen images of her a few times. I think she was the one who left the footprints that I thought I saw that one night when I was so shaken. And most recently I saw her on the stairs at the bar. That's why I fell."

He nodded, and she couldn't read his expression.

"Do you think I'm crazy?" She had to ask, because she certainly felt like she was.

He shook his head. "No. I don't."

They were both silent for a few moments.

"I think you should lay down for a while." He started

tucking the covers tighter around her still shivering body, but she shook her head, sitting up.

"I can't. I want our evening out."

Maksim shook his head. "You are too shaken. I think you need to rest."

She did feel drained, but she didn't want to be here. She was too nervous. Too afraid it would happen again.

"Can we spend the night at your place?"

Maksim nodded. "Of course. Why don't you get some things together and we'll head over there now?" He offered her a comforting smile. "We'll order in and watch a movie."

She knew he was trying to act as normal as possible and she appreciated it. Still there was a look in his green eyes that she couldn't read. Something guarded and distant.

Maybe he didn't believe her quite as much as he would lead her to think. But she didn't question it now. She wanted out of this place. She did not feel comfortable. Even the air seemed heavy with foreboding.

What did Kara want from her? Did she blame Jo for her death, too?

Maksim watched Jo get dressed and toss some clothing and other items into an overnight bag. She was seeing ghosts and he knew he'd done that to her. He was willing to bet money on that fact. There was always a consequence of entering a person's mind and this was hers.

And that consequence was terrifying her. And putting her at risk. And the baby, too. Disgust tightened his throat, making it hard for him to breathe.

This was a firm reminder that he was a demon. Demons could never be good for a human. Demons weren't good for anyone.

"Okay, I'm ready." She offered him a tremulous smile and he felt like even more of a dick because he was trying to be strong for her. For the individual who did this to her. And for purely selfish reasons.

He wanted to shout out his own anger with himself, but

just gritted his teeth and held out a hand to take the bag from her. She handed it to him, and then he followed her down the hall, not missing the way she skirted around the bathroom.

He ducked inside, turning off the shower he'd left on in his hurry to get her out of the freezing water.

When he got to the kitchen, he found her looking at the huge bouquet of flowers now forgotten on the counter. She fingered the petals of one of the large orange daisies.

She turned to look at him, her eyes misty. "You remembered they are my favorite."

Somehow that bouquet seemed silly and inadequate now compared to what he'd done to her. How did he give her a gift to fix that? There wasn't one.

"We have to bring them with us," she said, gathering them up in her arms. She smiled again. "Thank you. I'm sorry I've ruined your hard work and special night."

"You haven't ruined anything," he said, his voice adamant.

She smiled again, but he could tell she didn't believe him. But how the hell did he tell her that it was he who ruined their night? It was he who hurt her. And brought all this pain over her lost sister back. In vivid ghostly detail.

"This is nice," Jo said as they got out of the cab in front of one of the shotgun cottages that lined the street. "Although I wouldn't have guessed these would be your colors."

She smiled over her shoulder at him.

He raised an eyebrow at the cotton-candy colors of the siding and shutters. "Yeah, not my choice. This is my sister's place."

Jo looked back at the house. "Oh, I didn't realize you were staying in her place."

"Yes. I keep hoping she'll return or someone will show up here who knows something. But so far I'm not having much luck with that."

Jo watched him as he unlocked the front door, trying to read him. Over their past week together, she'd considered him an easy man to understand. But not tonight. It was as if something inside him had shut down.

Again, she wondered if he really believed her.

His sister's home was nice. "Cheerful" was the first word that came to mind as she walked through the living room and kitchen as he brought her stuff to his bedroom. Obviously the guest room, if the size was any indication, since the queen-sized bed took up most of the space in the room.

Realizing he was staying in here, waiting for his sister to return, made her feel awful. And selfish. She hadn't even asked him much about her.

"What does your sister do?"

"She's a writer."

He placed her stuff on the bed, then led her back to the living room.

"What does she write?"

"Mostly books on the paranormal. Demons in particular." He studied her as he told her, seeming to be gauging her reaction, though she couldn't tell why.

She wrapped her arms around herself, suppressing a chill. "I think I'll pass on reading those for the time being." She tried to soften her comment with a smile, but she still couldn't tell what he was thinking. And it was getting very unnerving.

"How about we order in Chinese?" he said, heading to a pile of takeout menus tossed in a basket near the phone.

"That sounds great."

Jo watched him sort through them. Something rubbed up against her ankles, making her jump and cry out.

Maksim spun toward her, dropping several of the menus to the ground. "What the hell?"

A cat rubbed up against Jo's legs, and Jo was certain it was Erika's cat, but it couldn't be.

"What the hell?" Maksim repeated.

"Is this your sister's cat?"

"No, I think it's Erika and Vittorio's cat. But how the hell did it get in here?"

His words caused a chill to return to her finally warmed skin.

"I must have left a window open somewhere," he concluded, but his explanation for the cat's appearance did little to soothe her.

"Why would it be Erika's cat?" Jo asked, staring down at the animal like it was one of the demons Maksim's sister wrote about in her books.

"I just think it is. It's showed up here before. Or least I think it's her cat."

Jo moved away from the black creature, who stared at her with those golden eyes she knew altogether too well.

"I think it is, too." Another chill prickled her skin.

"I'm putting it out in the back courtyard. I'll bring him back to Erika and Vittorio's in the morning." He scooped up the cat, who yowled indignantly.

Jo watched as he disappeared down the hallway. A few moments later he returned. She still stood in the middle of the room, her arms wrapped protectively around herself. Like that would guard her from the creepy vibe in the air.

"It's been a weird night," he said, shaking his head.

"Yes, it has," Jo agreed. They stared at each other for a moment, then smiled.

"Let's order Chinese and watch some stupid comedy," Maksim suggested.

She nodded. "That sounds like a great plan."

When Jo woke up with the sunshine streaming down onto the bed, the events of last night seemed far away. She and Maksim had watched a silly comedy starring Will Ferrell. They'd eaten lots of moo goo gai pan and szechwan. And then they had made love, which had been toe-curlingly wonderful as always.

Although Jo had to admit there had been an almost desperate quality to Maksim's touch, which seemed weird to say, because Jo couldn't exactly pinpoint what had made it seem that way. But that was the only way she could think to describe Maksim's behavior.

She did feel calmer today. And today was her last day of mandatory relaxation. Tomorrow she could go back to work— just for the morning. It was Saturday, but she was going to go in and get caught up on e-mails and other odds and ends, so she'd be ready for a normal Monday.

She was looking forward to the work, even though the rest had done her some good. Clearly it had not cured of her of her visions, but she did feel healthier, at least bodily anyway.

And she did feel hungry, plus she wondered where Maksim had gone. Then she remembered that he'd had to go in this morning to help Cherise. He'd be home at noon, then they would probably laze around reading, making love.

Oh yeah, her time off had spoiled her. Sighing, she rolled out of bed and padded to the kitchen. There wasn't much in the fridge. Mostly old takeout. She opted for some of the pork fried rice, which she ate cold out of the container.

While she wolfed down her dubious breakfast, she wandered around the apartment. The Easter-egg color choices for the walls wouldn't have been her first choice, but they oddly worked with the other decorating and furniture Maksim's sister had.

She browsed her artwork. And her cool furnishings. Finally she reached a room Maksim hadn't shown her last night. The room was clearly Ellina's study. She had an ornately carved desk with a new computer set up on top. Stacks and stacks of papers littered the rest of the desk.

Bookshelves took up one whole wall. Many appeared to be research books, all of them mostly about the occult. Several shelves were filled with Ellina's books, her name bold on each spine. And Maksim was right. Demons seemed to be her favorite subject matter. *The Everyday Guild to Demons. Demon Do's and Don'ts. Demons For Dummies.*

Jo set down the Chinese food container on the edge of the desk and pulled one of the books off the shelf, flipping through it.

Identifying your demon. Demons' names and their meanings. The Circles of Hell, Satan's Subdivisions.

Jo shook her head, Maksim's sister had some unusual interests. She continued to flip through the book until she reached the back cover.

Then she froze.

"Oh my God."

Maksim knelt on a dirty linoleum floor with shoelaces in his hands, and a small child with a runny nose attached to them.

"Right," he said, quickly finishing the task. Even double knotted them. Then he pulled a tissue out of his pants pocket and handed it to the little girl.

She took it, and mostly smeared the snot around her face, but Maksim accepted that as a start. For the first week she'd just wiped her nose on him.

The little girl darted off without so much as a thank-you.

You gotta love these little heathens. Although he didn't feel nearly as disgusted by the little creatures and their pretty revolting habits.

Maksim stood and surveyed the room. The kids were broken up in groups of five doing what Cherise referred to as "free choice centers." Which meant the kids got free playtime, moving between stations that were designed to get them to use different skills. One station was colors and sorting. Another was puzzles. Another was a kitchen area with fake food and a table. Yet another had books to play library, getting them familiar with letters and words. One was a store to play with numbers and money. Most of the stations had limited toys, but Cherise did her best. And the kids loved it.

He watched as the kids interacted, the room filled with noise, loud talking, laughter, some bickering, others singing.

It was chaotic and overwhelming, but not in the same way it had been when he'd first offered himself up to this torture.

"The kids love you," Cherise said, smiling at him approvingly as she came over to stand beside him.

"Well, they are great kids." Did he have to sound so sincere?

Just then the little girl whose shoe he'd just tied came running back. She tugged on the pant leg of his jeans. He leaned down to her level.

"Thanks, Mister Mak'im for tying my shoes." The little girl with a multitude of braids banded with multicolored ponytail holders gave him a quick kiss on the cheek before running off again to join the others.

He remained bent forward, a little taken aback by the child's spontaneous show of affection. In fact, it took him several moments to even realize that it was snot that had made the quick kiss extra sloppy.

When he did, Cherise reached into her pocket and pulled out a tissue, holding it out to him, grinning. She was where he'd learned the tissue trick.

"See what I mean. You are adored."

Maksim looked back to the kids, wondering why on earth they would like him so much. He certainly hadn't like them for much of the time he'd been here. But somewhere along the way that had changed.

He accepted the tissue and wiped his cheek, still watching the odd little creatures intermingling in front of him. What odd beings.

"Why would they like me so much?" he couldn't help himself from asking.

"Because you help them and listen to them and keep them safe when they often don't get any of that outside these walls."

Maksim frowned, considering them again. Really? This was the best their lives got? His gaze picked out Damon. He still wore that silly "E" necklace, valuing the gaudy thing like a family heirloom. Maksim supposed in his life it was.

And how would he be as a father? Could he really offer his child anything better? Self-centered, excessive, indulgent, ruled solely by his own wants and desires. Yeah, he'd be a great dad.

Then he thought of Jo. Look what he'd done to her. She was terrified, seeing her dead sister. She'd fallen down a flight of stairs and could have lost her baby. All because of his self-ishness.

And to top that off, he was a demon. Last night, he'd made love to her, because yet again, he couldn't deny himself. But he'd realized it was the last time. He was going to let her go. He was no better than Jackson Johnson. He couldn't really offer her a life she deserved.

And the truth was, he loved her. He wanted her, but he was going to do the first unselfish thing of his life. He was going to let her go. She could never accept what he was, and he didn't want her to accept it, she deserved better.

He had to let her go.

Chapter 29

Jo stared at the picture in the back of her book. That was her! That black-haired woman with the pale eyes. She was seeing Maksim's sister. Jo's first thought was that she needed to tell him. But then her excitement vanished. If she was seeing Ellina, then she must be dead.

How could she tell Maksim that?

She stared at the picture again. But that was definitely her. Just then, she heard a noise at the study window. Jo started as Erika's cat hopped up onto a flowerbox outside the glass. He pawed the window.

Ellina and that cat. Jo hadn't ever seen one without the other. Again she toyed with the idea that somehow Maksim's sister and the black cat were one and the same.

You're nuts, she informed herself. But then she was seeing her dead sister. So why couldn't her boyfriend's sibling be a cat? Nothing was out of the realm of possibility at this point.

Jo set aside the book and crossed to the window. The cat batted a paw against the glass again, the action distinctly impatient.

Jo unlocked the window and struggled to push it up, the old and swollen wood not making it easy. Finally she raised it enough for the cat to slip inside.

"Are you Maksim's sister?" she asked the golden-eyed feline, then felt decidedly stupid. But the cat meowed, making her consider the animal understood.

"How can I help you?" Again this behavior was going to get her committed, but she had to know.

The cat meowed again.

Then the feeling in the room seemed to shift. The same feeling she'd experienced in Erika's apartment. The air snapped with electrical current. The hair on her arms stood on end, and she felt like the air was somehow closing in on her.

She waited, trying to stay calm.

Then it happened. The woman appeared. Ellina appeared, standing next to her desk. She smiled at Jo, and Jo instantly felt calmer. Even though she was seeing something she shouldn't be.

"Ellina?"

The woman nodded, relief clear on her face.

"Are you dead?"

She shook her head.

"Are you in the cat?"

Ellina pulled an almost comical face, then nodded.

Jo felt another rush of relief. Maksim's sister wasn't dead. She was just stuck in a cat. Wow, that was beyond weird.

"How can I help you?"

Ellina glided across the room and pointed at a book on the shelves. Jo followed her, keeping a little distance between them. After all, could you ever really trust a spirit or whatever trapped in an animal?

Jo wasn't sure. But she followed Ellina's ghostly finger. She pointed at a book entitled *The Tricks and Trade of Being A Demon*. Jo carefully moved forward to pull it off the shelf.

She found the index, reading through the topics.

"Possession. Inciting lust. Transporting souls to Hell. Stealing souls. Placing souls into inanimate objects."

Ellina waved her hands, gesturing for Jo to continue.

"Placing souls into other living beings."

Ellina clapped, although it made no sound.

Jo smiled at her excitement. At least she seemed to be a good-natured trapped soul.

"Page 139." Jo flipped through the pages, finding the excerpt they needed to rescue Ellina. She read it aloud, fumbling through a lot of Latin and finally getting to the main point.

"This says you need a demon to do this spell or curse or whatever. And you need one to reverse it, too."

Ellina nodded, rapidly. Then she mouthed something.

Jo frowned, not understanding. "Again?"

Ellina mouthed the word again, and Jo said what she thought she saw. "Maksim?"

Ellina nodded.

"Maksim knows a demon?" Okay, this was getting weirder by the minute. And if she was making all this up, Jo realized she had one hell of an imagination.

Ellina shook her head.

"Maksim—is a demon?"

Ellina's eyes widened and she nodded. Jo grinned, glad she'd guessed right so quickly, then her smiled disappeared.

"Maksim is a demon?"

Ellina gave her a pained look and nodded again.

Great, she'd managed to go from a relationship with a married man to a demon. What was next? A vampire?

"Okay," Jo said, deciding if she was going to be crazy she might as well give it her all, "I'll go get Maksim. You stay here."

Ellina nodded.

Jo ran back to her bedroom and threw on some clothes. Then she hurried toward the Community Center.

Maksim was just finishing up lunch with the kids when Jo raced into the daycare room.

"Jo, what's going on?"

"You have to come with me." She grabbed his hand, tugging on him to follow her.

"What's going on?" he asked, even as he allowed her to lead him out of the center.

"You wouldn't believe me if I told you. Well, maybe you would."

Maksim shook his head, not following. "Where are we going?"

"To your sister's apartment. Hurry. I found your sister."

"What?" Maksim stopped, forcing Jo to stumble to a halt too.

"You heard me. I found her. Come on."

Both of them broke into a sprint, reaching the shotgun cottage in no time.

"Where is she?" he asked.

"In her study."

Maksim strode down the hallway, a smile on his lips, expecting to see her in her chair grinning at him. Happy-go-lucky Ellina home with some crazy story of travel for her research or some silly thing.

Instead he was greeted by Erika's stupid cat. It sat on Ellina's desk, looking like some sort of Egyptian statue.

"Where is my sister?" Maksim asked, confused, when Jo entered the room.

"She's in the cat."

"What?"

Jo pointed at the animal. "The cat. She's in there."

Maksim frowned. Maybe Jo was losing it. Did pregnancy cause bout of—hopefully—temporary insanity?

"You're a demon, and you're looking at me like I'm the one who's nutty."

Maksim gaped at her. "You know I'm a demon?"

Jo nodded. "Yeah, Ellina told me, which really you should have done."

Maksim blinked, then shook his head. "Wait. You talked to Ellina?" He turned to look at the cat. "Does it talk?"

"No. Apparently not only can I see ghosts, I can see people trapped in animals."

Maksim looked back at Jo. "You are taking this all very well."

"Yeah," Jo agreed, "I'm thinking I'm probably going to freak out afterward."

"I'm thinking you're right."

Maksim tilted his head, studying the cat. "So how do we get her out?"

Jo walked to the desk and handed him the book. "It looks pretty simple actually. Page 139."

Maksim took the book and found the correct page. He raised an eyebrow. "Hmm, I had no idea demons could do this."

"Oddly, I find it reassuring you haven't put anyone's soul in a house pet before."

"You really are taking this remarkably well," Maksim said, a little shaken by her unruffled reaction.

"It will sink in eventually."

Maksim didn't doubt that. And perhaps sooner than she thought.

"Okay," he said. "I can do this."

"Good."

"But—"

"Oh no," Jo groaned, "is this going to be something else disturbing?"

Maksim nodded. "I have to transform into my demon self to undo this curse."

Jo stared at him for a moment. "You don't turn into a thing like the Incredible Hulk or something? Like, you know, I have to run for cover, because you get all crazed and violent."

"No. I just don't look as good."

Jo made a face. "You don't look at good? You are quite conceited, you know that?"

"I'm supposed to be. I'm a demon, and my sins are seduction, deceit, and treachery."

Jo didn't respond to that, which didn't surprise him. She

may be able to accept that his home address was Hell, but she couldn't accept what he really was. A deceiver, a seducer, and disloyal. All the things the man who broke her heart and left her pregnant had been. Except to the extreme.

A loud meow brought both of their attention back to the task at hand.

"Jo, maybe you should leave the room." He suddenly didn't want her to see him in his true form. She was already getting too much of the truth at the moment.

But she shook her head. "No. I want to see you."

He hesitated, then nodded. He closed his eyes, and willed his true nature to appear.

He heard Jo's gasp, his first clue that he'd changed.

When he opened his eyes, Jo was staring at him, her jaw dropped, her dark eyes like obsidian orbs.

He glanced down at himself. Red scaled skin, bulging muscles, his spine popped out like blunt barbs. Small horns curved out from just above his temples.

She took a step toward him, reaching out a tentative hand to touch the skin on his arm.

She shook her head. "Amazing."

It was Maksim's turn to gape at her. "The ghost of your dead sister terrifies you, but I don't faze you."

She blinked at the guttural, unnatural change of his voice, then she said, "I know."

She appeared as confused as he was. "I guess I don't understand her intent. I don't understand what she wants, and I'm afraid she hates me because I didn't save her."

He understood that, but he still couldn't understand her lack of fear of him.

As if she'd read his mind, she said, "I know you wouldn't hurt me."

He stared at her for a moment longer, wondering how she could be so sure. Then he turned to the book.

He started to recite the Latin curse, willing the words to work. To restore his sister to him.

*   *   *

Jo watched Maksim, her mind not really wrapping around what she was seeing. Anything that she'd seen since wandering in here this morning. Part of her still thought it had to be a dream. That was the only explanation.

But she wasn't sure. She touched Maksim, felt his thick, scaly skin, his rock-hard muscles. For someone who had always pooh-poohed the occult, she was sure getting thrust headlong into it today.

Yet, she wasn't scared. Which as Maksim pointed out, made no sense. Kara terrified her.

Maksim finished the incantation, then closed the book and waited. Jo frowned. Nothing seemed to be happening. No flash of lightning. No eerie green smoke. No choking scent of brimstone.

"Did it work?" she asked.

Suddenly, Ellina was just there. Sitting cross-legged on the desk. Boris beside her, looking downright miffed. The cat leapt down off the table, found a patch of sun, and began to clean himself.

When Jo looked back from Ellina and the cat to Maksim, he, too, had returned to the Maksim she knew—and despite all the intense weirdness—loved.

"Ellina." Maksim stepped toward her. Ellina hopped down and flung herself into her brother's arms.

"Oh, I was really beginning to believe I'd never see you again," she said, her voice matching her beauty. Lilting and lovely.

"Me, too," he said, and Jo heard deep emotion in his voice.

Jo started to slip out of the room. The siblings need time alone. Ellina had been gone a long time, and surely she wanted to tell Maksim what had happened to her to get her in that predicament.

But Ellina stopped her. "Jo. Thank you."

"I didn't do anything. Just saw you."

"Which is more than anyone else could do."

Ellina hugged Jo, and Jo found herself hugging her back as if it was the most natural thing in the world.

"Okay, I really am going to leave now and give you two some time to catch up." Jo looked at Maksim, but he didn't look at her in return.

She knew what she'd just seen was insane and she should be terrified of the man—or the demon—or whatever he was, but she wasn't. She just recalled what she'd shared with him. How many times he'd protected her. He'd helped her. He'd made love to her with such tenderness and caring. She didn't care what he claimed to be. She'd already seen the real Maksim. Many times.

"I love you," she said to him, knowing he wouldn't answer her. But also knowing she couldn't leave it unsaid.

Then she left.

Chapter 30

"I like her," Ellina said, after Jo exited.

Maksim didn't respond, nor did he look toward the empty doorway, though every fiber of his being wanted to look. To go after Jo. To tell her he loved her, too.

"So you have gone and fallen in love while I was away. I can't believe it." Ellina giggled, thoroughly pleased.

"Don't believe it, then," Maksim said. His sister was always annoyingly perceptive.

"So you are denying it?"

"Yep."

Ellina sighed. "That's silly."

"Well, you know me, silly to the bitter end."

"You are going to have a bitter end, if you don't get a clue."

"Where's that cat?" Maksim said, pretending to search for the animal. "I'm going to put you back in him."

She laughed, undaunted by his threat.

"How did you end up in a cat anyway?" he asked, glad for another topic than his feelings for Jo.

"I'm not sure, honestly. I was on my way to find Vittorio, to warn him about his mother. Do you know this woman, Orabella? She's Vittorio's mother and she's crazy."

Maksim nodded, albeit noncommittally. He wasn't about to reveal he'd had a relationship of sorts with the woman. Of course, only to find out what happened to Ellina, but that hadn't worked out terribly well.

"Anyway, I was on my way to find Vittorio, to warn him his mother had learned how to make demons do her bidding, when I suddenly found myself in a cat. And a male one at that. Not pleasant."

"Do you think this person is still a threat to you?" he asked.

Ellina shrugged with her usual blithe spirit. "No. I think it was a practical joke. Probably those twin brothers of ours."

Maksim had his doubts about that, but didn't bother to say anything.

"So are you going to go find Jo and tell her you love her, too?" Ellina asked casually.

"No."

"Well, that's silly, because it's clear you do love her."

"No, I don't."

Ellina placed her hands on her hips, suddenly reminding him of Cherise. The realization he wouldn't see her again made his chest ache.

"Okay. I do love Jo."

"Ha! I knew it."

"But for the first time in my existence, I'm going to do something unselfish. I'm going to walk away. Jo deserves better than me."

"How can you say that?"

"She does. I can't be a father to her child. Not a good father."

"Jo's pregnant? I'm going to be an aunt?" Ellina's eyes lit up.

"It's not mine. It's a long story."

"Oh." She seemed slightly disappointed, and he understood that feeling all too well.

"Why do you think demons can't be fathers? Our father was a demon." Ellina pointed out.

"And would you call him a good one?"

Ellina shrugged, giving him a look that said he had a point.

"Besides, I can't even read Jo's thoughts to tell whether she really wants me or not."

Ellina made a face at him, stating she thought he was a moron. "You don't need to jump in her head. She told you how she feels. And after seeing you all red and in need of serious lotion."

Maksim shook his head. "That's the other thing. I jumped in her head once, which was selfish enough given what I knew it could do to her. I knew I couldn't read her thoughts. Yet, I did it again—and for the same damned selfish reasons. I've hurt her. I'm the reason she could see you. And she's seeing her sister because of me. How can I tell her that I did that to her?"

"Easy. Just tell her."

Ellina had a way of making things sound so simple. But how could Jo forgive him for making her see the sister whose loss devastated her once. Now it was devastating her all over again.

"No. I'm doing this. It's what is right."

With that he focused, willing himself back to Hell, back to where he belonged. He disappeared in a puff of smoke and lingering scent of sulfur.

Three weeks later . . .

Jo attempted to focus on her work, but she kept thinking about Maksim. She was furious with him, frankly. Every day she kept waiting for him to come to his senses, but so far he seemed determined to be stupid.

While Jo had learned so many things from her experience with him. Not the least to let go of her fears. Fears of failure, fears of losing control, fears of the past.

She'd even confronted seeing Kara again—with the help of Ellina. Kara had come to her because she'd known all this time Jo blamed herself. She'd just been trying to contact her, even though her attempts had seemed scary at the time. They were just a little girl's way of trying to get her attention.

Now Kara was gone. Both of them at peace.

Well, except for the fact that the man she loved was being ridiculous.

"Hey," Ellina appeared in the doorway of her office. Since Maksim's departure, Ellina had stepped in to help Cherise. It was wonderful, but the kids still missed Maksim.

"Hey," Jo greeted the exuberant woman. Ellina seemed to have the energy of three people.

"I discovered something in my research last night."

"Oh yeah, what's that?"

"You and Maksim are bonded."

"Excuse me?" Jo said, confused and not sure she wanted to hear anything else that would make her feel awful about him letting their relationship go.

"You are bonded. That's why he couldn't read your mind. That's one of the ways it manifests."

Jo shook her head, still not understanding what Ellina was trying to say.

"You two are meant to be together."

See, that was just what she didn't want to hear. She already knew they were meant to be together. More validation did nothing to make the loss any easier.

"And since you are bonded, you can call him to you."

"What good will that do if he doesn't want to be with me?"

"Well, I can't help you with that. All I can do is tell you how to get him there." Ellina smiled a cute, naughty little smile. "You'll have to do the work to make him stay."

Jo considered that information, then nodded. "Okay."

She was miserable. She had to try again.

Maksim sat in a bar on Bourbon. He'd gone back to Hell for a while, but couldn't seem to stay away from Jo. Oh, he hadn't seen her. That would have been too difficult for him, but being in the same city was enough.

Well, no, it wasn't enough, but it was all he was going to allow himself. She was better off without him.

He sat in Lafitte's drinking his usual whiskey on the rocks, when suddenly he felt very strange. Like he was dematerializing, except he wasn't doing it.

Next thing he knew he was in Jo's apartment. She stood in the living room wearing a dress that had a plunging neckline showing the gentle swells of her breasts. The high waist tightened over the swell of her belly, which he was surprised to see had grown noticeably since he last saw her. The material was covered in bright flowers, reminding her of the bouquet he'd bought her just a day before they were no more.

"Jo? What's going on?" He frowned, trying to understand what was happening.

She walked up to him, the sway of her hips, the sight of her lush body all holding him captive. Especially the enigmatic smile curving her lips.

"I brought you here."

"You? How?"

"Well," she stopped in front of him. "It turns out that you and I are bonded."

Bonded? He'd wondered if that could be the case, but it still didn't matter.

"Jo, bonding doesn't mean we have to be together. It just means we have a connection. You can be with anyone you want. I won't stop that."

Jo shook her head, laughing slightly. "You are the silliest demon I've ever met."

He raised his eyebrow. "And how many demons have you met?"

"That's not the point," she touched him, her fingers running along his jaw, down his neck. The caress sent fiery raging need throughout his entire body.

"The point is," she said slowly leaning up to kiss the same path her fingers just did. "Is that I want you. And as a bonded female, I can have you."

Maksim groaned. "Ellina told you?"

"Mmm-hmm." She nipped his neck and he groaned. Damn, he'd missed her. The smell of her, the feeling. He turned his head and caught her lips, kissing her hard.

She moaned, melting into him.

They kissed for several minutes, hours, hell, he didn't know. Finally he managed to gain a little sense and pulled back.

"Jo, how can you really want to be with a demon? One who was created to embody all the traits of someone who has hurt you?"

She smiled, gently touching his face. "Because of that very reason. You were formed to exist only that way, yet you have been better to me than any man. You turned away from your old nature to be what I needed. That's more than any woman could possibly ask for."

"But what if old Maksim returns?"

"Has he yet?"

"No," he admitted. He hadn't seduced, deceived anyone. He really was turning out to be a failure in the demon department.

"I can't be disloyal to you. I love you."

"Well according to your sister, once a demon loves, all his sins reverse."

Maksim raised an eyebrow. "Is that so?"

Jo nodded. "That's what she said and she does research demons for a living."

"Well, I think she may be mostly right. But I'm pretty sure my seduction techniques are still working fine."

Jo laughed, the sound throaty and sexy as any sin he knew.

"As long as the seduction is only directed at me."

"Only you." He kissed her lingerly.

"I love you," she murmured against his lips.

"God knows, I love you, too."

Epilogue

"I think we succeeded in having a very unusual wedding," Jo said, snuggling up against her new husband, pressing a kiss to his bare shoulder.

Maksim chuckled. "Oh, I think we did."

He cuddled her closer still, his hands stroking over her large belly. The man was obsessed with her pregnant body, which she had to admit she liked. Maksim always made her feel beautiful, even with swollen feet and a popped-out belly button.

"And you know which part I thought was the most unusual?"

He lifted his head to peer at her in the shadowy light of their bedroom, a huge master bedroom in a gorgeous house in the Garden District. Maksim's wedding present to her.

"Let me see, was it the fact that you, very pregnant with another man's baby, married me, a demon?"

Jo laughed. "No, that wasn't what I was thinking about."

"Could it be that most of our wedding party were lampirs?"

"And a half-demon," she added.

"And a half-demon."

"No." Jo grinned.

"Hmm. How about the fact that the wedding band was all vampires?"

"And one werewolf," Jo added.

"Right, and one werewolf."

"Nope," Jo said again with a little giggle.

Maksim smiled too, clearly enjoying her merriment. "Well, I can't imagine what else could have made it more unusual."

"That we went with devil's food cake instead of the usual white cake with buttercream frosting."

Maksim stared at her for a moment, then laughed. "You are too much."

Jo laughed, too, then stopped when the baby kicked her hard. Maksim lifted his head, watching her bare belly. Both of them never ceased to be fascinated by the little person growing inside her.

"We are going to have, like, five more of these," Maksim said, shaping his hand over her belly, smiling when their daughter kicked again. They'd been together for the sonogram that revealed Jo's intuition had been right. They decided to name her Kara. Kara seemed to approve—because she had not reappeared to Joe.

"Let's have this one first," said Jo, although she already knew she wanted more, too. Maksim, who now admitted he'd originally only volunteered at the community center to be near her, turned out to be one kid-crazy guy. And he could now honestly sway he was a member of Big Brother/Big Sister. Damon was his little brother.

"You're sure you don't mind being married to a demon? Having a demon's children?

Jo lifted her head to look at him. "Of course I am. And your sister seems fine."

Maksim made a face at that. "Most of the time, when she's not writing books that incite other demons to curse her into a cat."

Jo raised up on her elbow. She frowned. It did seem Ellina had ticked off some powerful beings. More strange things had happened to her since escaping Boris. Not that Ellina took the occurrences as anything serious.

"Just the usual mishaps," she'd said. Like nearly being run down by a car—not once but twice in as many weeks—was normal. Or that fact the her apartment had been ransacked.

Jo sighed, knowing Ellina's heedlessness worried Maksim a lot.

"I have no regrets," Jo said, wanting to draw his attention away from fretting. "I love being married to a demon. Even when you're red and scaly."

"Oh, we are not going to even speculate on how much you like my demon self. You kinky thing."

She laughed. "Plus you are a pretty reformed demon these days."

"Shh, you're ruining my reputation."

She laughed again, but the sound died on her lips as his hand sloped down over the swell of her belly, heading to the place on her body that always ached for his touch. He leisurely stroked her, her arousal slicking his fingers.

"Mmm," he moaned. He loved her reaction to him.

"I do have one concern," she managed to say, even though it was darn near impossible to focus when he swirled his finger like that—with just the right pressure.

Said finger paused.

"What's that?"

"Well, you are never going to age and I will," she said.

He was quiet, then said in a strained voice, "I will figure that out. We will be together forever."

She smiled. "Well, I do have a plan."

"You do?"

"Well, I do have four best friends who are lampirs. So I figured they could help me out. Would you be okay with being married to a lampir?"

"As long as the lampir is you. Then definitely."

He kissed her and that talented hand of his started moving again. Oh, being married to a demon *was* unusual, but she was loving every minute of it.

If you liked this book, you've got to try Amy Fetzer's latest, FIGHT FIRE WITH FIRE, out now from Brava . . .

"You don't have time for that."

Instantly Riley scooped up the pistol and spun on his knees, aiming.

A figure stood near the blown out entrance. Shit. He hadn't heard a thing.

Still as glass, the man's head and shoulders were wrapped in dark scarves over a once green military jacket, now a dull gray like the weather. The only skin exposed was his eyes. Around his waist, a utility belt sagged, and the sniper rifle was slung on his shoulder, the weapon held across his body, ready to sight and fire. Yet he stood casually, without threat.

"If I wanted you dead, I wouldn't have wasted bullets to see you two safe and alive."

The sniper, Riley realized with a wee shock, was a woman.

She advanced with easy grace, stepping over piles of rubble to hop down at his level. Her rifle looked all too familiar.

"Yes, it's American," she said, noticing his attention. He lowered his weapon. She stood a couple feet away, staring down at Sam. "He doesn't look good." She unwound her head scarf and a braided rope of shiny dark hair spilled down one shoulder. She met his gaze. Beneath arched brows, whiskey colored eyes stared back at him.

"Sweet mother a' *Jaasus*." She was younger than him.

"I get that a lot." She gestured at Sam. "What do you need to do?"

"Set his leg again and get a tighter splint on it."

She nodded as her gaze bounced around the interior. "Let's get busy. I don't know how much time we have."

Though the pop of gunfire was lazier now, Riley wasn't ignoring the help, or the danger of staying put too long. He instructed, glad Sam was unconscious or he'd be screaming to the heavens. After unbuckling her utility belt, she got behind Sam, her legs and arms wrapping his torso and hips as Riley grasped his calf and ankle. On a count, he pulled. Even drugged, Sam arched with silent agony. Riley ripped the flight suit more and pushed the bone down, forcing it to align closely. Blood oozed from the gash. He met her gaze and nodded.

"It's set. Well . . . better than it was."

She eased from Sam and unclipped her canteen, offering it.

He cleaned his hands and the wound, then Riley worked against the cold. With the needle poised over Sam's flesh, he shook too much to stitch. "For the love of Mike." He dropped the needle, sanding his hands, blowing on them. She quickly grasped them both, wrapping her scarf around them, then brought his fists to her lips. She breathed hotly against the fabric, and Riley felt the warmth sting his icy skin. She rubbed and breathed, her gaze flashing up. He felt struck, her soulful eyes hiding so much.

"Better?"

He nodded, unwound the scarf. "The rest of me is a bit chilly still."

It took a second for that to sink in and she made a face. He chuckled, then said, "Get yourself on the other side, woman, and let's make some quick work here."

She snickered to herself, yet obeyed, holding Sam's skin closed as he stitched. She still wore gloves and though she was dressed warmly, he noticed everything was cinched down, nothing to catch, and her rifle would collapse. It was a weapon he'd seen in spec, a prototype of the MP5. Not in production, yet she had one. And if the bodies outside indicated, she knew how to use it. It was at her right, by her knee with a bullet chambered.

"You're Company." CIA. Probably attached to NATO.

He had to give her credit, she didn't look up or make even a single nuance. If she was any good, she wouldn't give anything away.

"Tell me how an Irishman got to be in the Marines."

Okay, he could go that direction. "I was a runner for the IRA and my older sister caught me. Dragged me home by my ear, she did." His lips curved with the memory as he took another stitch. "My parents, fearing for my immortal soul, sent me to America to live with relatives." He shrugged.

"So dodging bullets comes easy, huh?"

"Yeah, I guess."

Then he went and chose a career in it. He glanced at Sam, knowing this would cost him what he held dear. His Marine enlistment. But he couldn't let the one man who treated him like a friend instead of his superior die in the frigid Serbian forests.

"I saw the jet go down."

His gaze briefly slid to hers.

"He was doing some amazing flying before the missile hit. I've been behind you for a day."

"So you're the reason the patrol didn't catch up to us?"

Bless her, that blank expression didn't change a fraction.

"Thank you for our lives." He clipped the thread. "I'm Riley." He held out his hand. She bit off her glove and shook it. Her skin was warm, her palm smooth and dry.

"Safia," was all she offered with her disarming smile.

He wondered why someone so young was in the field alone. She helped him work the inflatable air cast over Sam's upper thigh, then wrapped him in rags and curtains Riley'd found to keep him warm. Sam's fever would spike and he had to get him some antibiotics. He'd used his last just now.

The woman unwound from the floor, strapped her belt back on, then dug in her pack like a purse and blindly reloaded her magazines. He recognized C4 packs and some gadgets he didn't. She was a little fire team all by herself, he thought, smiling. Armed, she went to each opening. He reached for his gun when she disappeared out a gap in the wall. He waited, chambering a bullet and aiming.

Tell me I can't be that much of a sucker. Icy wind spun through the building. Seconds ticked by. She reappeared and stopped short, then cocked her head. She smiled almost appreciatively, and he lowered his weapon. She moved to him with an elegance that defied her crude surroundings and the two pistols in her belt. Her exotic features and tanned skin puzzled him. Without head scarves, she looked completely out of place.

Then the radio hooked on her belt buzzed and she brought it to her ear, listening. The language sounded Albanian. She didn't make contact, only listened, then said, "We need to go."

Don't miss Alison Kent's NO LIMITS, out this month from Brava . . .

By the time his guest returned, freshly showered and shampooed and dressed in his things, Simon had thrown together a breakfast of scrambled eggs, bacon, coffee, and toast. He didn't immediately turn around and greet her but focused on piling the food on paper plates, digging into his box of grub for sugar and powdered cream.

Concentrating on what was simple kept him from facing the complications that came attached like baggage to Michelina Ferrer. It was a different sort of baggage than what he'd been dealing with the last few weeks, but her being here was still going to weigh heavy on his mind.

Dealing with Bear and Lorna and the property would be enough to try any saint. Add King to the mix, and, well, Simon's patience wouldn't pass the first test. And now he had a mystery on his hands, a crime that needed more explanation before it would begin to make sense.

That was the only reason he finally turned around, the only reason he lifted his gaze from the food he carried to the woman standing in the frame of the kitchen doorway toweling dry her dark hair.

Her face was the same one he'd seen on *Page Six,* on magazine covers, on TV. The same one from his billboard. The same one . . . but not.

Her skin was scrubbed clean. She wore nothing glossy on her lips, nothing colored and glittery on her eyes, nothing to smooth out her cool ivory skin. She had freckles on her nose, two small red zits on her chin.

And her eyes were sad and scared, not sassy or sultry or seductive. A big problem, her eyes. An equally big one, her unbound breasts beneath his gray T-shirt, the curve of her hips and thighs in his long-legged briefs.

He set the food on the table, cleared his throat, went back for the Styrofoam cups filled with coffee and for plasticware. He didn't turn back toward her until he heard her sit, the chair legs scraping across the worn linoleum, the creak of the wood beneath her weight.

The table hid most of her body. He could still make out the shape of her breasts, the fullness, the upper slope that made him wonder about the weight he'd feel beneath. But there wasn't a damn thing he could do to avoid her face, so bare and exposed, or her eyes.

He had to look at her to get her story. He had to watch her expression, see the truth, her fear, find out how much she knew or had guessed or thought about what had happened. This is what he did—gathered information, ferreted out intel, zoned in on the pertinent details, used it all to come up with a plan of action.

He needed one. Desperately. One that had nothing to do with her body being naked under his clothes, one that addressed the fact that she was Michelina Ferrer. And she was miserable, frightened, and lost.

He couldn't help it. He feared that juxtaposition—what he knew about the celebrity versus what he sensed about this woman with her armor washed away and fearing for her life—was going to make it hard to keep this job from turning personal.

And be sure to catch Lucy Monroe's new book, WATCH
OVER ME, coming next month from Brava . . .

"Dr. Ericson."

Lana adjusted the angle on the microscope. Yes. Right there. Perfect. "Amazing."

"Lana."

She reached out blindly for the stylus to her handheld. *Got it.* She started taking notes on the screen without looking away from the microscope.

"Dr. Ericson!!!"

Lana jumped, bumping her cheekbone on the microscope's eyepiece before falling backward, hitting a wall that hadn't been there when she'd come into work that morning.

Strong hands set her firmly on her feet as she realized the wall was warm and made of flesh and muscle. Lots and lots of muscle.

Stumbling back a step, she looked up and then up some more. The dark-haired hottie in front of her was as tall as her colleague, Beau Ruston. Or close to it anyway. She fumbled with her glasses, sliding them on her nose. They didn't help. Reading glasses for the computer, they only served to make her feel more disoriented.

She squinted, then remembered and pulled the glasses off again, letting them dangle by their chain around her neck. "Um, hello? Did I know you were visiting my lab?"

She was fairly certain she hadn't. She forgot appointments sometimes. Okay, often, but she always remembered eventually. And this man hadn't made an appointment with her. She was sure of it. He didn't look like a scientist either.

Not that all scientists were as unremarkable as she was in the looks department, but his man was another species entirely.

He looked dangerous and sexy. Enough so that he would definitely replace chemical formulas in her dreams at night. His black hair was a little too long and looked like he'd run his fingers through it, not a comb. That was just so bad boy. She had a secret weakness for bad boys.

Even bigger than the secret weakness she'd harbored for Beau Ruston before he'd met Elle.

She had posters of James Dean and Matt Dillon on the wall of her bedroom and had seen "Rebel without a Cause" a whopping thirty-six times.

Unlike James Dean, this yummy bad boy even had pierced ears. Only instead of sedate studs or small hoops, he had tiny black plugs. Only a bit bigger than a pair of studs, the plugs were recessed in his lobes. They had the Chinese Kanji for strength etched on them in silver. Or pewter maybe. It wasn't shiny.

The earrings were hot. Just like him.

He looked like the kind of man who had a tattoo. Nothing colorful. Something black and meaningful. She wanted to see it. Too bad she couldn't just ask.

Interpersonal interaction had so many taboos. It wasn't like science where you dug for answers without apology.

"Lana?"

The stranger had a strong jaw too, squared and accented by a close-cropped beard that went under, not across his chin. No mustache. His lips were set in a straight line, but they still looked like they'd be Heaven to kiss.

Not that she'd kissed a lot of lips, but she was twenty-nine. Even a geeky scientist didn't make it to the shy side of thirty without a few kisses along the way. And other stuff. Not that the other stuff was all that spectacular. She'd always wondered if that was her fault or the men she'd chosen to partner.

It didn't take a shrink to identify the fact that Lana had trust issues. With her background, who wouldn't?

Still, people had been know to betray family, love and country for sex. She wouldn't cross a busy street to get some. Or maybe she would, if this stranger was waiting on the other side.

The fact that she could measure the time it had been since the last time in years rather than months, weeks or days—which would be a true miracle—wasn't something she enjoyed dwelling on. She blamed it on her work.

However, every feminine instinct that was usually sublimated by her passion for her work was on red alert now.